SURROUNDED

The creatures seemed to be all around Maggie. They were circling her, she suddenly realized with chilling certainty, circling as though she were some kind of prey.

"Go away!" she hissed.

The circle seemed to be closing in on her. Suddenly she felt claustrophobic. She couldn't breathe.

"Away, I said! Please!"

At last her paralysis broke, and she ran the rest of the way toward her husband. "Keith!" she screamed as loud as she could. She shook him violently until she was certain he was awake, then she screamed again.

One of the creatures had touched her.

Other Leisure Books by Edmund Plante:

Seed of Evil
Transformation
Garden of Evil

EDMUND PLANTE

TRAPPED

For Harry Mugrditchian,
and the memory of his wife, Muriel.

Book Margins, Inc.

A BMI Edition

Published by special arrangement with Dorchester Publishing Co., Inc.

Printed in the United States of America.

PART ONE

PART ONE

CHAPTER ONE

Maggie Hunter's first thought was: this is a mistake.

It was true that she wanted peace and isolation, time to be with her family, time to mend things. Now she wasn't sure if she'd chosen the right place. The lake was too big, the woods surrounding it too thick, and the air too silent.

Turning to the others as they lugged suitcases out of the Ford wagon, Maggie forced a smile. "Lovely, isn't it?"

Her husband Keith grunted as he disappeared inside the small, wood-shingled cottage. Following him was their son, nine-year-old Brice, with his dog Commander at his heel.

"It's not all that bad," Maggie added, as

though trying to convince herself as well.

"I bet this place is loaded with bugs, frogs, snakes, and God knows what else!" Fourteen-year-old Toni Hunter grimaced as she struggled with her baggage. Her best friend, Lisa, merely shrugged indifferently, made a pink bubble with her gum, then sucked it back in.

Last to leave the car was Maggie's mother, Vivian. It had taken Maggie hours to persuade her mother to join the family on this so-called vacation. Vivian had lost her husband three months ago and was still hurting. Maggie didn't want to leave her alone at this time.

"Isn't the lake beautiful, Ma?"

Vivian squinted at the land across the water. Only one other cottage could be seen, a hazy miniature in the distance. "You could scream for help here and not be heard," she said.

"Why would anyone want to scream?"

"Who knows, dear. I'm just saying that this place looks so lonely, that's all."

"You don't like it here, do you?"

Vivian patted her hand. "I didn't say that. It's lovely, dear. In fact, your father and I used to come to a place like this when we were first married, although it wasn't this far out into the woods."

"I wanted us to be as far away as possible."

Finding this place hadn't been easy. When she had suggested to Keith that they get away to sort things out, he hadn't been

exactly enthusiastic. He hadn't objected
either, perhaps because he was relieved that
she hadn't demanded a divorce or thrown
him out of the house. He simply went along
with everything she said and told her to do
whatever she felt was right. So she called a
realtor and asked for the most private
cottage on the lake.

Now she wished she had seen this place
before renting it.

A bird cawed somewhere deep in the
woods. Maggie hugged herself. This should
be romantic and peaceful. So why was she
feeling uneasy? Was it because she knew her
mother was right? You could scream for
help and not be heard?

Vivian patted Maggie's hand again, then
picked up her luggage.

"Let me help you, Ma."

"No, no. I refuse to be a burden."

"You're no burden. Now let me—"

"No, I said!" Her voice was surprisingly
firm for a 63-year-old woman.

With a sigh, Maggie relented. Since her
father had died her mother had been
adamant about taking care of herself.
Sometimes her determination to do this was
unreasonable and ridiculous.

Carrying her own luggage, Maggie started
toward the cottage. The small, sagging
structure had an oversized open porch and
stone chimney. For a 100 feet between the
cottage and the grassy shore, the land was
clear, its ground covered with pine needles.

Beyond this were countless trees—hemlocks, pines, and oaks. They grew so close that one would almost need to walk sideways to penetrate the woods.

Inside the bungalow there was one large room, one side furnished with sofa, rocking chair and small portable TV, and the other with refrigerator, gas stove and dinette set. Beyond this were two bedrooms and a bathroom.

"Not bad," she commented.

Only her son and the dog seemed to agree. They were looking everywhere at once, as though they had embarked on a new planet that demanded exploration.

"We'll make the best of it," Maggie said to the others, then, looking directly at her husband, added, "We have to."

That evening the wind whined softly around the cottage. The treetops, black silhouettes against the night sky, swayed hypnotically. Maggie stared at them from the bedroom window for a long moment, wondering if a storm were brewing. It's so different out here, she thought. The night was never like this in the city, never—as her mother had said—this lonely.

You could scream for help and not be heard.

The wind stopped and the treetops ceased to sway. Silence and stillness surrounded the cottage. Maggie had to admit she did not like this place. Where was the serenity she sought? Something was wrong with this silence. It was too heavy, more like the calm before a storm.

"Honey?" Keith called from the bed.

Tensing at the sound of his voice, she turned away from the window. Perhaps the dread she was feeling had something to do with her husband. Intuitively, she knew tonight they would make love for the first time since the horrible night she'd found him in bed with that other woman. Since then Maggie had managed to avoid him. Now she would have to let him touch her. After all, they had both agreed to give their marriage another chance.

Naked under the covers, Keith watched her. He made no move, for it was tacitly understood that the first move would be hers. It was up to her to forgive, and Maggie knew if she didn't forgive him the marriage would end.

Slowly, with trembling hands, she began to undress. She felt as though she were a virgin, exposing herself to a man for the first time. She had mixed feelings. She didn't want her husband to make love to her after what he had done, but she didn't want to turn him away either and push him back toward the other woman.

She removed her top, then her jeans. Hesitantly, she took off her bra and stepped out of her panties. A chill rippled through her, although the air was warm.

She covered her breasts with her arms

until she realized what she was doing. She'd been undressing in front of him for 17 years, for God's sake! So why the sudden Victorian modesty? With some difficulty she let her arms drop, then she slid under the covers to join her husband.

An awkward moment ensued, but it was brief. Maggie had failed to move close enough to Keith, so he slid toward her, filling the gap between them. No words were exchanged. They stared at each other, searching for answers that would explain why they had strayed from each other. Then Keith's lips covered hers.

Maggie fought a sudden urge to pull back. "I love you, honey," she heard him utter in a deep, muffled voice. For the first time since they'd been married she wondered if his words were sincere.

She contemplated repeating the three words, but somehow could not utter them. Her lips, however, began to respond to his. Soon she was enjoying the feel and taste of him. His hand cupped one breast, and this time she felt no desire to recoil. At last she was melting and truly responding.

When it was over he kept her in his arms and lavished her with small, affectionate kisses. "I love you," he said for the second time.

Tears filled her eyes. This idea of hers was working after all. The isolation and the different environment were putting her marriage back together again. Maybe it would bring her family closer also, for she had grown apart from her children as well.

"I love you, too." At last the words came easily.

He gave her another kiss. She closed her eyes and smiled inwardly, knowing now she had forgiven her husband. It would be a while before she'd be able to forget, but at least she had forgiven him.

"I'm really sorry," he said softly, sensing her thoughts. "I never really meant to . . . well, you know, hurt you."

Maggie let the contrition penetrate and peered into his soft brown eyes. "And I'm sorry for being away so much," she replied, her voice equally soft.

A sound caught her attention. She looked toward the window. Was it the wind? The night here is so unlike the city, she thought again. She found herself wishing a car would blare its horn or a dog would bark.

"I do miss you, honey," Keith was saying, unaware of the sound outside the cottage. "I know I never should have done what I did, but . . ." His mouth was open, ready to say more, but he changed his mind and fell silent.

"But what?" she prompted.

"Well, you're gone so much, and . . ."

"Things are going to change," she said confidently.

"Yeah?"

"Yes. I've been doing some thinking, and I've decided to forget about the store."

"But it's your dream, honey. You've put in so many hours trying to learn everything about running the business."

He was right; it *was* her dream. She had always wanted to own and run her own business, and when the small department store where she worked went up for sale, she had jumped at the chance. Her friend and employer, Connie McCarthy, had agreed to wait until Maggie could learn every aspect of the business. Now the dream would have to wait—or be forgotten.

"If I buy the store I might have to put in even more time," she pointed out to Keith.

He said nothing, only kissed her nose, then her cheek. She could tell he was readying himself for another round. Sometimes she suspected he was oversexed.

"It wouldn't be fair to you," she sighed.

"Huh?"

"To run a store and have no time for my family."

"Oh, y'know, I hate to make you give it up." He kissed her earlobe.

"There'll be other stores, other chances. Maybe I should wait until Toni and Brice are on their own."

"You sure?"

"Yes. My marriage and family are more important. Much more."

Wordlessly, his warm mouth rose to meet hers, and soon she found herself responding again. She clung to him, knowing together they'd rise to another wonderful climax.

Blood pounded in her ears. She heard a moan, then a gasp. It was confusing to determine who was making these sounds. Was it Keith or herself? Then she heard something else, something too high-pitched to be human.

And there was something about this sound that made Maggie take notice. She tensed to listen.

"Keith, did you hear that?"

"Huh? The wind," he muttered without pausing.

Maggie tried to ignore the sound, telling herself that he was right, that it was the wind. She tried to concentrate on their lovemaking, and the feel of his male hardness inside her, but the passion she'd felt moments earlier was ebbing rapidly. The odd high-pitched sound was still discernible.

Maybe it was a whistling train in the far distance. Or maybe it was a tornado! Hadn't she heard or read somewhere that tornadoes sounded like freight trains?

"Keith . . ."

He ignored her, now increasing his rhythm.

"Keith!" She pushed against him.

"Wha—"

She extricated herself from under him. He looked at her incredulously, as though she had slapped him. Then his brows came together, and she knew he was furious, demanding an explanation for the abrupt withdrawal.

"Listen," she said.

He complied but continued to glare at her. After a few seconds, he shrugged. "So, it's windy. Big fucking—"

"How can you say it's the wind? It doesn't sound like that at all."

"Well, what the hell else could it be out here?"

"Tornado, maybe?"

"I don't think so," he said after listening. "Tornadoes are supposed to be loud, aren't they?"

"I guess so."

"Besides, they're rare around here."

But not nonexistent, she thought, then slid out of bed and reached for her robe.

"Where are you going?" Keith asked.

"To see what it is."

"C'mon, forget about it. Let's just finish what we—"

"Aren't you curious?"

"Not really. We've never been out here in the woods before. We're not familiar with the night sounds around here. Maybe this is something common."

"But what is it?" she asked, pulling her robe tighter and peering out the window.

"Maybe it's the cry of the banshee," he suggested in a mocking, sepulchral voice.

"Why can't you take anything seriously?" The view outside the window was disquieting. The sky, lake and trees were all black, seemingly blacker than the last time she had looked out. Never had she seen such darkness and stillness. Shouldn't the trees sway a little, especially if it was the wind that was making the strange sound?

Keith said something she didn't catch.

"What?"

"I said you take everything too seriously."

She ignored him, debating whether or not to open the window.

"Come back to bed," Keith demanded again.

She remained at the window. "The sound won't go away." When he made no reply, she asked, "Aren't you interested at all?"

"I've already told you what I'm interested in." A hard edge in his voice showed he was losing his patience with her.

She began to move away from the window. Maybe he was right, she thought. Maybe she was taking this sound thing too seriously. Maybe it really was only the wind. Perhaps it was the numerous trees that made it whine so eerily, made it sound so different from the wind in the city.

Keith leaned back against his pillow, waiting eagerly for her to return to his arms and pick up where they'd left off.

As Maggie crossed the room, the sound changed pitch. She halted, her head tilting toward the ceiling. The sound was now above them.

"It's over the house, Keith!"

Keith followed her gaze. Together, they stared at the ceiling, listening intently. The pitch was much higher, almost shrill, and it was definitely hovering above them.

"A helicopter?"

Keith shook his head, still looking upward.

Maggie returned to the window.

"Maybe you shouldn't—"

But he was too late, for she had started to push the window upward.

"You don't know what could be out there," she heard him say as she poked her head out the window. The air was cooler than inside the cottage. The smell of water and pine was intense; the noise above her was louder, suddenly no longer faint or muted.

She looked up at the shadowy clouds scudding across the black sky. No stars were visible, and the moon, almost full, was an incandescent blur straining to penetrate the clouds. Then she saw something else.

Rather than rolling across the sky, it made wide sweeps, circling the air. Like the clouds, it was dark, barely discernible against the sky. She tried to determine its shape, but couldn't. It was only because it was moving that she could see it at all.

What on earth was she looking at?

The object moved slowly, yet gracefully. It seemed to take a full minute to complete a revolution above the cottage. It reminded her of a vulture in the way it hovered so persistently. Why was it staying in this area? What did it want? What was it?

A hand fell on Maggie's shoulder, and she jumped, startled.

"What do you see?" Keith said behind her, dropping the hand.

"God, you scared the hell out of me."

"Sorry." He moved beside her, poked his head through the open window, and looked up at the sky. "Don't see anything."

"There's something up there, Keith," she said.

"Where?"

She was ready to point out the hovering object, but to her surprise found it gone. She stared harder, thinking maybe her eyes needed to adjust. Only the clouds and the feeble moon were above her.

"Well?" Keith was waiting.

Numbly, she looked back at him. Had she imagined seeing something? Had her eyes played tricks on her?

"What did it look like?" he asked.

"It was too dark. I couldn't see it too well."

"Then maybe you didn't see anything."

"I could see it move. I just couldn't make out its shape."

"Was it big?"

She thought about it, then nodded.

"How big?"

"About the size of a plane, maybe. A bus. I don't know. I couldn't tell how far away it was."

"Hmmm." He rubbed his chin and gave the sky another quick look. Maggie couldn't tell if he was being pensive or was amusing her. At length she decided it was the latter, for he abruptly retreated from the window and returned to the bed.

"We've got unfinished business," he said, patting the mattress beside him.

Hesitantly, she closed the window and started toward him. Couldn't he think of anything besides sex?

Forcing a smile, she joined him. Then the smile vanished as something occurred to her. "Keith, the noise . . . it's gone."

"Big deal. We've got other things to think about."

"What do you think it—"

She couldn't finish. His mouth was on hers, drowning out the words.

CHAPTER TWO

Maggie woke up disoriented. It took her a moment to realize where she was, and with this realization she felt the heavy, unpleasant ache in her heart that she was experiencing every morning now, ever since she had caught her husband with another woman. She wondered if the hurt would ever go away, or if it would be something she'd have to learn to live with.

She looked over at her husband who was sleeping and snoring softly. As she studied his face, that ache returned. Although his hair was thinning and graying and he had added a few pounds through the years, she still found him attractive. She still loved him, although not as strongly since his infidelity.

Most women, she knew, would tell her to

throw the bastard out, but she still was certain the blame was partly hers. If she hadn't been so busy with the store, he would have found no reason to stray.

Moving closer, she kissed his cheek. He stirred, but didn't awaken. She kissed him again, this time letting her lips linger on his stubbled cheek. He grunted in response, but still did not open his eyes. Instead, he turned away from her, tucked his hands under his pillow, and snored louder.

Sighing, Maggie gave up, donned her robe and looked out the window. It was a gray morning with fog rolling in from the lake. She strained to see the other side, where the water ended and the trees began. The pale mist was too thick. At length she turned away from the window and went into the spacious kitchen and living area.

Brice was on the floor in his sleeping bag, watching cartoons on TV. Lying faithfully beside him was the golden retriever. Vivian and Toni were at the kitchen table, and Lisa was still sleeping, curled up in a fetal position on the couch.

"Good morning," Maggie said as cheerfully as she could.

Toni returned the greeting around a mouthful of Honey Smacks. Vivian, absently dipping a tea bag into a steaming mug, gave a distracted smile.

"You want breakfast, Ma?" Maggie asked, heading toward the refrigerator.

"No, dear, I'm not hungry."

"What about you, Brice?"

"I ate, Mom," the boy said without looking away from the TV screen.

Maggie pulled out some eggs and a carton of milk. "Come on, Ma," she insisted, turning back to Vivian. "You can't live on tea. How about some scrambled eggs?"

"Oh, no." Vivian shook her head. "Please don't go through the trouble."

"I'm making some for myself."

"Well . . ."

Knowing this would be the closest she'd get to an assent, Maggie proceeded to make breakfast. "You want any, sweetheart?" she asked her daughter, who shoved another spoonful of cereal into her mouth, then shook her head.

"Did you all sleep well?" Maggie asked, after the eggs and milk were mixed and poured into a pan.

"There are a lot of bugs around here," Toni complained.

"The bugs kept you up?" Maggie said, surprised.

"Well, not exactly. Thinking about them kept me up."

"Oh, sweetheart." Maggie restrained from smiling. Past experience had taught her not to take her daughter's fears or problems lightly, no matter how exaggerated they may seem. "The bugs are part of nature, but I'm sure there aren't any around here that would hurt you."

"Yeah, I suppose you're right. But I just

hate spiders." She shuddered, then lifted her bowl to her lips and drained the milk.

"What about you, Ma?" Maggie asked, turning back to her mother.

"What?" Vivian had been in deep thought, still dipping the tea bag into the tea.

"Did you sleep well?"

"Yes . . . as well as can be expected, I guess." She blinked, then looked over at the eggs cooking on the gas range. "Oh, dear, I must help you with that," she said, quickly rising.

"No, Ma. It's all right. I'll cook it."

"But I should help if I'm going to eat—"

"It's all right," Maggie repeated. "I want to cook." She smiled, hoping this would convince her.

The other woman hesitated, then sat back down. "I don't want to be a burden," she murmured.

Stop saying you are and you won't be! Maggie thought, but said nothing.

"I hope the weather turns out nice," Maggie said when her mother was back to dipping her tea bag. "You think the fog will burn off?"

"If it doesn't, what are we going to do?" This thought horrified Toni. "We won't be able to lay out in the sun or go swimming, although I'm not sure if I want to go in the water. God knows what kind of things live in there. Blood suckers, frogs. Snakes! God!" She shivered again.

"Maybe you shouldn't go in the water,"

Maggie agreed.

"Then why are we here, if we can't do anything?"

"Just so we could be together and be away from everything."

Toni stared at her, as though trying to grasp this. After a long pause, she sighed, shaking her head. "I don't know. I just don't know." Before coming here, she had pleaded with Maggie to have Lisa join them. Now she seemed to regret having done this. "I don't really mind, Mom," she whispered so that her friend wouldn't hear her, "but Lisa's gonna be bored out of her mind. What am I going to do? Lisa's popular. She's used to excitement."

"There's a rowboat tied to the wharf," Maggie said. "The two of you could go out and take turns rowing."

"Ah, Henry took me rowing when we were first married," Vivian said.

Toni and Maggie looked over at her. Vivian was staring past them, a wistful smile on her face. It was apparent that she wasn't talking to them, but to herself.

"Or you could play some games," Maggie said. "We brought along Trivial Pursuit, Scrabble, and playing cards."

"I guess," Toni said, unenthusiastically.

"You'll survive."

"Maybe I will, but"—Toni dropped her voice even lower—"will Lisa?"

"She'll survive, too," Maggie assured her.

"Noise," Vivian suddenly said.

Again Maggie and Toni looked at her, and this time found Vivian staring at them.

"What did you say, Ma?" Maggie asked, momentarily turning away to stir the eggs.

"Noise," Vivian repeated. "I heard a strange noise last night. Didn't any of you hear it?"

Maggie looked back at her. Up until now she had forgotten about the strange, high-pitched sound and the black object circling above the cottage. "Yes, I heard it. Keith and I both did."

"Heard what?" Toni asked, glancing at Vivian, then at Maggie.

"We decided it must have been the wind in the trees," Maggie said, not wanting to upset anyone.

But Vivian felt differently and said, "Wind in the trees doesn't make sounds like that. I should know. Henry and I stayed in a cabin during some windy nights, and I can assure you no wind ever sounded like that."

"Well, it's gone now," Maggie said firmly, hoping her mother would catch the abruptness in her voice and drop the subject. Already Toni's eyes were widening in a mixture of curiosity and burgeoning alarm.

Vivian, however, did not notice. She took a sip of her lukewarm tea, then set the cup down. "To be quite frank, dear, I was petrified, but I didn't want to bother you." She turned to Toni. "You heard nothing?"

Toni shook her head, eyes widening even more. "What did you hear?"

Maggie sighed. The alarm button had been pressed. "I don't know what it was, but whatever it was, it's now gone," she emphasized.

"I certainly hope so," Vivian said, "although, how can you be so sure?"

"Because I saw it go away," Maggie told her before she could stop herself.

"You *saw* it?" Tony immediately picked up on the word. "Saw what?"

Now both Toni and Vivian were staring at Maggie, waiting for an explanation. What could she tell them? She didn't even know what it was she'd seen. It had been something dark, camouflaged against the night sky. It had been something that moved. What on earth could she say that wouldn't upset them?

"Saw what?" Toni pressed, her voice rising.

"I . . . I don't know what it was, sweetheart."

"But you said you saw something. What did it look like?"

"It was dark," Maggie explained slowly. "It was hard to see. Maybe it was a plane near the house—"

"It didn't sound like a plane," Vivian interrupted.

Maggie shot her a look that said: Thanks for nothing, Ma! It was a look she quickly regretted, for Vivian turned pale and turned away.

"I'm sorry," the older woman murmured.

"I'm making trouble, aren't I? I didn't mean to—"

"No, Ma," Maggie assured her, suppressing an exasperated sigh. "It's all right. Really, it is."

"What did you see?" Toni demanded.

"I told you, I don't know. It could have been anything. Maybe it was a blimp. Maybe a large bird."

"A giant bird!" Toni gasped, eyes now the size of golf balls.

"I said large, not giant," Maggie clarified. "It probably was a hawk, or something like that."

Toni mulled this over, then said, "How come I didn't hear anything?"

"It wasn't loud, sweetheart. If you were asleep you wouldn't have heard it." To her mother, she said, "I'm surprised you heard it, Ma. You went to bed before all of us."

"Couldn't sleep."

Maggie turned back to the eggs on the stove. Now smoke was filling the pan.

"Dammit!" She'd burned the breakfast. Frantically, she tried to move the eggs around with a spatula, to keep them from sticking to the pan. It was useless. She lifted the pan from the stove and stood indecisively with it in her hand.

"What should I do with this?" There was simply no saving the eggs. She'd have to dump them somewhere and start fresh.

"I think I saw a garbage can out back somewhere," Toni said.

Gripping the smoking pan tighter, Maggie hurried out of the cottage.

Thick fog greeted her, momentarily startling her. The pan at the end of her extended arm was almost invisible. Was it like this at the lake every morning? Tentatively, she stepped forward into the gray, misty gloom. Would she ever find the garbage can in this murkiness?

After several steps, she stopped and looked back. The cottage behind her was shrouded in a mist. If she traveled another foot or so it would disappear completely. Not wanting this to happen, for it would just be her rotten luck to get lost, she followed the outside walls of the bungalow. Stepping over and skirting rhododendrons, laurels and broken tree limbs that hugged the house, she reached the corner and rounded it. More gloom sprawled before her. This was the side that faced the lake, but for the life of her she couldn't see the water. She heard a soft splash. A fish? Then a bird cried out from the gray depths, briefly startling her with its shrill, hollow sound. Then the bird was silent.

Everything was silent.

This is how one feels when one is blind and deaf, Maggie thought, suddenly feeling uneasy. Stillness was all around her, and each step was filled with uncertainty. Frequently, with her free hand, she touched the coarse, shingled surface of the cottage.

Where was the damn garbage can? Had

Toni only thought she'd seen one?

Once more she followed the length of the house and rounded a corner. Then her foot hit something metallic. Looking down, she could vaguely make out something circular, something gray like the surrounding fog. Stooping to investigate, she found it was the aluminum lid to the garbage can. She picked it up and continued to search for the can itself.

At last she found it, about five feet further on. She turned the frying pan upside down over the can and banged it against the rim until all the burnt eggs were shaken loose, then she covered the can with the lid.

The fog prevented her from seeing anything, except dark shadows and shapes. Vaguely she could make out tree trunks, then suddenly noticed there was something else—a dark bulk. She stared, straining to see more clearly.

The bird she had heard earlier shrieked again, this time farther away. Then the silence returned, seemingly thicker. Maggie took several steps toward the strange bulk in the fog, then stopped to stare intently at it again.

She wasn't sure, but the object she was looking at seemed to be halfway between the cottage and the forest. And it seemed rather large.

For a long moment Maggie didn't move. She couldn't decide whether to continue forward and satisfy her curiosity, or go back inside and wait for the fog to lift. But as she clutched the now empty frying pan, feeling its weaponlike solidness in her hand, she mustered up her courage and proceeded toward the dark object.

As she moved closer, the object became more visible. Its shape, she gradually saw, was cylindrical. Again she stopped, frowning in puzzlement. The cigar-shaped object was sitting horizontally. It looked to be about ten feet high and as wide as a yellow school bus.

Where had it come from?

Certainly she would have noticed it before. She had looked out all the windows many times yesterday. So there was no doubt that this thing had just come here during the night.

Gathering more courage, she moved closer. The fog swirled around the object, creating a disquieting, ghostly atmosphere. For the third time the damn bird pierced the silence with its startling cry. This time she heard its wings flap and knew it had finally decided to fly away.

Eventually she was close enough to touch the surface. The side facing her seemed to be smooth and metallic. Yes, she decided, this must be a bus. Then she noticed there were no windows—and no wheels.

She frowned. What was it? Some kind of tank, then? A giant gas tank? A missile?

Oh, God.

Her hand trembled, and the frying pan dropped to the ground. It made a soft thud as it landed on a bed of pine needles. She continued to stare at the object before her, wanting to touch it, yet afraid to do so. A voice inside her urged her to get away from here, but curiosity left her paralyzed.

Where did this missile come from? Had a truck deposited it here during the night? Had it dropped from the sky?

She recalled the noise she had heard last night. Was this thing before her what she had seen circling the cottage roof? As she studied it she grew more confident that it was.

She extended her hand to touch it, then changed her mind. Perhaps she should wait until she could see it better. She had no idea what she was dealing with here. What if mere contact should trigger something and blow it up?

This time she took a step back. No, she firmly decided. She did not know what she was dealing with. This was something she had never seen before, something unknown, and she found it alarming.

She hurried back to the cottage, not bothering to retrieve the pan.

CHAPTER THREE

Keith was up when Maggie ran back into the cottage. Clad only in pajama bottoms, he was leaning against the refrigerator, a cup of coffee in his hand. Lisa was up and sitting at the table with Toni and Vivian, covertly glancing at Keith's naked torso. She quickly looked away when Maggie burst into the room.

"What's the matter, honey?" Keith asked, seeing the alarm on Maggie's face. He set the coffee down on the counter, ready to pull her into his arms and calm her.

"There's . . . there's something strange out there, Keith."

"Like what?"

"I don't know. I-I couldn't see it too well because of the fog," she stammered.

"What's out there, Mom?" Brice asked, scrambling out of the sleeping bag to join the others. The retriever followed.

"What is it, Mom?" Toni asked, her voice unnaturally loud. Maggie knew she was alarming everyone, but she couldn't help herself. She didn't like what she'd seen outside, and she had an awful feeling about it, a feeling she couldn't mask.

She said, "It's something big. Something shaped like . . . like some kind of missile."

"Missile?" Keith frowned, a small incredulous laugh in his voice. "Come on, show me." He took a quick swallow of his coffee, then followed Maggie back outside. Everybody else joined them.

Pale, gray fog enveloped the group. Toni and Lisa clutched each other's hands, and when Toni bumped into her father ahead of her she emitted a startled gasp. Then she giggled as she realized how silly her reaction had been. Brice kept a firm grip on his dog's collar. "Stay near me," he commanded, not wanting to lose him in the thick mist. Behind them, Vivian kept at a distance, one hand on the coarse siding of the cottage as she walked gingerly forward.

"How come it's so foggy?" Brice asked no one in particular.

"Because of the warm weather and the lake, I guess," Maggie answered. Then she fell silent as she tried to remember exactly where she had found the object.

"Mornings are creepy around here, aren't they?" Toni remarked. When no one answered, she too became silent.

At length they reached the spot. The object was still there, most of it concealed in the fog. No one could perceive its entire bulk at once. When one stood at the front, the rear faded out of sight, and when one stood at the center of the horizontal cylinder, both ends disappeared. If one stood far back, hoping to absorb its entire shape, it couldn't be seen at all. It became just a vague shadow in the gloom.

"What do you think it is?" Maggie whispered to her husband.

He didn't answer. Instead, he touched its surface, first with a finger, then pressing his palm against it.

"Don't!" Maggie cried. He ignored her, running his hand across the object.

"Metal," he commented. "And it's warm."

"Warm?"

"Yeah, like . . ." Keith replied slowly, "like the hood of a car that's been running awhile."

"You think maybe this is a vehicle of some kind?"

"Could be."

"Then you don't think it's a missile?"

"Who knows what it is," Keith said frankly, then left her side to follow the length of the puzzling object.

Maggie walked beside him. At first she

made certain that her hands, as well as the rest of her body, did not come in contact with the metallic surface. She was uneasy about touching something she knew nothing about, something she could not fully see. As Keith continued to explore its contours, however, her curiosity conquered her trepidation. Tentatively, she touched the object.

As Keith had said, it was warm. Also, she found the metallic cylinder smooth and slippery, as though highly waxed. She let only her fingertips make contact, then pulled her hand back. She wished the fog would lift.

"Why don't we come back later," she suggested, "after—"

"No doors, no windows," he remarked, cutting her off. "So I guess that rules out a vehicle."

"Keith, did you hear what I said?"

"Yeah, I heard." But he continued to feel the surface.

Toni caught up to Maggie. "Mom, what is it?"

"We don't know, sweetheart."

"'Y' think it's a nuclear weapon? Think it's— a bomb? Think it could blow—"

"You're scaring yourself needlessly," Maggie told her, wishing she could reassure herself the very same way. "I doubt very much if this is a bomb or a missile."

"Wow!" Brice exclaimed as he reached the object.

"Don't touch!" Maggie ordered.

"Then what is it?" Toni demanded.

"Maggie!" Vivian's voice, shaky and fearful, suddenly cried out in the fog. "Maggie, I can't see you!"

"Over here, Ma." Judging from the direction and distance of her mother's voice, she could tell the woman was clinging to the cottage.

"What are you all doing?" Vivian asked. "What is that over there? I can't make it out too good."

"We don't know yet, Ma," Maggie replied as patiently as she could. She wished she had insisted that everyone, except Keith, stay in the house. She hadn't wanted to alarm anyone, especially prematurely, but she had reacted hastily.

Vivian, as if aware of her daughter's thoughts, suddenly stated, "I'm going back into the house. I don't like it out here."

Maggie turned to the others. "Why don't you all go back with her."

"Aw, Mom," Brice whined, "I wanna see what this—"

"Please," Maggie added, her tone demanding obedience.

The boy groaned, then said to his dog, "Come on, Commander, let's go."

Maggie waited, listening to the sounds of footsteps receding into silence, then turned back toward Keith and the metallic object.

"Look," Keith said. "I found something interesting. There are grooves here and there. You can't see them, but you can feel them. Here, put your hand over this and you'll be able to trace an outline."

"No," she said. "I'll take your word for it."

"Hmm. Interesting. I think these are outlines of windows or doors. Maybe this is a vehicle, after all. Maybe these doors or windows slide open."

Maggie felt a chilly breeze. She pulled her robe closer at the neck, then crossed her arms tightly over her stomach. "I'm cold, Keith. Let's go back into the house."

"But I thought you wanted to find out what this thing is."

"I do, but I think we should wait until the fog lifts."

"No harm in doing a little investigating now. A little fog never hurt anybody."

There was that faint chuckle in his voice, and Maggie knew he was mocking her again, letting her know she was overreacting.

Didn't he realize that the windows and doors could open at any time? You don't know what you're dealing with here, she wanted to shout at him. Something could be inside this thing. And something could—

A sound froze her thoughts. It was a slow hiss, a sound of something sliding, a sound of something opening.

"Keith!" Instinctively, she reached for his hand and yanked it away from the metallic surface. She struggled to pull him back with her.

But he was slow to react. He stared dumbly at the spot where his hand had been and watched in awe as a gap developed on the otherwise featureless surface. At first it was a thin black line, about two feet in width. Then the line thickened, gradually rose to a square, then to a rectangular orifice.

"Keith!" Maggie shouted again, and at last he responded. He broke away and joined Maggie who was frantically waiting at a slight distance.

Together they stared at the new opening, which was an ebony mouth in the midst of the swirling grayness.

Was something about to come out?

Was this some kind of alien vessel? Was this actually a UFO?

Maggie's hand rose to her lips, as though in slow motion. She couldn't believe what she was seeing. UFOs didn't exist, she told herself. They were only something that science fiction writers had dreamed up in the forties and fifties. This thing before her had to be something else. But what?

What was inside?

Aliens?

Suddenly there was so many things Maggie wanted to do. She wanted to laugh at her crazy thoughts, and at the same time scream. She wanted to hold on to Keith, and she wanted to run back to the cottage. But she did none of these things; a sense of wonder and fear kept her mesmerized.

She and Keith waited.

They'd have time to run, Maggie told herself. They weren't really in danger—not yet.

Nothing stirred inside the dark opening. Why weren't there any lights? And why wasn't anyone—or anything—coming out to greet them? That was how they did it in those old science fiction movies, wasn't it?

Then with sudden, chilling certainty Maggie knew the answer. Whoever or whatever was in there was watching her and Keith. They were hiding in the dark and were watching.

"Keith . . ." She could barely speak. " . . . let's get out of here."

He ignored her, too fascinated with the thing before him.

She reached for his hand, but he didn't let her pull him away. His feet were firmly rooted.

"Please . . ." Fear was not coated with wonder anymore; it was naked and raw. "Come on."

It was a long moment before he responded. "Aren't you curious?" he asked.

"I'm scared is what I am, Keith."

Again he ignored her. He continued to stare at the opening, then to Maggie's disbelief began to move toward it.

"Keith!" She tried to pull him back, but he was stronger and too determined. Her hand slid loose. "Keith, for heaven's sake, you don't know what this thing is!"

"I just want to see it better, that's all."

But as he took another step forward, the opening began to diminish. The top half dropped smoothly, and quickly, until it was again a thin line. Keith stopped in surprise. The line, no more than two inches in thickness, remained this way for a long moment, as though something from within were peeking out, then the dark band disappeared altogether.

Keith was stunned and looked back at Maggie. "What the hell was that, you think?"

"Somebody—something—is in there. And I think we should get out of here!"

Keith looked back at the now featureless object, then again at Maggie. He nodded decisively and started toward her. "Yeah, you're right. Let's go."

He hurried ahead of her, and Maggie tried to catch up. When she reached the cottage, Keith was already on the phone, dialing. The others in the room could see he was upset, and they infectiously became alarmed. They watched him for a second, then looked questioningly at Maggie.

"What happened, Mom?" Toni asked. "What's going on?"

Be calm, Maggie told herself, be calm.

She gently shook her head, silently telling everyone there was nothing to worry about, but she knew no one was convinced. The fear was evident in her face.

"Great!" Keith shouted, then slammed the receiver down. "Just like in an old clichéd movie—the line's dead!"

Maggie hurried to his side. Somehow she'd have to calm him down, keep him from getting out of control. He was scaring the others.

"Easy, Keith," she whispered, so that only he would hear her. "Let's not lose our heads, all right?"

He glared at her, as though she had insulted him, then he sighed, nodding. "Yeah, right," he said, rubbing his forehead. "Christ, honey, what the hell do you think that thing is out there? Some kind of UFO?"

"UFO?" Brice exclaimed. "You're kidding!"

"I don't know," Maggie replied, "and I don't care. I think we should just pack up our things and leave."

Wordlessly, Keith went into Vivian's bedroom and looked out the window. The fog was still too thick. "In a way I'd like to see that thing when it's clearer," he said when Maggie joined him.

"But it could be dangerous." Maggie kept her voice low.

"I know," he agreed, "but that still doesn't stop me from being curious. Aren't you curious at all?"

She remembered she hadn't run when the strange cylinder had opened; she had remained frozen. Why? Curiosity? "Yes," she admitted reluctantly, "but—"

"You're afraid," he finished knowingly. "And so am I. So let's get the hell out of here."

Before she could respond he was out of the room, throwing an empty suitcase onto the bed in the master bedroom. "Everybody start packing!" he ordered.

Vivian, Brice and the girls seemed confused, standing in the large living area. When they turned to Maggie, wondering if she would confirm the command, she gave them a nod.

Keith was the first to finish and was the first in the car. "Come on, hurry up!" he shouted impatiently to the others. The fog was beginning to lift. Part of the lake could be seen, but not the shore on the opposite side. When everyone was finally in the car, he gunned the engine and shot forward.

"Great vacation," he muttered as he maneuvered the car down the narrow, gravelly driveway. Tree limbs from the sides slapped violently against the vehicle.

Maggie was tempted to tell him to slow down, but she remained silent, not wanting to upset him more than he already was. She turned around and looked out the rear window. From the back seat the others did likewise. The fog shrouded most of the view, but they could make out the cottage—and the strange thing near it.

They don't go together, Maggie thought. The cottage looks old, wooden and cozy, and the object looks futuristic, metallic and cold. Now she wished Keith would hurry faster. The sooner everyone was away from this scene, the better.

Maggie turned her head back to the front, and as she did so, she felt a powerful jolt and let out a startled cry. Then she experienced an explosion of pain as her head slammed against the windshield.

After the impact, a series of thoughts ran through her mind as she covered her face in agony. We shouldn't have been going so fast! We should have known better than to rush in such a fog! We should have known better than to speed when there are so many trees around us.

But when Maggie dropped her hands from her face, she didn't see any trees before her. She couldn't see anything at all.

So what on earth had the car hit?

CHAPTER FOUR

"What happened?" Maggie asked, dazed. Already her head was beginning to pound. Though in a hazy cloud of pain, she managed to turn around to see if everyone else was unharmed. Brice was clutching his dog, hiding half of his fearful face in the animal's fur. The teenage girls seemed frightened, hands over their mouths as though to stifle their gasps, and Vivian was rubbing the back of her neck, her face ashen.

"Ma, are you okay?" Maggie asked.

Vivian made an attempt to smile, but faltered. "I—I'll be fine, dear."

"You hurt your neck, didn't you?"

"I've been hurt worse. Now don't you start fretting about me." She ceased rubbing and looked around her. "What on earth happened?"

Maggie, who had asked the same question, could not answer her. She checked the girls and her son again, and when she saw that they were shaken but not hurt, she turned her attention to Keith. He was already out of the car, investigating the cause of the accident.

At first Maggie couldn't believe what she was seeing and blamed it on her hazy vision. She closed her eyes to clear it, but when she looked again she saw that nothing had changed. For a fleeting moment Keith reminded her of a mime she'd once seen performing on a sidewalk. The mime had pretended to be trapped behind an invisible wall and was searching for an exit.

Maggie stared, still unable to believe what she was seeing. Was Keith playing games? Why was he behaving like that mime? His palms were flat against an invisible surface, pressing and roaming.

"Keith, what are you doing?" Maggie finally got out of the car, followed by the others. "Keith?" she called again.

As usual, he ignored her when he was preoccupied. His countenance, she noted, was that of bafflement, while his hands continued to explore what looked like a flat surface.

Haltingly she walked up to him, then stopped as though suddenly afraid to go any further. She didn't like this; it was all too damn bizarre. Keith was not playing games.

He had no reason to. The car, she saw, was damaged. The front bumper, the grille and the headlights were crushed, folded and flattened against—air?

The pounding in Maggie's head intensified. She pressed her palms against her skull as if to still the horrible throbbing.

"Keith?" she repeated, this time in a faint, sickly whisper.

At last he responded, dropping his hands and stepping back toward her. When he turned around, she saw not only wonder in his face but panic as well. A nerve pulsed at his jaw.

"Well, what is it?" she demanded softly, inwardly bracing herself. "What did we hit?"

He stepped aside. "See for yourself."

She hesitated, then slowly moved forward. As she walked, she could feel the others watching her, experiencing the same sense of confusion and fear that she was feeling. Her steps were small, as though she were stalling, playing for time, but within seconds she found the answer to her question.

Her left toe hit something, abruptly stopping her. Then, as if refusing to accept what had just happened, she brought her other foot forward. It made a soft thud as it slammed into something solid, something invisible.

Still unwilling to accept this, she reached out, fingers splayed, palm open. She touched a flat surface. Next, she did the same with her other hand and again touched something.

She pressed, first gently, then firmly, but she couldn't move forward. It was as though she were pushing at a wall of glass.

"What is it, Mr. Hunter?" she heard Lisa ask her husband, her voice shaky.

"I don't know," Keith said. "It seems to be some kind of shield."

"Shield? What do you mean shield?" Lisa's voice rose, panicking.

He didn't answer her, his hands probing the invisible barrier. The transparent wall rose higher than he could reach, even on tiptoes, and it extended to both sides of him. It threaded the trees and continued upward in a gradual curve.

"It's all around us, isn't it?" Toni said, her voice also shrill with fear. She and her friend clutched each other's hand as they watched Keith and Maggie. The retriever sniffed at the barrier while Brice explored its surface. Vivian remained close to the car in stunned silence.

"I don't know if it's all around us," Maggie answered when it was apparent that Keith wasn't going to reply.

"We're trapped, aren't we?" Toni asked.

"Sweetheart, let's not jump to—"

"We *are* trapped!"

Toni's eyes quickly filled with tears, and her chin began to quiver. Seeing this, Maggie hurried over to the girls and wrapped her arms around both of them. "You're panicking needlessly," she said. The girls seemed grateful, for they leaned against her.

"I'm sure we'll find a way out, and I'm sure it's not as bad as it appears."

Peering past the top of their bent heads, Maggie watched Keith continue his exploration. He was now on his knees, digging at the base of the transparent shield. Brice and the dog were doing the same in another area.

Vivian still hadn't moved from the car.

"You sure you're all right, Ma?" Maggie asked.

"What?" It took her a moment to realize someone was speaking to her. "Oh . . . yes. Yes."

Maggie appraised her, wanting to be sure she was not too frightened or on the verge of a heart attack. When she was somewhat convinced that her mother, indeed, was all right, she returned her attention to the girls in her arms. One of them was sniffling and beginning to wipe her eyes.

"Everything's going to be fine, you'll see," Maggie reassured them, wishing she herself were more certain. When she felt the teenagers were at last in control of themselves, she dropped her arms and went over to Keith.

"What do you think?" she asked.

He looked at her as though she had asked the stupidest question he'd ever heard. "What do you mean what do I think?"

She forced herself to ignore his caustic tone, telling herself he was understandably fighting panic. "What kind of shield is this?

What do you think it's made of? Why do you think it's here?"

"How should I know?"

"You think it's been here all along?"

"Nothing was blocking the driveway when we arrived," he reminded her.

Of course, how stupid of me, she thought. Her own struggle to keep terror from surfacing was clouding her mind, causing her to ask foolish questions. "So this took place after we came here." She looked over at the cottage and the cigar-shaped object beside it. Fog still swirled around it, but she could see most of its metallic surface. It was as dull as the surrounding air. Was the dark entrance open? she suddenly wondered. Were they being watched?

"This happened during the night, and that thing over there is responsible," she said with sudden, sickening certainty.

"Brilliant."

She gave him a sharp look. Why did he have to be so sarcastic? Was he blaming her for this?

He caught and understood the look. "Sorry," he muttered.

She nodded faintly, accepting the apology. "Did you find any opening at all?"

"No. I tried to dig a little to see if I could make a tunnel under it, but as soon as I made a space the air . . . well, hardened. Weirdest thing. It's as if each hole I'd made was like a bowl or mold. It instantly filled up and turned to plastic."

"Plastic?"

"Something like it." He knocked at what looked like empty air, but his knuckles made a sharp, rapping sound. "Something damn strong." He kicked at the shield with his foot. "As strong as metal, I bet," he added.

"But so transparent," she said incredulously.

"If you really study it, you can see it." He tilted his head upward, tacitly urging her to do the same.

Maggie complied and soon discovered he was right. At certain angles she could discern the plasticlike shield above her. It seemed to curve in an arch, not above the trees but through them as though they didn't exist. The transparency of this shield, however, was almost absolute, for whenever Maggie shifted her eyes she'd lose sight of the shield and would have to experiment with various angles before she could find it again.

The shield reminded her of an inverted bowl.

"Keith, what do you think is the reason for this?"

He looked at her, but said nothing. Then without a word he started toward the cottage.

"Keith, where are you going?" Why did he have to do things so impulsively?

"To see if the phone's working now," he said over his shoulder.

Maggie glanced over at the others. Brice was still fascinated with the shield, apparently more curious than fearful. Vivian and the girls were watching Maggie, but they seemed all right—no sign of hysteria—no heart attack. Satisfied, she rushed to catch up with Keith.

Back inside the cottage, Keith tried to phone again, and again found it not functioning. "Dammit!" He slammed the receiver down. "Of all the fucking time for it to quit!"

"Maybe it never worked," Maggie said. "Maybe it was down before we even came here."

Keith wasn't listening to her; his attention was on the small refrigerator at the other side of the room. "Damn quiet, haven't you noticed?" he said, heading straight for the appliance.

Maggie frowned, puzzled. When he yanked the old refrigerator open, it suddenly dawned on her what he was saying. The appliance had been noisy when they first had arrived, humming and rattling loudly. Now no sound at all was coming from it.

"Thought so!" Keith said. The light inside the appliance was out. Furiously, he slammed the door shut; it scarcely made a sound as it kissed the rubbery seal. "The power is off!"

"But it was on when I made breakfast."

"Well, it's not on now," he snapped at her.

Maggie rubbed her arms, as though to warm them and at the same time smooth away the goosebumps. She couldn't blame Keith for being upset and angry. This was how he usually reacted whenever he was frustrated and scared. Anger was his outlet, but she wished he wouldn't direct it at her.

"Please, we've got to be calm about this," she pleaded. "If we don't, the others will panic."

"What do you think they are—stupid? They already know we've got a problem here."

"Yes, but if we stay reasonably calm, they probably will, too. But if we get hysterical, so will they."

Keith said nothing for a moment, but his eyes burned into hers. It couldn't have been more obvious if he verbally told her that this was all her fault.

"And we've got to think calmly," she added, turning away from his disdainful gaze.

"Miss cool, calm and collected." He sneered. "You try to get us out of this calmly. Me, I'm going to find out why the hell the phone and the power are out."

Once again he was outside, abruptly leaving Maggie behind. This time she didn't hurry to catch up, for she needed a moment alone. Her composure was slipping, the panic surfacing. She hugged herself and squeezed her eyes shut. Please God, help us. You must help us.

Keeping her eyes closed, she tried to will peace into her body. Mentally, she commanded her muscles to relax and her heart to slow its beat. No matter how hard she tried, though, she couldn't rid herself of the feeling she was trapped.

"Hey, Maggie!" Keith shouted from outside. "C'mere!"

Maggie's eyes sprung open as hope surged through her. When she saw Keith's grim face, however, her hope vanished. His head was tilted back, looking at something near the roof of the cottage.

Maggie followed his gaze as he said, "Something happened to the wires on the house." It was true, for she could see that two wires had been disconnected and were dangling loosely against the side of the cottage. The wires, she noted, hadn't been severed cleanly; the tips were melted blobs, as though something had seared them.

She looked questioningly at Keith.

"Our friend or friends in that thing over there didn't use clippers," he said dryly.

"What did it—they—use, you think?"

He gave her another how-the-hell-should-I-know look, then, as though suddenly aware he was being too hostile, muttered, "Beats me."

"What does this mean?" a voice suddenly asked behind them. It was Vivian, and beside her were the two teenagers, still clutching each other.

Maggie opened her mouth slowly, wanting to find the right words, the gentlest words, but Keith beat her to it.

"It means we've got no phone or electricity," he said bluntly.

Maggie closed her mouth, pulling in her

lower lip and biting it. She wouldn't have spoken so callously if given the chance, but the damage was done. Fear was growing rapidly now on Vivian's and the girls' faces.

Maggie looked around for Brice, who was at the cylinder, touching its surface.

"Brice! Get away from there!"

Quickly, he dropped his hand.

"Come over here!" Maggie demanded.

Reluctantly, he obeyed.

"You mean . . ." Vivian began in a faint voice " . . . we're forced to stay here?"

"Yeah, something like that," Keith replied.

Maggie shot him a cold glance, wanting desperately to silence him, but he ignored her.

"But why?" Vivian asked. "I don't understand. What is happening?"

"Ma, take it easy," Maggie urged gently. "I'm sure we'll find a way out of here." Brice reached the group. "And you, young man. I want you to stay away from that thing, at least until we know more about it."

"But Mom, how can we get to know more about it if we don't go near it?"

"Did you hear what I said?"

"Yeah, Mom." He pouted, dropping his head.

"Is the barrier all around us?" Vivian asked.

"We don't know for sure."

"Why is there a barrier?" Vivian's voice rose, cracking.

"We don't know," Maggie answered as

calmly as she could, stroking her son's hair. "But we're not going to panic. We're going to keep our heads. Right, dear?" She turned to Keith as she said this, her tone sharp, demanding agreement.

"Yeah, right. We gotta keep our heads here," he said disgruntledly.

"But what are we gonna do without the phone or electricity?" Toni asked, her eyes still wide and fearful.

"We're going to make the best of it. That's what we're going to do," Maggie replied. "We've got a gas stove, canned food, and a manual can opener." She managed a reassuring smile. "Yes, we'll make do."

Later that morning when Keith was alone with Maggie on the porch, he said, "If it weren't for you, we wouldn't be in this goddamn mess."

The remark momentarily stunned her, then his words began to infuriate her. "Me? What about you? You're the one who . . . who . . ."

"What I did has nothing to do with us being inside this fishbowl."

"It has everything to do with it! We came here to sort everything out, to be together!"

"We're together now."

"Damn you, Keith, you're not being fair." Tears threatened to fill her eyes, but with determination she willed them away. "I was trying to save our marriage. I thought a peaceful vacation would help. It would be what we desperately needed. How was I to know something freaky like this would happen?"

She stared at him, waiting for an answer, but he avoided looking at her, a dark scowl on his face. He gazed unseeingly at the driveway ahead of him. The car was still where it had come to an unexpected halt, a short distance away.

Damn, damn, damn! she thought. Why couldn't he comfort her, and she comfort him? They were in this together, so why couldn't they fight it together?

At length she got up from the aluminum patio chair and started toward the front door. Before she could reach it, she felt his hand on hers.

"I'm sorry," he said, now looking up at her from his chair. His dark eyes pleaded for forgiveness.

"You've been saying that all day."

"I know, and this time I mean it." He pulled her toward the empty chair beside him. "Sit down. Stay close to me. Please."

This sensitive side surprised her. She stood uncertainly, then let herself return to the chair.

"I really am sorry," he said again. He wrapped his arm around her, and after a brief hesitation she leaned her head against his shoulder.

"I don't know why I keep hurting you," he said, his voice deep yet soft. "Please forgive me, honey."

The tears that Maggie had been fighting to repress started to spill. She made no move to wipe them, not wanting to bring attention to them. She let herself cry silently.

"Do you forgive me?" he asked.

She nodded against his shoulder.

After a moment, he added, "I got angry at you because . . . well, I'm scared."

"I know. I'm scared, too. We're all scared." Maggie paused.

"Keith?"

"Yeah, hon?"

"What do you think is going to happen?"

"I don't know. It looks like we're going to have to wait and see."

CHAPTER FIVE

Keith spent the rest of the morning and part of the afternoon in search of a break or opening in the transparent shield. The fog had eventually lifted, and now the sun glared in a blue, cloudless sky. The day turned uncomfortably warm, the domelike shield trapping and containing the heat in a greenhouse manner. Sweat ran in rivulets down Keith's naked back and dripped into his eyes from his brow, but he refused to stop. He was determined to find a gap somewhere.

He had followed the barrier on land. The shield was definitely circular, evenly bordering the cottage and the cylindrical vessel. He had tried to penetrate the barrier with his car, strapping himself securely with the safety belt, but it was as though he were trying to break through a concrete embankment. He only caused more damage to the car while getting nowhere with the barrier. With his hand he had touched the surface where the car had hit and found the area still smooth, free of any indentations.

Now there was the water and the sky left to explore. Not in the mood to climb trees in the debilitating heat, he chose the lake. He lowered himself into the boat that was tethered to the wharf and rowed straight out.

Although he could not see the shield, especially in the harsh sunlight, he knew almost exactly where it would be. The barrier was about 200 feet away from the cottage on land, and since the barrier seemed to be a perfect circle, it would be 200 feet away from the cottage on the lake. So when he suspected he was nearing the 200 mark, he slowed, slicing through the dark water gently.

As he expected, the boat bumped against the invisible shield. The boat fell back, drifted forward, then bumped again. Keith rowed toward another section, toward the right. Once more he came to a gentle but firm halt. This time he let go of the oars and leaned over the boat, arms extended. His hands touched the smooth shield, but they could not press against it without pushing the boat and himself away. Unlike the firm footing on land, it was impossible to remain in any one spot and explore. Most of the time was spent drifting away from and rowing to the barrier.

After 20 frustrating minutes of this, Keith decided to continue the search underwater. Maybe the shield did not extend beneath the surface. But after diving into the water he discovered that the transparent wall descended to the lake's bottom, some 10 feet below.

Underwater, he pressed against the shield, momentarily flattening his face while his hair billowed like an undulating cloud about his head. Now more than ever, he felt like a fish in a bowl, and this realization triggered a fresh rush of terror. How long would he be confined this way, circling a see-through prison?

He pushed both hands against the shield while his legs kicked desperately in the water. Then, as though he'd been too engrossed to remember he was in an airless environment, he shot toward the surface in a frantic need to breathe. The instant he broke surface he let out a violent gasp, then collapsed, clinging to the side of the boat and panting laboriously. He waited until his breathing was again normal, then he struggled back into the boat, almost capsizing it. He began to row back to the shore, too exhausted to resume the search. Right now he could use a can of beer.

When he reached land, the beer was forgotten. From the shore he could see a portion of the metallic cylinder. A dark entrance was partly opened.

It was not the same opening he had seen earlier, but another one at another section of the cylinder. But once more the opening was directly facing him—and watching him?

Absently, Keith tied the boat to the wharf while he kept his eyes on the black entrance. He stood at the end of the wharf for a long time, trying to grasp what was happening. Here, at this slight distance, he felt it was somewhat safer to study the object.

Nothing moved. The water behind and on each side of him had gently slapped against the wharf when the boat came in but was now motionless. There was no sound and no wind. Dimly, Keith knew this was because of the surrounding shield which seemed to make everything stagnant.

What do you want? his mind shouted as he stared at the object, which was no longer dull like pewter but gleaming like polished chrome under the sun. In contrast, the opening was a stark, ebony square.

Why are you here?

The square continued to watch him.

Keith found himself trying to outstare it, slightly lifting his chin and tightening his lips in defiance. When he realized he was foolishly trying to outstare an inanimate object, he looked away. It would be best to ignore it, he told himself. Maybe it would go away.

And for a minute he succeeded. He glanced

back at the boat to make sure it was tied securely to the wharf, when he looked upward at the sky, shielding his eyes from the sun with his forearm. He tried to discern the shield's domelike shape, but the sun was too bright. He saw a bird in flight and wondered if the small creature was inside or outside the barrier. The question was promptly answered as the bird crashed into the shield and slid down an invisible slope toward the water. The bird had been flying toward Keith, thus was outside the barrier.

Keith stared dully at the limp bird, which was now floating in the water, then he slowly looked back at the black, gaping cavity in the metallic object. His mouth was dry, although his body was drenched in sweat.

He saw something.

He blinked, and the something disappeared. What had it been? He kept his gaze riveted to the opening, waiting for it—whatever it was—to recur. After a few minutes, he saw it again.

It was a faint flash of light, greenish-yellow in color. This time there were two flashes, a beat apart. Frowning, he waited to see it again. To his disappointment, the opening began to shrink, dwindling to a thin line before disappearing completely.

Jesus, what had he just seen?

He continued to gawk at the silver hull for a moment longer, until something in the periphery of his vision distracted him. He turned his head and was surprised to find

Lisa at the end of the wharf, watching him. She was hugging herself and shivering. Although she was clad in cut-off jeans and a skimpy top that covered only her breasts, Keith knew this was not why she was shaking. She, too, had caught a glimpse of the glinting light inside the cylinder.

"What do you think that was inside, Mr. Hunter?" she asked when she realized she had his attention.

Keith's eyes took in the curves of her hips in the tight cut-offs. Then they rose to her tiny waist and then to her breasts which, bunched together between her arms, were large—especially for a 14-year-old. She was more woman than kid, except when you looked at her face.

"Mr. Hunter?"

"I'm sorry. What did you say?" He started toward her, at the same time chiding himself for his sexual thoughts.

"What do you think that was inside there?" she repeated.

"I've no idea."

"None at all, Mr. Hunter?" Her eyes were large and fearful—and a pretty shade of green, the color of grass.

"Please don't call me that," Keith said. "It sounds too formal. Call me Keith . . . Lisa."

"Keith," the girl said, complying readily, "what do you think is gonna happen to us? Think it'll be something bad?"

"I wish I knew. But whatever is inside that thing is either shy or just doesn't want to be sociable," he said, making an attempt at humor.

But Lisa only hugged herself tighter, squeezing her breasts closer. "I feel so alone, Mr. Hun—I mean, Keith. You've got your family, but I'm not part of it. I'm alone, and . . . I'm scared." She began to cry, raising her hands to bury her face.

"Hey, everything's going to be all right." He wanted to pull her into his arms and stop her from crying, but he wasn't sure how she'd respond to his embrace. "If we ignore it, it might go away, Lisa. Maybe it just wants to see us squirm and panic. If we show no reaction, maybe it'll get bored with us and go someplace else."

"You really think so?" She lifted her face from her hands.

Keith's mind replied "No," but he nodded as he watched a tear slide down her youthful face. Sexy face, he thought. Once again he was filled with an urge to soothe this girl in his arms. He cleared his throat and said strongly, "Yes, I do."

Their eyes locked. Except for their breathing, there was silence. Lisa stepped closer.

"What if . . . what if you're wrong?" she said.

"Then . . ." his voice drifted away. He had no answer to give her. Lord only knew what would happen, what was in store for them.

Fresh tears blurred the girl's green eyes. "Oh Mr. Hunter, I'm . . . I'm so scared."

"Keith," he said.

"What?"

Gently, he put a hand on her shoulder. "Keith. Call me Keith," he reminded her.

"Oh." She didn't flinch or pull away from his touch. "Keith, I'm scared," she repeated.

He tenderly clutched her other shoulder, waited a bit, giving her a chance to reject him, then drew her closer.

"Don't be afraid," he said softly. "I wouldn't let anyone or anything hurt you."

She felt warm and soft against his bare chest, her tension gradually relaxing.

"I don't want to be alone," he heard her say as he concentrated on the feel of her shapely, youthful body against his.

She made him feel ten—no, 20—years younger.

From inside the cottage Maggie watched her husband and the teenage girl. As the couple drew closer she experienced a tightness around her heart even though there was no reason to be upset at what she was seeing. If anything, she should be proud of her husband, for the poor girl was obviously frightened and Keith was doing his best to comfort her.

Maggie pushed herself away from the window. Would she ever forget that night when she had found Keith in bed with that woman? If only she hadn't come home early that night. Toni and Brice had been at their grandmother's; they visited her almost every

evening since their grandfather died.
Business had been slow, and she had had a
headache that wouldn't go away. She had
called the owner and had received
permission to lock up the store an hour
early. She had planned to make herself a cup
of tea and go straight to bed. She had the
shock of her life when she found someone
else in her bed—a stranger, a woman much
younger than she, a woman prettier than she.

God, please let her forget. Maybe time
would eventually turn it into a hazy memory,
or would it always be vivid like this?

She must learn to control her thoughts.
Most of the pain was mental, and if she could
control her mind, she'd also control the pain.
It was rather simple, wasn't it?

And besides, she reminded herself, there
was something else to worry about,
something more important and urgent. This
was no time to be weak. She was sure that
everybody was in danger here.

And it was her fault that everyone was in
this predicament. It was she who had
insisted on this stupid vacation.

The dog pushed his nose against Brice's
arm, whimpering softly.

"Mom, Commander's gotta go to the
bathroom," Brice said. Without waiting for
an answer, he jumped up off the couch and
headed for the front door. The retriever
followed him.

"Wait," Maggie called to him from the

kitchen table. "Where are you going?"

"I told you where. Commander's gotta go to—"

"Can't he go alone?"

"He never did before. I always walked him."

Maggie looked worried. She glanced at the others in the room; each seemed to be lost in his or her own thoughts. The sun was sinking rapidly now, creating lengthy shadows. "Well . . ."

"Aw, come on, Mom. I'll only be gone a minute."

"All right. But be quick about it."

Brice went outside, shaking his head. How the heck could he be quick about it? It was up to the dog.

The dog immediately sprinted ahead of him, stopped to sniff at the base of an oak, then bolted onward.

"Hey, don't go too far!" Brice shouted.

The moment the words left his lips, the retriever hit the invisible barrier. The dog seemed momentarily stunned, then it crept closer to the barrier and began scratching at it.

"Piss on it," Brice said, then turned toward the cylinder about 40 yards away. He knew he should be afraid, yet he wasn't. He was too curious about the object and the transparent dome it had created. Did this thing come from another planet, another galaxy, or was it from the future?

Yeah, maybe that's it, Brice thought as he

moved toward the cylinder. It's a time capsule. He bet somebody was inside it right now, somebody from the year 3000.

After covering 20 yards, he looked at the cottage. Nobody was looking out the windows. He looked back at Commander, who was watering a bush.

Brice crept closer toward the cylinder. Close enough to touch it, he studied the surface. He wanted to run his hand across it, but suddenly lacked the courage. The cylinder seemed to be aware of his presence, aware that he was alone, and it seemed to be waiting. Or was this only in his head?

"Commander, c'mere!"

The retriever looked over at Brice, hesitated a beat, then bounded toward him. Brice dropped to his knees and wrapped his arm around the animal's neck. Immediately he felt better and braver.

"What do you think of this, Commander?"

The dog licked his face.

"No, Commander. This." He turned the dog's head toward the silver object.

The dog drew back.

"What's the matter?"

The dog whimpered.

Brice held him tighter, not wanting him to run off and leave him alone.

"Do you think it's from another world? Or from another time zone?"

A growl rose from somewhere deep inside the dog, his lips pulled back.

"Hey, what—" Brice loosened his grip on

him.

Before the dog could do anything more, a partition slid upward on the cylinder's surface and light shot forward. Like lightning, the bolt of light was rapid and blinding. To Brice, the world had suddenly turned white and bright. Though everything seemed to be in slow motion, it all was happening too quickly for him to respond. He heard Commander yelp, and he knew the dog was beside him, still in his grip. Also, it occurred to him that if his dog was being struck by lightning, the electricity would surge through him, too, but nothing like this happened.

Then, as fast as it had begun, it was over. The world was no longer blinding with white light. The surface of the cylinder was as before—unbroken. The only thing different now was—

"Commander!"

Brice frantically looked around him. Where was the dog? Had the object taken him?

"Commander!"

He was panicking, screaming hysterically. He couldn't help it; he was sure they had taken his dog. He pounded at the cylinder. "Give me back my dog! Give me back my dog!"

Something was pulling him back. He wrenched himself loose and continued hammering at the cylinder.

"Stop it, Brice!" his father was shouting.

This time Brice couldn't pull himself away. His father was holding him firmly and was half-carrying and half-dragging him back toward the cottage.

"What on earth were you doing?" Maggie demanded.

"They took Commander, Mom. He's inside that thing!"

"Why were you banging on it like that?"

"Because they've got him in there. Mom, Dad, we gotta get him back!"

"Take it easy, son," Keith said. "We don't know what we're dealing with yet."

Inside the cottage, Keith locked the door.

"But Dad! Mom!" Brice wailed.

"I thought I told you to stay away from that thing," Maggie said. "Your father's right, you know. We don't know what we're dealing with here. Banging on it like that could have . . . well, done something."

"You don't understand!" Brice cried. He told them about the burst of light. "And then Commander was gone!"

"Maybe he's just out there somewhere," Keith said. "Want me to look for him?"

"Yeah, Dad! I'll go with you."

"No, young man. You stay right here."

"But—"

Keith was gone before his son could say anything else. Brice looked pleadingly at Maggie, who in return embraced him.

"I'm sure Commander will be all right," she said, resting her cheek against the top of his head.

"He's inside that thing, Mom. Dad isn't gonna find him."

"Try to calm down, sweetheart. We all must try to calm down."

Brice forced himself to obey. His cheeks were damp with tears, which surprised him for he hadn't realized he'd been crying. He sniffed back the remaining tears and buried his face in his mother's shoulder. His father would never find the dog—not unless he went inside that thing.

When Keith returned a half hour later, Brice's conviction was confirmed. His father never said anything, but the expression on his face was enough.

The retriever couldn't be found anywhere.

Vivian had made herself a fresh cup of tea, hoping the warm brew would soothe her nerves, but she found herself unable to drink it, for her stomach was queasy with fear. At length she pushed the cup aside and tried to think of something pleasant.

Her gaze fell on the fieldstone fireplace at the other end of the room. It was not lighted, but she envisioned warm, romantic flames with Henry and herself sitting near it, embracing each other.

With Henry she was never afraid.

Then she heard Maggie say something about everyone being calm. She looked away from the fireplace to her daughter. She could see that there was doubt in the young woman's face, could even detect it in the voice.

Fear was everywhere in here. You could almost smell and taste it. Perhaps in another room it wouldn't be overpowering.

Getting up, she started toward her bedroom. As she walked, pulling her cardigan closer around her, she could feel Maggie's eyes on her. She knew they were eyes filled with worry, as well as fear.

Vivian paused and looked back at her daughter. She gave her a smile, wanting to tell her to stop worrying about her. She didn't want to be any more of a burden than she already was. The smile, unfortunately, was too stiff, hardly comforting.

Inside her room, she closed the door softly after her. Here, alone, she wouldn't be a burden to anyone. Here, alone, she would be with her thoughts. She'd be with Henry.

Fear was absent in this room. Henry was strongly in her mind, and with Henry she was never afraid.

CHAPTER SIX

As the hours passed, the tension thickened. The lake turned to ink. Stars appeared, faint at first, then bright. The moon, almost full, glowed, splashing its pale light onto the cylinder and illuminating it. The night was clear and warm.

There was no electricity inside the cottage. There was only one oil lamp—Keith had fetched a flashlight from the car, only to discover that it needed fresh batteries—so there was scarcely enough light to brighten the cottage as much as everyone would have liked. Burning wood in the fireplace was considered, then dismissed; it was already too warm.

For a while everyone was silent. Vivian sat at the kitchen table. She had wanted to stay in the bedroom, where she said she'd be out of everybody's way, but Maggie had insisted, wanting everyone to be together. Brice, at last, had fallen asleep in Maggie's arms and was now in his sleeping bag on the floor. Toni and Lisa sat on the sofa while Maggie sat opposite them in a rocking chair. Between and around them Keith paced, frequently glancing out the window at the huge cylinder. Everyone, it seemed, was waiting. Certainly there had to be a reason for the metallic object outside and for the surrounding shield.

Maggie rocked, hoping to relieve some of the tension, but the chair creaked gratingly against the wooden floor. She stopped, and the silence returned. She looked at the girls across from her and soon found herself wondering how they had become good friends. They were exact opposites. Toni was underdeveloped in comparison to Lisa. She scarcely wore any makeup, whereas Lisa's face was usually buried under it, although now most of the makeup had faded. Maggie wondered if this was the longest the girl had gone without cosmetics.

"Mom?"

Maggie blinked, then focused on her daughter. "Yes, sweetheart?"

"Please don't stare at us like that."

Maggie flushed. She hadn't realized she'd been staring so openly. "I'm sorry." She looked away, quickly searching for something else that would occupy her mind. She'd just wanted to think of something else besides . . .

Her eyes paused on a small bookshelf in a corner. There were only a few paperbacks that had been left behind and a stack of games that they had brought along.

"Anyone care to play a game?" she asked.

No one answered, too lost in his or her thoughts.

"How about Scrabble?" Maggie spoke louder. She didn't want everyone to sit around and grow more and more afraid. "It'd be good to get our minds on something else."

At first it looked as if no one would answer her again, then Lisa said, "I like Scrabble, Mrs. Hunter. My brother and I used to play it all the time."

"Good." The decision was made. Maggie pulled the Scrabble box from the shelf, opened it, and spread the playing board on the coffee table.

Lisa dropped to her knees before the table, and a few seconds later Toni reluctantly joined her.

"Ma, would you like to play?" Maggie turned to Vivian at the other end of the room. The elderly woman was mostly shrouded in shadow, the feeble light from the oil lamp scarcely reaching her.

"What?"

"Would you like—"

"Oh, no. I'm a terrible speller. I'll only slow the game down, be in the way."

"Don't be silly."

"No, not tonight."

Vivian looked away, and Maggie knew there'd be no persuading her. She turned to Keith, who had just glanced out a window. "What about you?"

"Nah."

"Why not?"

"Because."

"Because why?" she pressed.

He opened his mouth to decline again, then he sighed with resignation. He looked once more out the window, then sat on the worn braided rug, joining the others around the coffee table.

The game began. Though no one's heart was in it, everyone continued to play.

A half hour passed. Toni was winning, but she was hardly enthusiastic about it. At length Keith got up and stretched.

"Go ahead and play without me," he said and was back at the window before anyone could object.

Maggie and the two girls watched him as he peered out into the night.

"See anything?" Toni asked.

Keith shook his head.

"Maybe they're not going to do anything. That's possible, isn't it?"

There was silence as he thought about this. "Maybe, sweetheart."

He sounded doubtful.

"What are you waiting for?" she asked.

Keith shrugged in reply. Toni turned back to Maggie, her eyes repeating the question she had asked her father.

"That's a hard question," Maggie said slowly. "We don't even know what they are, let alone what they're waiting for."

"But what do you think, Mom? You must have some kind of idea."

"I'm just as puzzled as you are."

"I saw something today," Lisa said before Maggie could reply.

Toni's head swung toward her friend in surprise. "Like what?"

"That thing out there was open, and I saw a light of some sort. It was quick. A blink or two, and then it was gone."

"That's all? Just a light?"

"Yeah, that's all, but it was still scary."

"What do you think it was?" Toni asked.

"I don't know. Maybe a machine."

"What's so scary about that?"

"Well," Lisa said slowly, apparently finding it difficult to put her feelings into words. "It seemed more than a machine. It seemed . . . well, it seemed as though it was watching us."

"Us?"

"Yeah, Keith—I mean, Mr. Hunter—and me."

Toni and Maggie simultaneously looked over at Keith.

"It was like she said," he agreed. "It was a flash of light, a green flash."

"Do you think it was a machine?" Maggie asked.

"I don't know what the hell it was. It's awfully dark inside that thing. You can't see anything, not even a faint outline or shape. Nothing. Just that burst of green light."

"Do you think the dog is inside that thing?" Maggie dropped her voice in case Brice wasn't fully asleep.

Keith didn't answer. He gazed out the window a moment more, then abruptly headed for the fireplace, selected an iron poker, and returned to the window.

"Keith, what—" Maggie began.

"Gotta have some protection, y'know."

"My God, do you think—" She stopped, suddenly realizing she was about to ask a foolish question. She wasn't being very realistic. She had been clinging to hope, desperately trying to convince herself that they were not in danger, that the dog had found a hole in the shield and merely run off.

She turned back to the Scrabble board. "Come on, let's keep playing."

"Mom, I don't feel like it," Toni said.

"We've got to do something. It's not good to just sit and dwell about what may happen."

Toni stared at the game board as though it were something distasteful. She didn't make a move until Lisa wiggled closer to the table in a show of renewed interest in the wooden tiles before her.

"Guess you're right, Mom," Toni mumbled, also moving closer to the table.

They played for another half hour. Maggie periodically glanced over at her mother, who was still at the kitchen table, sitting in the semidarkness. When the game was over and the girls were back on the sofa, their eyes at last heavy with exhaustion, Maggie got up and checked on her mother.

Vivian was asleep. Her hands were still folded on her lap, but her head was bent slightly forward, and her eyes behind the spectacles were closed. Maggie thought of leaving her like this, then decided against it. The woman would be stiff and in pain if she remained asleep in this upright position, so she gently nudged her awake and walked her to the bedroom.

When Maggie came back out to the main room she was surprised and relieved to find the girls asleep on the sofa, each at one end. Brice was still asleep, deep inside his sleeping bag with only the top of his head exposed, and Keith was still at the window, watching, poker in hand. Maggie glanced at her watch. It was close to midnight. It had been a long, long day.

"You should go to sleep, hon," Keith whispered to her. "I'll stay on watch."

"You sure?" She was tired. Her eyes were burning and her lids kept drooping.

"Yeah, I'm sure. Go ahead."

"You need to sleep, also."

"I'm not tired."

Maggie hesitated. She was the one who

should be on watch. After all, it was her brilliant idea to come here in the first place. But her eyes were so heavy. She yawned. "Well, just a little snooze," she decided, returning to the rocking chair. "If you get tired, promise you'll wake me up."

"Promise." He nodded curtly, then went back to looking out the dark window.

As Maggie watched him she felt a sudden urge to cry. This was all her fault. Why hadn't she chosen a heavily populated resort, a place where they could summon help? Here no one would hear or notice them, at least not for two weeks. I'm sorry, she silently whispered to Keith and everyone in the cottage. I'll make it up to all of you. If we get out of here safely, I most definitely will. It's a promise.

She closed her eyes, holding back tears that were beginning to surface, then fell asleep.

Maggie awoke with a start. She had been dreaming about finding Keith with two women in his arms, and she was surprised to find him in the chair by the window, sleeping. The chair had not been there before, so she was momentarily confused. As she rubbed sleep from her eyes, it occurred to her that Keith must have grown tired of standing and therefore had dragged a chair to the window. He had probably wanted to continue the vigil while sitting but had dozed off. She could hear him snoring softly.

Other than this, the room was silent.

Maggie let her eyes sweep the interior. The oil lamp emitted a weak, yellowish glow, leaving too much of the room in darkness. The furniture created elongated, distorted shadows on the floor, walls and ceiling. She could see her husband in the chair clearly enough, but his face was a dark patch.

The darkness and shadows were as thick as the silence. Maggie angled her watch toward the light. 3:12. She looked at the window from where she sat and saw nothing but more darkness. She wasn't sure why, but suddenly she felt very alone and very afraid.

She thought of awakening Keith, then quickly changed her mind. He needed his sleep, and nothing was happening—was there?

Once more her eyes swept the room. Somehow she was certain something was wrong. It was as if an alarm were shrilling inside her. She told herself it was her imagination that was triggering the warning bell, but she was not appeased.

She scanned the walls, but could not see too much of the wood panels or the cheap paintings of autumn landscapes and farmhouses that she knew adorned them. She wished it weren't so damn dark. Of course she could brighten the lamp, but the lamp was halfway across the big room, and she was reluctant to leave her chair.

No, not reluctant, she corrected herself. She was afraid.

But why? She was letting the darkness and stillness frighten her for no reason.

No reason except that she knew there was something strange still outside the cottage, something that had abducted the family dog, something that was waiting.

She heard a sound. Or was this only her fear and imagination again? She listened intently, turning her head toward the fireplace, for that was where she had heard—or thought she had heard—the noise. It reoccurred, and this time the sound made her think of flapping wings or something beating the air. Then it stopped as abruptly as it had started, as though it suddenly knew she was listening.

Vaguely, Maggie could make out a form. It was dark and squatty, and was in the air, halfway between the floor and the ceiling. She squinted to see clearer, but most of the form blended with the surrounding shadows. Then she saw a greenish spark, and emitted a gasp, throwing a hand to her throat. Her heart accelerated. What had she seen?

The dark form slid away and the beating sound she'd heard seconds earlier returned, this time sounding more furious.

"Keith!" Her voice was strangled, barely audible. She tried to follow the sound with her eyes, but it seemed to move too quickly, to be everywhere at once. It was as though a bird had flown into the cottage via the fireplace and was frantically trying to get out.

It sparked its greenish, fluorescent light again and again, still moving too rapidly for its true shape to be discerned.

"Keith," she called again, her voice louder, but it was not enough to rouse him or the others. Maggie then rose from the chair, keeping her eye on the bird—or whatever it was—that was eluding her.

There was another flash of light. She was reminded of fireflies, those little, mystifying insects she used to trap in empty mayonnaise jars on warm summer nights when she was little. They used to blink like that, and their shapes could not be seen as they flew in the dark. It was only when they emitted light that they became visible, just like this creature that was darting around the room right now. Maggie noted it never came near the oil lamp. Was it deliberately avoiding it so that she wouldn't see it clearly?

Maggie hurried toward Keith, then halted as she spotted another dark form and a flash of light emerging from the fireplace. This flash was of a different color, more yellowish than green. Now, she realized with numbing horror, there were two creatures in the room.

"Keith, wake—"

Another flash, this one reddish purple, appeared before it shot into the room. Then there was another.

My God, how many are there? What are they?

The creatures seemed to be all around her, blinking at different parts of the room. They were circling her, she suddenly realized with chilling certainty, circling as though she were some kind of prey. Lights sparked at every angle, some lazily, some furiously.

"Go away!" she hissed.

The circle seemed to be closing in on her. Suddenly she felt claustrophobic. She couldn't breathe.

"Away, I said! Please!"

At last her paralysis broke, and she ran the rest of the way toward her husband. "Keith!" she screamed as loud as she could. She shook him violently until she was certain he was awake, then she screamed again.

One of the creatures had touched her.

CHAPTER SEVEN

The scream jolted Keith awake. He was startled to find Maggie so close, her hands clutching at his shirt. The hands, he noted instantly, were frantic, almost clawing at him.

"Honey, what—"

"They're after me!" she shrieked.

"Who?"

"Can't you see them?"

Keith was ready to ask her where, but she abruptly ran away from him, as though a hornet were after her. She spun around, ducked, then ran near the lamp.

"They're everywhere, Keith!" Her voice was still shrill with fright. "Everywhere!"

From the couch Toni and Lisa woke up and looked at her with confused, groggy eyes.

Brice did the same from his sleeping bag on the floor. Keith rose from his chair, clutching the iron poker that had been on his lap. Maggie's panic was infectious.

"Where, for God's sake?" he demanded. Before she could respond, he saw the familiar greenish flash. It was hovering not too far from his wife, but too far from the lamp's glow for him to see it clearly. Then, almost simultaneously, he spotted another glint of light. This one was faint, pulsing softly rather than flashing at a frenetic rate. As he tried to focus on this it ceased to blink, and a different light, bluish white, began to throb in the periphery of his vision. When he pivoted toward it, it zipped into another part of the room, winking on and off as it went.

"Mom, what's happening?" Brice was also aware of the creatures in the room. Toni drew closer to her friend and together they held each other as their heads swiveled to follow the numerous sparks exploding in the shadows around them.

"What are they doing?" Maggie asked Keith as she hugged Brice, who now had his small arms tightly around her waist, pressing his face against her breasts.

"Damn if I know," Keith replied, hefting the poker in his hand, readying to swing it.

He tried to count the flying beings, but whenever he thought he'd seen them all, a new one would appear. There were at least a half dozen of them, and one, he noted, was coming closer to him. At each blink it would be a foot or two nearer.

Clenching his jaw, Keith waited until he was certain the creature was only an arm's length away, then he swung the poker at it, like a baseball player swinging his bat. He struck out, hitting only empty air.

But it was enough to create pandemonium. A mixture of sounds exploded in the room. Maggie let out a loud gasp, unwittingly squeezing Brice tighter. One of the girls shrieked, and glass exploded. Keith found himself spinning in various directions as he tried to follow all these sounds that were happening at once. He saw the girls hug each other, saw Maggie and Brice grasp each other, and saw blinking creatures flee the house, some through a window they had shattered and some via the fireplace.

Keith ran to the broken window and saw the creatures flee toward the cylinder in the yard. With the aid of the moon, Keith could see the opening in the object and see the beings' dark, squatty forms, when not blazing, bolt for the entrance. When all the creatures were inside, the opening began to close. Keith remained at the window, praying the object would now disappear, take off, do in reverse whatever it did when it had come here. But the object, gleaming in the pale moonlight, went nowhere.

As he stared at it, wishing he could will it away, his hand holding the poker trembled. He squeezed the iron instrument to steady his hand, then he turned to the others in the room. Toni and Lisa, still in each other's arms, seemed hysterical, hugging each other and crying. Maggie's and Brice's eyes were on him, frozen with fear, their faces as pale as the moon outside.

"Are you all okay?" he asked everyone, then focused his attention on Maggie.

Numbly, she nodded.

"What happened?" Keith asked gently. He had never seen Maggie looking so fragile, so breakable. He remembered thinking how tough she was when she had found him in bed with Sheila Moody. He had thought nothing could make Maggie fall apart, at least not completely, but now a sudden noise or gust of wind would probably make her run, shrieking, all the way to the mental hospital.

Maggie took in a deep breath and nodded once more, perhaps this time to assure herself she was all right, that everything was under control. "I was sleeping," she began, "and when I woke up I saw . . . saw them all around me. I think they came in through the fireplace. I tried to get your attention—"

"My fault," he interrupted. He hadn't meant to fall asleep, but since nothing had happened, the inactivity had eventually caused him to drift off.

"—but I was afraid to move," Maggie went on, as though he hadn't spoken. "I couldn't figure out what they were doing. They kept circling the room. I tried to yell, but couldn't—not at first."

"You screamed," Keith reminded her.

"One of them touched me." She shivered, remembering, then shook her head, trying to push the horrible incident from her mind.

But Keith wanted to know more. "Were you attacked? Nudged? What?"

"No, I wasn't attacked, just touched, but it felt so horrible—not normal."

"What do you mean?"

Maggie hugged herself, looking away, then looking back at him. "I don't know. It sort of patted my arm. The touch felt warm, but slippery and sticky."

"It patted your arm?"

"Yes."

"Why, do you suppose?"

"I don't know. Maybe it wanted to see what I felt like."

"You don't think it was trying to . . . well, hurt you? Abduct you?"

She thought about this, then shook her head, still keeping her arms wrapped around herself. "It didn't use any force."

"Did you see what any of them looked like?"

"No. I tried, but they blended with the dark, and they kept away from the lamp. I noticed that."

"Bats!" Toni suddenly declared, startling everyone. "They're vampires, Mom! Vampires come out at night, and they don't like lights, and one of them was trying to suck blood from your arm!"

"No, no, sweetheart." Maggie, seeing her

daughter was getting herself worked up, quickly denied that. "I'm sure they weren't vampires."

"And that thing out there is their coffin," Toni added, not listening. "Oh, God, what are we going to do?"

"We're . . . we're not going to panic is what we're not going to do," Maggie declared. A moment ago her voice was weak and tremulous; now it was surprisingly firm.

"What else did you notice?" Keith asked, wanting to steer her back to the original topic.

"They were fast," she replied after a thoughtful pause. "That's why I couldn't see them. But they lighted up on and off, like fireflies."

What made fireflies luminous? Keith tried to remember what he had learned in ninth grade biology. He knew the luminosity of fireflies was the result of a complete chemical reaction of enzymes and some other substances in the organisms. Also, he vaguely remembered learning that bacteria, algae, and fungi were similar, bioluminscent species. Also, some deep-sea fish were equipped with glowing organs to attract their prey. Were the creatures he'd just seen speeding around the room something like these species from biology?

No, not quite, an inner voice told him. Those species he had read about in biology books were from Earth. The creatures he had just seen here were from—

space, another dimension, Hell?

Maggie, as though suddenly remembering something, turned away from him and disappeared into Vivian's room. "Ma," she said, "are you all right?"

The older woman was awake, but her face was pale. Her hands, on her chest under the covers, could be seen wringing nervously, rippling the blankets. "I—I'm fine, dear," she replied in a raspy voice. But it was evident she was petrified. She had not seen anything, but had heard the commotion in the other room.

"Ma, do you need a drink of water or something?" Maggie asked.

"No, no. I'm fine. Really."

"Ma, everything's going to be all right."

Vivian said nothing, and only gave her a ghostly smile.

"Why don't you come out into the other room with us," Maggie said.

"No, no. I would only be in the way."

"Don't be silly. I think we should all be together."

"No!" This time the woman spoke sharply. Then, as though realizing she'd been too harsh, she repeated in a softer voice, "No. Please. I like to be alone. You know that, dear."

"Ma, you will not be in the way. I wish you'd believe that."

"No, no. I'm fine, dear. Really."

Maggie sighed, yet did not leave her mother's side. She remained sitting on the bed while she looked through the open door into the big room. Keith was dragging the bookcase toward the broken window.

"Should have brought some nails and tools," he said, grunting. "There's nothing much here to board up the windows."

"Are they dangerous, Daddy?" Toni asked from the couch.

Keith, unable to decide whether to lie or be truthful, avoided the question. "Give me a hand with this, will you?"

Lisa jumped to his aid, while Toni hesitated.

"Think they'll be back, Daddy?" The girl sounded so young, more like a child of eight than 14.

"I'm blocking the window just in case they do," he told her as Lisa and he pushed and pulled the bookcase across the room.

"What about Commander?" Brice asked.

"What about him?"

"What are they gonna do to him? Are they gonna keep him? Kill him?"

Keith groaned inwardly. Questions. Questions.

"They could come back through the other windows," Toni said, as if her brother had never spoken. Her voice rose, sounding younger and younger. "What are you doing to do about them, Daddy?"

Keith rubbed his forehead with his arm. Christ, he didn't need this. It was hard enough to keep himself under control. "Take it easy, okay? Everything's going to be all right."

"Why did they break the window?" Toni asked.

"To get out," Keith answered. What other reason could there be? "So, y'see, they're afraid of us. Nothing to worry about."

"Why didn't they break a window to get in?"

"Because it was easier to use the fireplace. They probably went through the window in panic. So again, it's obvious they're afraid of us."

At length Toni helped with the bookcase. When the window was partly blocked with only about two inches exposed at the top, she said, "What about the fireplace?"

"We'll do what we should have done in the first place—close the flue."

"Daddy?"

"What?" he snapped. He hadn't meant to be brusque with her, but the questions were thinning his patience. Why, for Christ's sake, did she and Brice think he had all the answers? Everybody here was in the same fucking predicament. Everybody was scared shitless. "Sorry," he mumbled.

"They came here when we were all asleep."

"Yeah, so?"

"They're not afraid of us when we're asleep. They're sneaky, Daddy. They snuck in on us when we were asleep. If Mom hadn't woken up—" She paused, for her voice was beginning to crack. "If Mom hadn't seen them, what would have happened? Would they have killed us?''

"Come on, take it easy. You're scaring yourself.''

"But it's true, Daddy. They're dangerous. They want to kill us. We're gonna die, aren't we?''

She needs a good slap, Keith thought. Just like in those old, soppy movies. "Knock it off, I said—''

"We're gonna die! I just know it. We're gonna die!''

Keith spun toward Vivian's room. "Maggie!'' he called to his wife. It was not a cry for help but a demand, which Maggie quickly understood.

"Toni, come here,'' she said from the other room. Unlike Keith's, her voice was tender with compassion.

Toni obeyed and sat on the bed next to her mother. "We're gonna die,'' she sobbed. "We're gonna—''

"No, we're not, sweetheart,'' Maggie told her softly, cradling her in her arms.

"But they're gonna come back,'' Toni said, her voice muffled against the softness of Maggie's breasts. "And they're dangerous.''

"You don't know that for sure.''

"They took Commander.''

"You don't know that for sure, either. One of them could have hurt me, but it didn't.''

"But the next time it will.''

"No, it won't.''

"How can you say that, Mom? You don't

know for sure, either."

"We'll be on guard, sweetheart."

Toni didn't believe her. Vivian didn't believe her. Nobody did.

They all knew the horror had only begun.

PART TWO

PART TWO

CHAPTER EIGHT

They were agitated, squealing, blinking, and flying furiously in the dark hull. There were eight of them, and they were continuously colliding into each other, exciting themselves further. The Elder, the oldest and by far the largest of them, silently commanded them to stop. At first they paid no heed, but after the third command they gradually composed themselves and turned attentively to her.

The humans are weak, she informed them. She had observed and found them slow, ungainly, and defenseless, not at all like the dog. The man with the metal rod had not been quick.

A Little One pulsed frantically. The dog made a lot of noise, but the man had almost hit him, he told the Elder. The man had come so close.

The Elder explained that this was because The Little One had not been careful. Always be alert, she cautioned, and there will be no danger.

The Little Ones glanced at each other, and The Elder could see that they were still afraid, that they would not be easy to pacify. Most of them were still blinking in rapid succession, disrupting the darkness with dizzying spurts of lights.

A Little One showed The Elder he was bleeding. He had cut his arm as he broke through the window. The Elder wrapped her long talons around The Little One's cut and held the arm for a long moment. Warm, balming liquid dripped from the tips of the claws and seeped into the wound. When the bleeding was stopped, The Elder released her grip and once more cautioned The Little Ones to be careful.

There is nothing to fear, she assured them. The humans are at our mercy.

CHAPTER NINE

Maggie awoke to daylight and a painful stiffness in the back of her neck. She was in the rocking chair. It was no wonder her neck was tight with pain. She rubbed it until it was somewhat better, then she rose, looking around her. Lisa was slouched on the sofa, absently flipping through an old issue of *TV Guide* that someone had left behind. Brice was asleep in his sleeping bag. Toni was at the window that viewed the lake. Apparently Keith was somewhere outside, for Maggie couldn't see him anywhere, and Vivian was asleep in the other room.

"Where's your father?" she asked Toni.

"With that . . . thing out there."

Outside, Maggie found Keith talking to the cylindrical object.

"What do you want from us?" he was demanding. "Where are you from? What are you?" He moved closer to the object, then stopped when he spotted Maggie. He looked at her, then returned his attention to the silver hull. He hesitated a moment, then touched the metallic surface, first with one hand, then with the other.

"I'm not going to harm any of you," he spoke slowly. "*We're* not going to harm any of you. I'm—we're peaceful. You do not have to hide from us." He let a minute go by, and when nothing happened, added, "I think that's the least you could do."

There was silence, then a soft thump. Simultaneously, he and Maggie looked upward at the sky, where they had heard the sound. A blackbird, glossy and bluish under the sun, had crashed into the shield and was now diving unconsciously toward the water. It made a muted splash, then was still.

"That's the second one I've seen," Keith said, despair evident in his voice. He stared at the floating bird for a moment, then once more concentrated on the cylinder before him.

"Come on," he pleaded. "Tell us what you want. Maybe we can help you. Maybe we have what you want. Maybe—"

"Keith," Maggie interrupted softly.

"What?" he asked, without looking over at her, as though he knew she'd see not only fear in his eyes but terror as well.

Maggie stepped closer, but not too close,

sensing he did not want her near him. "What are you doing?"

"What does it look like? I'm trying to communicate with those damn things. Trying to find out what they want."

Maggie walked forward until she was beside him. "Can you hear anything inside?" she asked.

He shook his head. "It's as if the damn thing is empty. Not a peep in there."

"Maybe they're sleeping," Maggie said, suddenly remembering Toni saying the creatures were vampires and vampires sleep during the day.

"Maybe I should wake them up, then. They woke us up last night." He closed his hand into a fist and made an attempt to pound at the surface, but Maggie's voice stopped his hand in midair.

"Don't, Keith! They may be dangerous."

He thought about this, then let his fist drop to his side. "Christ, I wish they'd at least talk to us," he said. "Not knowing why they're here or what they're up to is damn . . . damn . . ."

Maggie knew he wanted to say "frightening," but at this moment his male pride would not let him.

Maggie reached for his fist, held on to it until she could feel it loosen, then slipped her fingers between his.

Together they stared at the object before them. It gleamed like polished metal, except for one end which was dull and dark in the shade of a pine tree. Although there was no more fog, the outlines of the doors or windows were still difficult to discern. One had to minutely examine the surface, which seemed smooth and flawless, something that was one solid piece. It was unmistakably a work of perfection, simple in design and devoid of blemish. There were no visible scratches or indentations, and that was a wonder in itself, considering the object must have undoubtedly plowed its way through numerous tree limbs before alighting on this site.

Looking around, Maggie found broken limbs here and there. Also, there were deep niches in several tree trunks, confirming her belief that this vessel before her had made a somewhat violent landing. The object must be of strong metal, she mused, or perhaps it was of a substance equally tough, like the shield surrounding them—something unknown.

"Do you think it's . . ." She found it difficult to say what was on her mind. She swallowed, then tried again. "Do you think it's . . . a spacecraft?"

He said nothing, and in the silence Maggie found herself thinking of all the ludicrous tabloids she'd seen in supermarkets and drugstores over the years. It seemed there were always stories about UFO sightings in them. She always had considered them silly, trashy stories, but now they didn't seem so absurd. Could some of them have been true?

"Who knows?" Keith eventually answered in a low voice, so soft that she almost didn't hear it.

"But . . ." She turned to look at him. "They don't exist."

"Spacecrafts? How do you know that for sure?"

"Because . . . because . . ." She really had no answer.

"Where do you think this thing came from?"

"Maybe it's some kind of government project."

"The creatures inside, too?"

"Maybe they're from . . . Oh, I don't know!" she blurted out frankly. "It's just that I never believed in UFOs before."

"But you believe in the devil."

She frowned at him, wondering what this had to do with anything.

"I remember you telling me that you thought demon possession was possible. You said it was why you found that movie 'The Exorcist' so scary. You said you believed there was so much about God and Satan that we didn't know about."

"Yes, but what has religion to do with—"

"It has to do with the unknown. No one is certain about God and Satan, and no one is certain about UFOs, about what is out there in space."

Space. Unknown. The words were like echoes, haunting her mind. Keith, she knew, was right. There was so much they didn't know. Mystery was all around them. Even the human body and brain were enigmatic in their functions. Creation was enigmatic. Space was enigmatic.

Nothing that could not be explained or understood should be hastily labeled absurd.

"Oh God," she moaned, wishing this thing before her would go away, wishing that everything would return to normal.

"When do you think they'll come back out?" she asked. "Do you think it'll be at night again?"

"Maybe. Maybe they're afraid of daylight."

Maggie remembered the creatures had avoided the oil lamp last night.

"We're going to have to be extra careful tonight," she said, her voice already weak with dread.

"Yeah. Too bad the electricity is out. We could use more lights. But then, it's no accident that we lost the power, I'm sure."

"We'll be all right," Maggie said, determined to be optimistic. "We'll be alert. In fact, I'm going to take a nap later so that tonight . . . " Her voice trailed away as she realized Keith was not listening to her.

She watched him for a moment as he pressed an ear against the cylinder. He listened, then moved to another section to listen some more. When it was evident that he was hearing nothing, Maggie turned away and headed back for the cottage.

She tried to take a nap that afternoon, but her mind and fear would not rest.

* * *

Brice could not stop thinking about Commander. What had happened to him? Was he inside that thing out there? It had all happened so fast, the memory of the incident a blur.

"What are we gonna do about him, Dad?" he had asked his father. When he received only a grunt in reply, he repeated the question. He knew his father would probably get mad, but he needed an answer.

"What do you want us to do?" Keith finally snapped at him.

"I want to find him."

"I already looked."

"He's inside that thing, Dad. I know he is. I just know it!"

"Well, there's nothing we can do about that now, son."

And that was the end of it. Brice knew he'd never get anything else out of him. Clearly, finding the dog would have to be all up to Brice.

In the bathroom, Brice closed the door and crawled out the small window. The sky was darkening, the sun had set. Everybody else was inside the cottage, fearfully waiting for night to fall. This would be the perfect time to approach the creatures, to make them give him back his dog.

Brice crept toward the hull and glanced back at the cottage. When will someone realize he was no longer in the bathroom? He would have to be fast. They would stop him if they knew he was out here.

They didn't understand his feelings toward Commander. Commander wasn't just an animal. Brice loved him more than he loved most anybody.

"Please, let him be all right," he whispered.

When he reached the cylinder, he searched for the exact spot from where the blinding light had flashed. When he found it, he ran his hand over the surface. Then he pressed his ear against it. Hearing nothing from within, he knocked gently.

"Open up."

His heart hammered. He was afraid, but he was also determined.

"Give me back my dog."

His voice was low, his mouth almost touching the metallic surface. He pounded softly yet relentlessly, wanting only the creatures inside to hear him.

"I want my dog. Did you hear me? I want my dog."

He paused to listen. Something inside had made a noise, a faint but shrill screech. Now he knew he had triggered a response. Maybe the creatures had been sleeping and he had awakened them.

He spoke louder, "I want my dog! I want my dog!"

He heard more sounds from within. They were getting excited. Now maybe they'd listen and give him what he wanted.

Suddenly, something on the surface began

to move. Brice jumped back. The door was opening!

Mesmerized, Brice watched the entrance now. When it was about three feet in height and width, it stopped. Brice waited, expecting something else to happen. He moved closer. Maybe he should go inside. Maybe this was some kind of invitation.

Swallowing, he bent to crawl through the small opening. Before he could reach it, however, white light filled the entrance, startling him. He scrambled away, as though the light had burnt him, and fell back onto the ground.

He stared in shock at the entrance. It was still open, but was hazy with brilliant light.

"My dog," he mumbled, feeling tears pressing behind his eyes. "I just want my dog."

The light brightened, then faded. When the entrance was once again a black, empty opening, Brice stood up. He roughly wiped a tear that had managed to escape, sniffed back the rest, and forced himself to return to the spot from which he'd fled.

He made another attempt to enter the cylinder. Again he found himself falling backward onto the ground. This time something hurled past him, narrowly missing him. He swung around on the ground to see where the mysterious thing was going. Blurry because of its incredible speed, it struck a tree with a soft, wet splat sound, then dropped to the base.

Brice looked back at the cylinder. It was closed. He returned his gaze to the clump at the bottom of the tree. Was it Commander?

He hesitated, then broke into a run toward the tree. The clump did not move, but maybe that was all right. Maybe Commander was unconscious. Maybe he was hurt just a little.

Dropping to his knees, he recognized his dog's golden fur and scooped him up into his arms.

"Commander!" he cried. "You're all right, aren't you? You're all right!"

He knew the animal was limp in his arms, even shapeless, but another part of him was convinced that this was okay. His dog was unconscious, that's all. It was normal to be shapeless when you were unconscious.

The clump in his arms was wet and sticky. Until now he hadn't looked but had only hugged the animal against him. He forced himself to gaze down at the face. It stared up at him, eyes huge and milky, a tiny network of blood crisscrossing them. The snout was flat and caved in (from when it hit the tree?) and its fur was matted with dark blood. Its mouth was open, letting pink froth bubble and trickle down its side to mat more fur.

"Commander, wake up!"

He shook the dog. He hated how limp it felt. It was like one of those stuffed animals you see in toy stores—soft, boneless, lifeless.

"Commander!"

He frantically shook, then squeezed the furry clump. Now he could feel the bones deep inside the body, but they moved with his fingers. They were loose—in little, fragmented pieces.

Brice buried his face into the fur. When he felt himself being yanked to his feet, he was momentarily disoriented. How much time had passed? His face and the dog's fur were wet with a mixture of blood and tears. Now his father was looking down at him.

"What are you doing out here!" he demanded.

"My dog, Dad!" Brice sobbed. "They . . . they killed my—"

"I can see that. Come on, let's get back in the house."

Keith propelled him toward the cottage, his big hand firm around Brice's upper arm, actually hurting it.

"Dad, we can't leave Commander!"

"I'll bury him later."

"Why not now?"

Keith didn't answer.

Night was falling fast.

CHAPTER TEN

"It's them," Keith said.

Maggie joined him at the broken window, most of which was hidden by a bookcase that had been propped against it. She couldn't see anything outside, only darkness. Keith reached for an iron poker from the fireplace.

"I don't see—" she began, then stopped. She saw a greenish spark, darkness, then the greenish spark again. Behind this was another small explosion of light, this one purplish.

Yes, it was them all right. The group was back, and this time they hadn't bothered to wait until everyone was asleep.

They were heading straight for the cottage.

Maggie clutched her elbows as she waited. She thought of moving away from the window and searching for something that could serve as a weapon, something like the fireplace poker, or searching for a place in which to hide. Instead, she found herself mesmerized, frozen to the window.

The lights moved closer. Actually, they're pretty, Maggie thought. Sometimes the lights would flash green, a pale emerald color; sometimes they'd be rubies; sometimes blue sapphires. Their loveliness, however, did not soften the dread of their presence. She didn't like their utter invisibility when they weren't luminous, especially when they would reappear in a different place. It left one feeling uncertain and vulnerable.

Suddenly Maggie realized why these monstrous fireflies appeared only at night. They did not want to be seen beyond the light they cast. They knew it would be difficult to catch them this way.

"We're not going to let them in the house this time," Keith said, his voice a low whisper, yet hard with resolve. He shifted the poker from one hand to the other.

He was ready for them, but what about her and the others? Maggie wondered frantically. What were they to do? Run and hide? There was nothing they could use for protection, except maybe the kitchen knives.

Maggie started toward the kitchen area, then changed her mind. If she took the knives out, the others would panic. They would be too frightened and possibly too hysterical to defend themselves. How could they attack beings that were invisible most of the time? No, the knives would not do.

"Hide," Keith abruptly demanded, as though aware of her difficulty in reaching a decision. "Go in the bedroom closet."

But the closet he was referring to was too small to fit five people, and the closet in Vivian's room had a curtain instead of a door covering the entrance—not much protection there. Besides, Maggie didn't want to leave Keith behind.

Keith looked at her, as though surprised she wasn't running to the bedroom.

"You might need some help," Maggie said.

"I'll be all right. I can handle those little mother—"

"Maybe they're not dangerous," she interrupted. "Maybe we're worrying needlessly."

She knew she was fooling herself. The creatures had killed the dog, hadn't they? They had put up an impenetrable shield to imprison them. Now they were coming toward them. Of course they were dangerous.

Lisa joined her and Keith at the window, then Toni joined them while Vivian remained in the rocking chair, sitting rigidly, scarcely moving. Brice, on the couch, seemed somewhat detached, his eyes red-rimmed and glazed.

"What's taking them so long?" Lisa asked, looking out the window.

The creatures, indeed, were flying slowly.

Last night they had moved with incredible speed. Now they seemed to be in slow motion, blinking intermittently, and rather than flying directly toward the cottage, they were hovering in the air. What were they doing?

"I've counted six of them," Lisa said when no one answered.

"Mom . . . Dad," Toni said, sounding like a frightened child, "what are they doing?"

Again no one answered.

"Seven," Lisa declared after a pause, then added uncertainly, "I think. I wish they'd stay lit, so I could tell how many of 'em there are."

"There are too many!" Toni cried. The exact count did not matter. "Dad, please don't let them in the house."

"Wasn't my intention."

"Hey, did you see that!" Lisa exclaimed.

"What?" Maggie had been looking at Keith and Toni for a moment.

"Yeah," Keith answered. "Christ!"

"What?" Maggie demanded. She stared out the window, but saw nothing different. The creatures were closer to the cottage, but were still hovering, erratically circling. "What did you see?"

"It was something big," Lisa finally replied. "Wasn't it, Mr. Hunter?"

He said nothing, apparently feeling there was no need.

"It's about three times the size of the others," Lisa went on, "and its light was white, wasn't it, Mr. Hunter?"

This time he responded with a small nod. A muscle pulsed at his jaw, which was clenched as though in readiness and defiance. Once more he shifted the poker from one hand to the other while he stared straight ahead.

Outside, the creatures continued to circle like a swarm. While they were circling and hovering, they were gradually approaching the cottage. Now they were more than halfway toward their destination.

"The mother," Lisa blurted out.

"What?" Toni frowned, glancing at her friend.

"It must have been the mother I saw," Lisa explained, "and those out there are her children."

"Where is this mother?" Maggie asked. Before the girl could respond, however, she glimpsed a large, pale light. It was near the dark cylinder, away from the other creatures, and it was, as Lisa had claimed, about three times larger than the others. Even its light was different; it did not flash spontaneously, but rather waxed and waned in a soft spectral glow.

Maggie waited for the light to return, but it didn't. Unlike the smaller creatures, it did not blink repeatedly. She wondered if this was because it was larger and, therefore, more time and energy were needed to pulse light.

Whatever the reason, Maggie had to agree

that this creature seemed motherlike. It seemed calmer than its children milling about in the air. Like a mother watching her children at a playground, she thought.

Is this cottage their playground? Are we their playthings?

Maggie felt her daughter's hands on her arm. The hands were cold and sweaty.

"Mom, I'm afraid. I'm—" She stopped, as though something had suddenly distracted her. She stared silently out the narrow section of the window for a long moment, her eyes wide and unblinking. Her lips parted, slightly at first, then noticeably. The fear she felt began to diminish until only wonder was left.

She let go of Maggie's arm and moved closer to the window. "Maybe they're friendly," she said in a soft yet steady voice. "Maybe they hadn't meant to hurt the dog. Maybe the dog had hurt them first. Maybe they're only curious about us, Mom. Curious like the way we are about them."

"I'm not curious," Maggie told her. "I don't care if I ever see them again."

"Mom . . ." She turned slowly to her, as though heavily sedated. "I want to go outside."

Are you crazy? Maggie thought. Her mouth opened to say this, but her mind grew cloudly before she could find her voice. She stared at her daughter, as though seeing her for the first time, then she looked out the window. The darkness was complete except for the occasional sparks of color—blue, purple, green, so pretty.

She touched her forehead, suddenly feeling a little dizzy. She closed her eyes a moment, then returned her gaze to her daughter. She struggled to remember what she had wanted to say to her. She knew it was something, but what was it?

Toni started to leave. She walked away while keeping her eyes on the window, as though unable to part with the creatures outside, even for a brief moment.

"Are you crazy?" This time Maggie remembered and found her voice.

Toni stopped in the middle of the room. She had been heading toward the front door. "They're friendly, Mom," she insisted, her voice thick. Her eyes were hooded as she strained to focus them on Maggie.

"You . . . you have no way . . . of knowing." It was so hard to talk. Her mind was so hazy, and her vocal cords seemed to be miles away from her brain.

Toni blinked. She, too, seemed to be having a difficult time thinking and talking. Her mouth worked soundlessly for a moment, then uttered, "Can't you . . . can't you hear their thoughts, Mom? Can't you . . . feel them?"

"Yes," Lisa agreed. The girl was nodding with slow, groggy enthusiasm. "I can feel 'em. Can really feel 'em."

"Can't you tell they're friendly?" Toni's

attention was still on Maggie. "Can't you, Mom?"

Maggie felt a strong urge to look out the window again, to see the pretty sparks, but she fought it. "No, Toni. Stay here. Don't open the door—"

"But hon," Keith interrupted without looking at her, his gaze still riveted to the window. "They *are* peaceful. We should welcome them, shouldn't we, Lisa?"

"Yes, Mr. Hunter. Peaceful."

"No, they're not!" Brice cried from the couch. "They killed Commander! They are killers!"

Keith and the two girls ignored him. They watched the creatures, who were now close to the window. The creatures still moved languorously, as though floating in the air rather than flying. One of them almost touched the window, glinting purplish light, then receded. Soon another came forward, pulsed pale green light, then disappeared.

"Peaceful," Lisa repeated, sounding like a faint echo.

"Let them in, Toni," Keith said.

No! Maggie's mind protested, but the word was faint, far away in a remote region of her brain. She was now too tired to fight the attraction outside the window, and besides, it made no sense that she should be the only one fighting.

Sighing, she capitulated and stared out the window.

"No!" This came from Vivian in the chair. "Don't let them in! Please don't!"

"Let them in, Toni," Keith said, as if Vivian had never spoken.

Maggie could feel something penetrate her mind. The more she stared at the floating beings, the more intense the sensation became. It was like warm, silky liquid slowly filling her head, as though her skull were a bowl. It was a lovely, tranquilizing feeling.

"Yes . . . peaceful," she said, now agreeing with Keith and the girls. "Let them in. Yes, let them in."

"You guys are nuts!" Brice said.

"No!" Vivian cried, struggling out of the chair. "Please, don't."

Toni, her head turned toward the window, reached for the door.

Vivian tried to hurry after her, to stop her, but the woman was too old, too slow. "Nooo," she whimpered.

Brice, realizing what his grandmother was trying to do, leapt from the couch. He was too late.

Toni opened the door.

A warm, pine-scented breeze wafted into the room, then the creatures began to float in, keeping to the low ceiling. They circled the air, and in the faint glow of the oil lamp their roundish, squat bodies could be vaguely seen. Their bodies were too dark, blending with the shadows, but this time, now that they weren't flying and zigzagging frenetically, their wings could be discerned. They were batlike and leathery. Sprouting from the tips of their wings were what looked like tapered fingers with lengthy nails—claws. And from below, as the creatures flew past, their bulbous bellies could be seen. Round and large, they spasmodically pulsed light, fleetingly illuminating and tinting networks of arteries and inner organs within the translucent bellies.

Their faces, however, managed to escape notice behind the flapping of wings.

"Oh, my God," Vivian moaned, a trembling hand over her lips. She staggered backward toward her room, keeping a cautious eye on the circling beings. She made a sign of the cross. "Our Father, who art in heaven, hallowed be Thy name . . ."

Her back bumped against the wall, missing the door to her bedroom by mere inches. But instead of turning toward this door, she stood, transfixed, gawking at the melon-size beings in the air. The words to the Lord's Prayer died on her lips.

"There's nothing to be afraid of, Ma," Maggie said, noticing the horror on her mother's face. "If you stop fighting it, you'll see how peaceful they are. So stop, Ma. Stop fighting it."

Whimpering, Vivian began to shake her head, refusing. Her hand at her mouth became a fist pushing against her lips, as though to keep a scream from erupting.

Brice had been terrified too, but now he was gawking at the creatures, his mouth gaping with wonder.

Maggie looked away from her mother and son and watched the creatures in the room. The fear she had felt toward them was completely gone. Somehow they had won her trust, made her open her arms to them, but to her disappointment they didn't come to her. They just continued to circle and circle.

They continued to fill her mind with sweet, peaceful liquid. Tilting her head, she smiled up at them, then became aware of a presence at the front door. It was this presence, she quickly realized, that was responsible for the serene sensation inside her.

The motherlike creature was watching everyone from a slight distance. It was standing in darkness, the light from the lamp reaching only a fraction of its frame. Unlike its children, the creature was tall and slender rather than rotund. And because its wings were not in motion, the feeble light from the lamp caught a reflection of an eye, a glint of yellow. It was this glint in the darkness that entranced everyone—even Vivian, finally.

Maggie stared in rapt fascination at this being with the yellow eye, wanting to step closer to receive more of the warm sensation it was feeding her. But it was as if an invisible hand, with its palm out, were stopping her. Undoubtedly, a force was at work here, keeping her and the others at a distance from the being in the doorway.

The mother glowed like a ghost, became shapeless with hazy brilliance, then dimmed until it was once again a solid form in the gloom.

"Wow," Lisa whispered. She, too, wanted to move closer, but the force kept her at bay.

The children flew toward the two girls, slowly circled them, like planets revolving around twin suns, then drifted toward Keith and Maggie. Maggie was aware of them around her, yet did not care. Nothing mattered anymore, only the wonderful feeling inside her. No drugs or any amount of alcohol could be as delightful as this. She found herself wishing this would last forever.

The children moved on to Brice, then finally to Vivian, who, occasionally whimpering, was still frozen in awe.

"Go away," she pleaded, although her voice was weak. She was losing the fight, succumbing to the pleasure that the mother was giving her. "Go . . . away . . ."

The trembling fist at her mouth rose to her temple. Here, it pressed against the skull. She was not certain what was happening within it. The sensation filling and coating her mind had been warm and delightful; now it was beginning to change. The feeling wasn't warm anymore; it gradually was becoming cold and painful, as though she'd drunk something icy too fast.

Vivian emitted a cry, now pushing both hands against her head. The pain was excruciating. "Stop!" she pleaded. The pain would not relent. "Stop! Stop!"

Maggie looked over at her. It was like watching someone on film, someone that wasn't real. She looked away and stared at the creature in the doorway. The creature glowed again. Maggie smiled, marveling at how pretty the spectral light was. So pure, she thought, so heavenly.

Vivian slid down the wall to the floor, hands still clutching her head. "Please! Go away! Stop!"

Brice and the two girls glanced over with mild interest, then back at the doorway. Keith did the same. The poker was now at his side, its heavy tip scraping against the floor. Vivian let out an agonizing sob, then began to whimper while the children floated around her. It was only she they circled now, only she that attracted them.

"Please . . . go away . . ."

Maggie found herself floating. Never had she felt so weightless. She drifted, as though she were a cloud in an endless sky. There was no sense of time or direction. She floated, going nowhere.

For a while she could feel herself dissipating, coming apart in gossamer strands as a cloud would. This made her feel even lighter and airier. Then the sensation began to reverse itself, and she began to feel heavy, as though the cloud were condensing. Gradually the floating feeling went away, and she could feel the hardness of the floor beneath her feet.

Then she noticed the doorway was empty.

"Grandma!" she heard someone scream. The sound jolted her. It was Toni, and at the girl's feet was Vivian, lying completely still.

"Ma!" Maggie cried, dropping before her mother's inert body. "Ma!"

The winged creatures were no longer in the room.

CHAPTER ELEVEN

Maggie repeatedly shook Vivian's body. She pleaded and sobbed, repeating that she was sorry, that this was all her fault. "We wouldn't be here if it weren't for me," she moaned as she rocked her mother's limp body, then cradled the woman's head in her lap. "Oh Ma, please wake up. Please don't be . . ."

Keith and the girls stood by helplessly. The room was dim, filled with deep, amorphous shadows cast by the oil lamp. The silence was as deep as the shadows, only broken by Maggie's sobs.

Finally Toni found the strength to ask, "Is she dead, Mom?"

Maggie couldn't answer. She shook her head vigorously, refusing to accept the possibility, and resumed rocking the older woman desperately.

"Ma, please, please . . ."

Keith knelt beside her. "Honey."

Maggie ignored him. "Ma, wake up!" she demanded. "Oh, God, please wake up."

Vivian's eyelids fluttered.

Maggie's heart accelerated, first with hope, then with relief. "Ma!" she sobbed, a smile spreading across her face. "Oh, Ma!"

Toni dropped to her knees. "Grandma!"

Vivian's eyes opened. She focused on Maggie's face, then looked at the others in the room. It was a while before she was able to recognize any of them. She made a feeble attempt to sit upright, but Maggie kept her firmly in her lap.

"What happened?" she asked.

Maggie wiped away a tear. "We thought you were a goner."

"Goner? Of course not!" Vivian made another attempt to sit up, and this time succeeded. She adjusted her cardigan sweater, pulling it tighter together, then with Keith's and Toni's help, she struggled to her feet. "Oh my!" she suddenly exclaimed, swaying until Keith tightened his grip on her arm. "I-I'm a little woozy."

"Are you all right, Ma?" Maggie asked, rising.

"Yes, I'm fine." The older woman managed a weak smile. "Please let me lie down for a spell." She started toward her room. Keith and Toni flanked her, hands on her arms. She shook them off as if they were pesty house-flies. "I'm fine," she insisted. "Fine."

Once inside the room, she began to close her door, but Keith stopped her.

"Might be too dangerous to leave you completely alone," he said.

"But I said I was fine."

He shook his head firmly. "We don't know what we're dealing with here, Ma."

Vivian sighed. Too weary to argue any further, she left the door ajar, then lay down on the bed. Never had her body felt so tired and old, and her head wouldn't stop spinning.

What had happened?

She couldn't remember too much, only that she'd been sitting in the rocking chair one minute, then was lying on the floor the next. But as she concentrated, closing her eyes, she remembered that when Toni had opened the door, the beings with batlike wings had flown into the room. She remembered them circling her and closing in.

Yes, it was clear now. She had been frightened and tried to run away from them, but there had been a strange attraction that rendered her motionless. They had reached inside her, had soothed her mind, had explored it.

Vivian felt as though she'd been used, as though her mind had been raped. She wept silently, wishing her husband were here. She needed his arms around her and having him assure her that nothing would harm her.

"Henry," she whimpered, just to hear his name. Then she drifted off to sleep.

She dreamed of her husband, when he was a young man. She was in his arms, looking up at his handsome face, at his thick moustache and the curved pipe protruding from a corner of his lips. She couldn't kiss him because of this pipe, but that was all right with her. It was enough just to be in his strong arms. Besides, the cherry aroma from the pipe was sweet yet delightfully masculine. He smiled down at her and dimples dotted his cheeks. "I love you," he said, then began to fade, gradually bleaching out like an old photograph. She began to weep, holding him tighter around the waist, but the waist shrank as his features faded.

"No, please don't go," she whimpered. "I love you, too. Love you so very much."

He disappeared, leaving her only holding herself. She stood alone, weeping. Time passed, yet the wound in her heart remained fresh and raw. The tears would not cease.

Then she heard something, and her eyes flew open.

Darkness was all around her. A moment of concentration was needed to remember where she was—in the bedroom of a cottage by the lake. She was not young anymore, and Henry was no longer with her. Still feeling weary, she closed her eyes again, wanting to slip back into another dream. She wanted to be in Henry's arms again.

She heard the noise once more.

She reopened her eyes and turned her head toward the closet, where the sound had emanated. Staring intently into the darkness, she could gradually make out the outline of the curtain hanging over the closet's entrance. It was swaying softly, although the air seemed heavy and stagnant.

Pushing herself up to a sitting position, she listened but there was only silence. She kept her eyes on the curtain. The thin, dark cloth was still for a moment, then it billowed, as though someone or something on the other side had let out a gentle breath. The curtain gradually became still once more, then billowed again.

Vivian's heart hammered against her chest. Who's there? she silently demanded, too much of a coward to utter the words out loud.

She watched the curtain breathe.

Maybe I'm still sleeping, she thought. Maybe I'm dreaming that I'm awake. She had had dreams like this before, hadn't she?

She heard the sound again. It was the rustling of clothes inside the closet.

Go away! her mind screamed. Leave me alone! I've done nothing to deserve this!

Something slipped through the curtain— something dark and round—and it was floating like a balloon in the air, drifting toward her.

No, not again. Go away!

Deep green light pulsed twice from its body.

Go away!

She felt something penetrate her mind. First she felt that comforting warmth, then the painful cold. She bit down on her lower dentures, straining to endure the agony. For a moment it was certain she'd crack her false teeth, then the pain began to subside, leaving her breathing laboriously. She opened her eyes.

Henry was at the foot of the bed.

She gasped, at the same time pressing her back against the headboard. Again she told herself she was dreaming, and this time she was certain of it. Henry was dead!

She stared at her dead husband, masked in the darkness though clearly outlined. He was slender and tall, and one shoulder was higher than the other because of the stance he always had. His head was tilted slightly to one side as he appraised her, as he had always done. Yes, there was no mistake about it. This was definitely Henry.

A cough sounded in the other room. She turned her head toward it and waited for the cough to recur. When it didn't, she returned her gaze to her husband. He'd be gone, she was certain. He'd be gone like a ghost.

His tall, black frame was still there.

When he saw that he had her attention again, he moved closer, gently bumping the bed with his knees. She pushed harder against the headboard.

"Why are you afraid, love?" he said in a deep whisper, as though out of deference to those who may be asleep in the other rooms.

It was Henry's voice. Yes, there was no mistake about it.

"You must be a dream," she said, not answering the question.

"Because I am dead?"

Vivian stared at him, then slowly nodded.

"Why do you think of me?" he asked.

"What?"

"If I am dead, why do you still think of me?"

Vivian frowned. The question did not make sense to her. "Because I miss you," she answered after a long silence.

He said, maintaining his low whisper, "Why do you miss me, love?"

Such foolish questions! "Because I love you, Henry. You know that. I'll always love you. I'll never stop." When he made no reply, tilting his head the way he always did whenever he looked at her, she added, "Don't you still love me?"

"But that should have ended when I did."

"What?" Suddenly the room felt cold. Henry flared greenish for a fleeting second, then faded, causing her to wonder if she had only imagined the burst of light. Dream, she reminded herself. Crazy things always happen in dreams. "What?" she said again.

"Your thoughts of me should have ended when I had ceased to exist."

"But why should it, dear?"

"Because it is pointless. I am gone, therefore your thoughts and love for me should be gone as well."

"So what you are saying is that you don't love me anymore, is that it?"

"I am only saying that it is pointless."

"I don't understand you, Henry. You used to be so romantic." This conversation is crazy, she thought, but she was used to crazy dreams. She used to have them all the time, especially when she was a little girl. "I remember when you said your love for me was as hard and as endurable as a diamond. Nothing would ever wear it away. Do you remember saying that?"

He was silent. Then that horrible, gelid sensation filled her head again. She clutched it, gasping. After the pain subsided, he said, "Yes, I've found the memory. Interesting indeed."

"Interesting? What do you mean?"

"It does not matter." He dismissed the question, straightening his head for a moment, then tilting it toward the other side. His movements, Vivian suddenly noted, were stiff, while Henry's had been smoother. That could only mean that this man standing at the foot of the bed was not her late husband.

"You're not—"

Again that agonizing cold pierced her brain. When it faded, she forgot what she'd started to say. She looked at the man before her, momentarily forgetting who he was. His face was in shadow, but his tall frame was clearly visible. Of course, now she remembered.

"Henry," she fondly whispered.

Her loving husband flashed green light, then moved to the side of the bed, closer to her. "I am dead and still you desire me." It was a statement, but it sounded like a thoughtful question.

"All the time, Henry dear. And I think about you all the time, too."

"Would you mate with a dead person?"

"Would I what?"

"Mate. Or as you would call it, make love."

"As I would call it?" she echoed uncertainly.

"Would you make love to a dead person?" the dark figure repeated.

"I love you, Henry."

"Then you would make love to a dead person." It was another statement that sounded more like a question.

"I-I don't know," Vivian answered hesitantly.

"But you think of me all the time, although I am dead."

"You don't look dead, Henry."

"But I am. You were there when I died. You were there when they buried me."

Yes, I was, she thought. And it had been horrible. She'd never forget the agony in his face as he had clutched his chest. They had been eating breakfast, and the morning had been sunny. There had been no sign, no warning. He fell off his chair, and his skin quickly changed to an ugly blue color. The end had been so abrupt, such a shock.

She had tried to breathe life into him and had pounded his chest, but nothing she did would bring him back. And all the while she sat with him on the kitchen floor the sun streamed in through the window, basking them with warm light. She remembered thinking how disrespectful that was. It should be raining, she had thought. The world had just ended for Henry, as well as for her. It shouldn't have looked so damn cheerful!

Now tears filled Vivian's eyes. She loved Henry so much, had never stopped loving him.

The dark frame opened its arms for her.

She missed him, missed being in those arms. It'd seemed so long since they'd been around her.

"Henry, hold me," she said, her voice now as soft as his. "Hold me and kiss me, like you used to."

The figure sat on the bed, paused for a moment, then wrapped its arms around her. The contact stunned her with its coldness. Vivian began to pull back, but the icy sensation quickly reached her brain and left her dazed. Henry, I love you so much.

The arms held her tightly, cold and dry—like a corpse would feel, she momentarily thought.

"Kiss me," she pleaded. Again there was

a pause, then the dark face moved closer.

Their lips met, but the kiss was not as she remembered. She reminded herself she was dreaming. She told herself that it did not matter that Henry's mouth felt leathery and thin against hers, that the taste of him was bitter and acrid, and that his odor reminded her of a green, stagnant swamp. She adamantly told herself that this dream was about Henry, that she was in his arms, and that was all that mattered.

They still loved each other. Death could not keep them apart.

He pushed her down on the bed. He wasn't as gentle as he used to be, but it didn't matter. Maybe it was because he was so eager. After all, it had been so long.

His hands and lips were all over her, moving quickly and roughly. The hands enveloped her, not feeling like hands at all but rather like wings—leathery wings.

She heard shrill, squeaky cries, and she knew Henry was aroused, even though it was deep grunts he had uttered in the past.

Crazy dream!

He scratched her with his long nails. He'd never done that to her before. He'd never been brutal with her.

She didn't like the way this dream was going.

For the first time in her life she wished he'd go away.

"Henry, you're . . . you're hurting me."

He paid no heed.

She tried to push him off her and found that his body was surprisingly spongy, not as firm as it looked. Alarm coursed through her.

"Go away!" she cried, pounding against the soft flesh. "Just go away!"

"But I thought you wanted me."

"Go away!"

There was a moment of silence, then he released her. He stepped away from the bed, cocked his head to one side for a long moment, then retreated from the room.

Vivian watched as her beloved husband disappeared and flickered with a strange green light. She saw something glow spectrally near the closet, something that she now realized had been watching her. Then she felt a sharp pain in her chest. She was going to have a heart attack in this crazy dream.

She was going to die in it.

CHAPTER TWELVE

Toni and Lisa were on the couch, sitting close together. They felt alone, for the silence was heavy around them and the darkness was kept at bay only by the feeble glow of the oil lamp. Keith and Vivian were in separate bedrooms, Brice was asleep in his sleeping bag on the floor, and Maggie was asleep in the rocking chair. It was 4:15 according to Toni's watch. Soon it would be daylight, but not soon enough to suit the girls.

"How could they all sleep?" Toni asked, shaking her head in stunned amazement.

"Your mother was trying to fight it," Lisa said, her voice a soft whisper. "I was watching her."

"Well, *I'm* not gonna sleep."

"Me neither."

"They come out only at night."

"Your parents?"

"No, no." Toni shook her head impatiently. "Them. Those . . . those creatures."

"Oh."

"They're vampires."

Lisa said nothing, as though not wanting to think about it.

"Well, don't you agree?" Toni demanded. "Didn't you get a look at them?"

Lisa looked back at her, hesitated, then nodded.

"And?'

Lisa shrugged. "And nothing."

"Didn't you notice that they looked like bats?"

"Well, their wings did," Lisa admitted reluctantly, "but not the rest of them."

"They had big bellies."

"Yeah, I saw."

"They were ugly, Lisa."

"I know."

"They killed Commander." When Lisa didn't reply, she said, "Why do you think they did that?"

"I never heard of vampires killing dogs," Lisa pointed out. "So I guess you can rule out vampires."

"Maybe they figured Commander would only be in the way at getting to us, so they killed him."

Lisa said nothing.

Toni shivered. "Aren't you scared?" Lisa

seemed so calm sitting next to her, casually looking at this and that. Didn't anything faze her? Didn't she realize what was happening? Didn't she know that they were all going to die?

"Of course I'm scared, silly!" Lisa said after a long pause.

"You sure as hell don't look it."

"That's 'cause I don't dwell on it like you do."

"I can't help it."

"Just don't think about it."

"Lisa, we're stuck here."

"Think about something else."

"They're going to kill us!"

"Shh!" Lisa shot a glance at Brice and Maggie. When she saw that they hadn't stirred, she said, "You're gonna wake everybody up."

"They *should* be up," Toni declared, although she dropped her voice anyway. After a moment of silence, she said, "What do you think happened, Lisa?"

"I said I didn't want to think about it—and that also means talk about it."

"You know what I think?" Toni said, ignoring her. "I think we are hypnotized. Vampires can do that, you know. They put their victims into trances and—"

"They're not vampires!" Lisa hissed, her voice suprisingly sharp.

Toni knew she was upsetting her friend by talking this way, but she couldn't help it. She was never one to bottle up her feelings. "How do you know they're not vampires?" she demanded.

Lisa sighed. "Because we'd already be dead with our blood sucked out of us, wouldn't we?"

"They did something to my grandmother."

"I think she got scared and passed out. I don't think they did anything to her. She's old, you know. Probably almost had a heart attack."

"They hypnotized us," Toni reminded her.

"So they did." Lisa shrugged.

"But why?"

Lisa let out another petulant sigh. "I don't know."

"I'm scared."

"Think about something else, dammit!"

Toni stared at her, then slowly nodded. Maybe her friend had the right attitude after all. Certainly she wasn't getting anywhere thinking about the creatures. She was only frightening herself more and more.

She said, "Okay, let's talk about something else."

The abrupt change surprised Lisa, rendering her speechless for a moment. At length, she replied, "Want to talk about our favorite subject—boys?"

Boys and sex were the farthest thing from Toni's mind right now. It was a subject that had been, less than two days ago, more important than anything else in the world, but now it seemed so insignificant, even silly.

"Did you do it with Chuck, yet?" Lisa

asked.

Toni looked at her.. The girl's eyes were wide, waiting for an answer.

"Toni!" Lisa demanded sharply. "Answer me!"

Toni knew it was sex she was talking about. In truth, Toni was still a virgin, although she had never admitted this to Lisa, lest the girl laugh at her. Lisa, she knew, had slept with more boys than Toni had kissed. "No," she finally answered. "Not yet."

"What're you waiting for? He's awfully cute."

Yes, he was cute. Toni was fully aware of that. He just wasn't the right guy, that's all. She wanted her first time to be very special. "I'm not sure if I like him anymore," she said.

"Oh? Who do you like now?"

"Nobody, really. Who do you like?"

"I like men now, not boys."

After a brief pause, Toni asked, "Is there any particular guy—man—you like now?"

A secretive smile spread across Lisa's face. A full minute passed before she answered. "Your father."

"Who?"

"Your father, silly."

"What?" Toni's mind refused to accept what the girl was saying.

"Your father's nice, Toni."

"But . . ."

"Please don't tell him, though."

"But he's . . . old, Lisa."

"Yes, I know—a man."

"I don't believe what I'm hearing."

"Oh, come on now, don't get so excited. I just think he's nice, that's all. It's not as if I'm gonna, you know, seduce him or anything."

"I should hope not!" Toni glanced at her mother in the chair.

"But he is nice," Lisa repeated wistfully.

"That's sick!"

Lisa shrugged, although she was clearly affronted. "I told you, I've outgrown boys."

"But why my father?"

"Oh, Toni," she sighed. "You're making a big deal out of this. I told you I'm not going to do anything. It's just a silly . . ." She rolled her eyes upward, searching for the right word.

"Crush?" Toni supplied.

Lisa thought about this for a moment, then shook her head. "That sounds so juvenile. No, it's a silly attraction. Yes, that's it— attraction."

Toni stared at her with disgust. She had thought she knew her friend quite well. Now she realized she didn't. Her best friend was actually a stranger.

She had always admired Lisa and envied her popularity with the opposite sex. But now, Lisa simply had gone too far.

"You think I'm horrible now, don't you?" Lisa said.

"No," Toni lied automatically, then began to wonder why she wasn't being truthful. She swallowed, then nodded. "Yes, Lisa. God, he's my father," she repeated emphatically.

"I know, I know." Lisa moved closer and sandwiched Toni's hand between hers, endeavoring to placate her. "I'll get over it, and I promise I won't start any trouble. I won't break up a marriage. I'm not like that."

Toni fought an impulse to pull her hand away. Lisa had touched her like this many times before, and Toni had never thought anything of it. Lisa was the affectionate type, she had thought. She was one who liked to touch and be touched, the hugging sort. Now Toni no longer found this trait as something sweet and moving. She found it phony.

After being friends for almost three years, why was Toni seeing the girl in a different light now? Did the tension and fear in the air have something to do with it? Was this bringing out the truth, no matter how ugly, because in a matter of days, maybe even hours, everyone was going to die?

Toni shivered visibly, but did not pull her hand back.

"Are you all right?" Lisa asked.

It took Toni a moment to respond. Her eyes, she realized with surprise, were filled with tears. "We're . . . we're going to die."

"No, we're not."

"But I'm sure of it. I can feel it."

"No, you can't."

"Why do you think they're here? What do you think they want?"

"I said I didn't want to think about it. We were talking about men and boys, so let's keep talking about them."

"No. I don't want to talk about my father. It's disgusting."

"Nothing will happen. I promise."

"Lisa," Toni said. She had heard something from her grandmother's room.

"What?"

"Shh." She pulled her hand free from Lisa's and listened intently. She could hear her grandmother faintly moaning. Was her grandmother talking in her sleep? Toni knew she should investigate, but she found herself unable to move from the sofa.

"What?" Lisa repeated, frowning.

"I think I heard Grandma."

Both girls fell silent and listened, turning their heads toward Vivian's room. The door was ajar, exposing only darkness. A gasp and something indistinct came from the bedroom, then a clear "Go away!"

The girls looked at each other.

"Having a nightmare," Lisa said.

Toni glanced over at her mother in the chair, then looked back at the bedroom door, thinking again that she should investigate. Again she found herself lacking the courage. Maybe it really was only a nightmare, she told herself. Maybe there was no cause for alarm.

She heard her grandmother again, this time an unmistakable outburst of agony.

"Something's happening!" Toni was suddenly certain. She jumped to her feet and rushed toward the bedroom. As she reached the door, it opened wider. She let out a cry and jumped back. Something had slipped through above her head, missing her by mere inches. She spun around to look.

It was one of the creatures, its leathery wings flapping rapidly as it flew across the room toward the front door. It hovered like a frantic moth at this door, banging repeatedly against it. The banging increased as it panicked and struggled to open the door.

Toni and Lisa watched, mesmerized. Maggie slowly awakened from the noise.

The creature began to screech. Green light pulsed from its body in a frantic rhythm. Then as quickly as it had all begun, the creature was calm. Its mother had joined it from Vivian's bedroom, and with ease its mouth turned the doorknob.

Instinctively, Toni bolted for the door, just as it was opening, and slammed it shut before the creatures could escape.

"Toni!" Lisa shouted in disbelief. "Let 'em go!" She ran toward the door and yanked it open.

Toni stepped back, uncertain as to why she had reacted the way she had. The creatures sped through the now open door and flew into the night, but not before Toni caught a glimpse of the larger creature's visage. Its sole, yellow eye had glared at her, and its mouth, still open after working the doorknob, was a circle of small, sharp teeth. Then the body pulsed white light and obscured the face, bleaching its features to resemble that of a bright moon. When both creatures were gone, Toni looked down at the brass doorknob and noted it was filled with numerous niches. Teeth had violently marred it.

"Oh God," she whispered.

"Why the hell did you try to keep them in here?" Lisa asked, staring at her as though she had lost her mind.

"It was automatic, I guess," Toni said, pulling her gaze away from the knob. "I knew they were running away from something, and it just seemed natural to stop them."

"That was dumb, Toni, really dumb."

Maggie joined them, alarm evident in her face and voice. "What happened? My God, I didn't mean to fall asleep."

"Two of those things were in Grandma's room—" Toni stopped short in sudden alarm. "Grandma! They must have done something to her!"

Simultaneously, the three of them broke into a run toward Vivian's room.

CHAPTER THIRTEEN

Through the darkness Maggie and the two girls could see that Vivian was still alive, for the frail form on the bed was moving—and breathing, although laboriously.

"Ma, are you all right?" Maggie asked.

"Yes . . . I'm fine," came the weak reply.

Maggie groped for her mother's skeletal hand and held it. It was cold and trembling, hardly fine. "What happened?"

"I think I had a dream, but I'm not sure."

"It was no dream, Grandma," Toni assured her. "We saw them coming out of the room."

"Henry?" Vivian's voice cracked. She struggled to sit up straighter, but could not find the strength.

"No, not him, Grandma—them. The creatures!"

"But it was Henry I saw."

"Who's Henry?" Lisa wanted to know.

"My grandfather," Toni quickly told her. Back to Vivian, she said, "No, Grandma, we didn't see him."

Disappointment and confusion were evident in Vivian's face as amber light suddenly spilled into the room. Keith had entered, carrying the oil lamp.

"What's going on?"

"I think they came back," Maggie said. She wished she could tell him more, but she had slept through it, something she hadn't meant to do.

"I thought I saw Henry," Vivian said, and Keith angled the lamp toward her. Her entire face appeared out of the gloom, yellow and waxen. Never had she looked so old or sickly. "Maybe it was a dream, but it seemed so real. I even felt him holding me."

"We're all here because of a dream?" Keith said incredulously. "From the sound of it, I thought somebody was being attacked or something."

"They came back, Daddy," Toni reminded him. "Lisa and I saw them come out of this room."

The scowl on Keith's face vanished. He looked over at Maggie, tacitly demanding details, but she had none to give.

"I was sleeping, like you," she said lamely.

"Christ," he cursed in a low voice. "I tried to stay awake, I really did, but nothing was happening. It was so dark and quiet."

"You don't have to explain," Maggie assured him. "The same thing happened to me. I fell asleep, too."

"So exactly what happened?" he asked, turning to the others around the bed.

"We heard noises in here, Mr. Hunter," Lisa said. "Then Toni and I came here to see what it was—"

"Not you and me," Toni interrupted. "Just me."

"And by the time we reached the door," Lisa continued, ignoring her, "two of those creatures flew out. One of them was that big one. You know, the white one. Toni tried to stop them from leaving, but I let them go. After all, why would we want to keep them in here with us?"

"I don't know why I did it," Toni stammered. "It's just that I thought they were running away and—and—"

"It doesn't matter, sweetheart," Maggie said, seeing that the girl was upset. "I'm sure I would have reacted the same way. What matters, though," she said, now giving Vivian her full attention, "is that you're all right. Do you know if they did anything to you?"

"I didn't see them," Vivian said. "I saw only Henry. It was Henry when we had first met."

"But you're all right now, aren't you?" Maggie didn't like to talk about her father— not because the memory was painful, for it certainly was that, but because it seemed to set her mother back. She wanted to help her move forward, not stay behind in the past. "It was only a dream," she concluded confidently.

"I could smell his pipe tobacco, Maggie. You can't smell things in dreams, can you?"

"You can imagine smelling things in dreams, I would think," she replied uncertainly.

"I'm not sure it was a dream. I felt him, I told you." She paused thoughtfully, then added, "Although it really didn't feel like Henry."

"Ma, what are you saying?"

Vivian stared at her for a long moment, as though she herself was uncertain what she was saying. She licked her lips before speaking. "He felt cold, Maggie. He felt . . . dead."

"That's because he is. So it definitely was a dream."

"He came back. Now that I think about it, I'm sure that's what happened. He came back, Maggie."

"But that's impossible."

"No, it's not."

"Ma, he's dead." Maggie made her voice firm, yet gentle. "The dead cannot come back. You know that as well as the rest of us."

Vivian began to shake her head, refusing to believe her. "It was not a dream, I tell you. It was Henry. I felt him in my arms. I smelt his pipe. It was real."

Maggie looked over at Keith, wishing he'd

say or do something, but he was staring at the woman with rapt bemusement.

"Ma," she began slowly, when it was evident she'd get no help, "it is impossible for Dad to return. He can only do that in your mind or dreams."

"But it was so vivid, so real."

"Sometimes dreams are very vivid."

Vivian gave this some thought, then dismissed it. "I don't think so. Henry was here," she declared adamantly. "Right here in this bed with me."

"Maybe *they* did it," Toni suggested. "Maybe they brought Grandpa back somehow."

"The main thing is that you're all right," Maggie said in a softer voice. "You're not hurt or anything?"

"No I'm fine."

"I'll stay here with you for a while."

"No need. I don't want to be a bother."

"No bother." Maggie sat on the bed and squeezed her mother's hand, hoping this would convince her. "No bother."

Slowly, Vivian began to relax. She leaned her head back, letting it sink deeply into the pillow, and closed her eyes for a moment. The room fell silent as the group around the bed watched her. No one wanted to leave the room, for it would mean leaving the light of the oil lamp, the only light they had.

A soft smile grew on Vivian's face before she opened her eyes. "It was wonderful seeing Henry again," she said. "I hope it wasn't only a first and last visit. It would be something to look forward to."

"Ma, you don't really mean that."

"Oh, but I do. I enjoyed seeing your father. It was as if he had never left." Her smile widened and became dreamy. "I miss him so much. Love him so much."

Maggie experienced a surge of sadness and sympathy for Vivian. She could see the wound was reopening, and she wished there was a way to stop this before it was again raw and painful. "Nothing good can possibly come of this," she said.

"But I need something to look forward to, Maggie."

"It's just not, well, healthy. You should try to find something else, Ma. You should—"

"People watch TV and read books," Vivian interrupted. "Sometimes they do this to fulfill their lives. These things they see or read are not real, but still they make them happy."

"That's different."

"Seeing your father made me happy."

"Ma . . ." Maggie began, then fell silent. Nothing she could say would change her mother's mind. Maybe I'm making an issue out of nothing, she thought. Maybe it'll be better not to argue. The less that is said, the sooner this will fade.

Vivian, aware that Maggie was no longer protesting, closed her eyes again, and this time did not reopen them. She drifted off to sleep, the smile still on her lips.

Looking over at a window, Maggie noticed the night was beginning to pale. The trees were black, but the sky behind their tips was a dusty gray.

Soon it would be daylight.

Brice had been dreaming about Commander when he heard his sister yell. When he woke up and crawled out of his sleeping bag, he saw his mother and the two girls run to his grandmother's room. Minutes later, his father came out, grabbed the oil lamp and joined the others. Now Brice was alone in the dark.

At first he was afraid. He sat on the floor, the bag under him, for a long while and listened to the conversation in the other room. He heard his sister talk about the creatures, and as he listened, the fear gave way to resentment, then anger.

The creatures had tried to hurt Grandma. The creatures had killed his dog.

Images of Commander's wet, matted body kept flashing in his mind. He knew he'd never forget the feeling of holding the limp, furry clump in his arms. He loved that dog. It wasn't fair that he was gone for good. Commander had never hurt anybody. He was a good dog—the best! No, it wasn't fair at all. Somebody should be punished for this!

Brice stood up and looked around the dark room, trying to decide what to do. His heart was racing. Yes, somebody should be punished, he thought again. The creatures should be punished.

He headed for the kitchen cabinets. Pulling out a drawer, he reached inside for a knife, the biggest his hand could find. When he found what he wanted, he went outside, closing the door quietly after him.

He moved straight for the cylinder. The hand holding the knife trembled, and his small frame shivered in the predawn chill. When he reached his destination, he drew in a deep breath.

The cylinder looked so big before him, its dull surface cold and featureless. He knocked on it. Of course there was no response, so he knocked again. When he realized he wasn't knocking hard enough, he started to pound violently with one hand as he held the knife with the other.

More than once he wanted to give up. Even if the creatures did come out, would he have the guts to use the knife on them? He remembered the creatures had been fast, so maybe he was crazy to even think of doing this. Yet whenever Commander's lifeless body flashed in his mind, the fear and insecurity vanished.

"Open up!" he shouted. "You ain't gonna kill my dog and get away with it!"

He kicked at the object. He wasn't going to let them ignore him. He'd kick and pound until they came out, and then . . .

"Open up!"

His face was wet with tears, although he was not sad; he was angry, angrier than he'd ever been in his whole life.

"C'mon, open up! Open up now!"

An entrance materialized, immediately silencing him. As he watched the door grow larger, as though in slow-motion, fear chilled his belly. He gripped the handle on his knife tighter.

He took a step back and waited. Confidence and courage were waning fast. He had never used a knife on anyone before, not even to skin a squirrel as some of his buddies had done to make caps. So why was he standing out here with a butcher knife in his hand now?

He took another step back. Suddenly he needed to pee. Maybe he should forget about this whole stupid thing and go back into the house. He'd think of another way to make them pay for what they'd done to his dog.

As he turned, he heard a sudden fluttering of many wings. He stopped, frozen in his tracks. The sound was surprisingly loud, beginning somewhere deep inside the cylinder and now rushing outward toward him. Like a tornado or a swarm of bees, he thought. His paralysis snapped when he saw the creatures shoot out of the cylinder and speed toward him.

He ran for the cottage. Halfway, he realized he'd never make it. Within seconds they were all around him. Wings seemed to be everywhere, violently fanning his face.

Their squeaky cries deafened him. He brandished the knife blindly, but it did no good. He felt them pull at his hair and at his clothes. He swatted at them, covered his face with his forearm, and ran in another direction.

They were after him like angry bees, except that they were a hundred times bigger.

He wanted to scream for his parents, but he was too intent in warding off the creatures. Again, he changed direction. This time he found himself heading toward the wharf on the lake.

He stumbled over something and fell to his knees. A sob swelled in his throat as he saw it was his dog's body that had tripped him. The creatures, reaching him, swooped down. Waving his arms wildly, he jumped back up and continued toward his new destination.

He leaped onto the wharf and raced down the length of it. At the far end he sucked in a deep breath and jumped into the water.

Silence engulfed him. Under the water the darkness was all-enveloping. Brice looked up, his cheeks puffing out as he held his breath. He could see nothing on the surface. He had no way of knowing if the creatures were hovering, waiting for him to surface.

He forced himself to wait as long as he could. Releasing his breath a bubble at a time, he swam to another spot, hopefully near the shore. He moved gently, so as not to cause a detectable ripple in the water. He didn't want to break surface with the creatures directly above him. They would have his head.

Stopping and keeping himself as motionless as possible, he looked up once more but still couldn't see anything. Were they still waiting for him?

His lungs felt ready to pop. He'd have to shoot to the top very soon. He was afraid to do this, but there was no choice.

Please don't be there, he prayed silently, then began to swim upward. Visions of the creatures plummeting toward his head filled his mind. Needing both arms to keep himself afloat, how would he protect his face? They'd slash at it, with either their teeth or claws, until the face was bloody and gone.

He broke surface, gasping, then quickly looked around.

The air above him was empty.

"What do you think really happened?" Maggie asked Keith two hours later, when they were alone. They were gathering twigs, planning to light the fireplace for the following evening, not for warmth but for light.

"What do you mean what do I think?" he replied gruffly. "I told you, there's no way I could bury the dog. I know it was stupid of me, but I forgot to bring a shovel along," he added.

He had stuffed the dog in the aluminum trash can and dumped it in the lake. Maggie had objected, but in the end had to agree with him. There seemed to be no other choice. As Keith disposed of the body, she and Brice remained inside the cottage. Earlier, Brice had come running to her, soaked to the skin. He told her the creatures had tried to attack him. It had taken him an hour to stop trembling. He said it was because the water was so cold, but she knew it was more than this. The creatures had terrified him. For two entire hours she had kept him on her lap, her arms tightly around him.

"No, I'm talking about Ma," she now said to Keith. "Do you think it was a dream she had?"

"I don't know."

"You must have some idea."

He dumped a load of twigs and branches on the porch, then returned to the trees to gather more. "I think the creatures had something to do with it, yeah," he said, then quickly corrected himself. "No, I think they had everything to do with it."

"But how?"

He gave her that how-the-hell-should-I-know look.

"You think they made her dream about Dad?" Maggie wondered.

He said nothing, only grunting.

"Or do you think they actually brought Dad back?"

Keith stared at her, and in his eyes she detected a flash of fear. "Who the hell knows about anything," he muttered, then looked away, searching for more twigs.

Maggie stopped helping him, letting him move away from her. Did they bring her father back? Could they do that? Could they bring back the dead?

If they could do that, then they could do anything, couldn't they?

"Keith, we've got to get out of here! Somehow we've just go to!"

"You've got us into this mess, so why don't you get us out of it?"

Once again guilt cruelly hit her.

It was almost noon when Vivian woke up. The room in which she slept was uncomfortably warm, the air thick and humid. This was because of the transparent shield outside the cottage, no doubt, but this was not the woman's first concern upon awakening. She was certain she actually had seen Henry rather than dreamed of him.

The smile that she had fallen asleep with returned.

It had been so lovely seeing him. He had come back so young, and she regretted that she hadn't been as youthful and attractive for her husband. What had happened to him? Did death make one regress and move backward in time?

You're losing your hold on reality, an inner voice warned her. Death is death. Death is final.

Henry did not come back.

"Oh, but he did," she whispered to the empty room, a desperate sob in her voice. "I don't know how or even why. Perhaps it's because his love for me is so strong, like mine is for him, but he did come back."

They did it, the stubborn voice said. They tricked you.

Somewhere far inside her she knew this may be true. The creatures had been responsible, and if so, this was something evil. But she ignored this faint awareness. She only wanted to think about Henry.

She wondered when she would see him again.

CHAPTER FOURTEEN

They were puzzled and intrigued. The Little Ones turned to The Elder, hoping she would explain, but she quickly informed them that she was equally surprised.

Humans, she agreed with them, are strange, indeed. They do things that seem to make no sense. But then, she reminded them, this is because they are different.

This explanation did not satisfy The Little Ones. They still could not understand why one would miss one who was dead. Why would one continue to love someone or something that no longer existed?

A Little One had wanted to see how far a human would go with one that did not exist. With the Elder's permission and guidance, he had experimented with the oldest woman.

He was surprised that the oldest woman had gone as far as she did. The Little One could have easily mated with her, and he would have, for it would have been a most interesting experience. But the oldest woman had begun to protest, and The Elder had commanded him to stop.

Yes, it was interesting, but it seemed so pointless. The Little Ones' bodies pulsed rapidly in the dark cylinder as their confusion and curiosity mounted. The Elder tried to explain that it was only pointless to them. She urged them to try to enjoy their findings, not be perplexed too greatly by them.

The Little Ones huddled together to digest this bit of advice. They flew to one corner, squealing and blinking while The Elder glowed patiently in another corner. She could not blame them for being so excited. They were so young, energetic, eager, and this was all so new to them.

As they huddled, the boy pounded at their vessel. He would not stop. They tried to ignore him, but in the end realized he would never go away. With the Elder's permission, they flew out after the boy. Otherwise, how else would they be able to concentrate and then sleep?

At length The Little Ones returned to The Elder's side. They circled her and expressed their desire to learn more about the strange humans. The dog had bored them, which was why they had tossed it back to the boy. Now they wanted to probe deeply into one of the humans' minds.

The Elder nodded, giving them the approval they sought, then she asked which human they wished to explore.

They mulled this over. The Elder was giving them permission to use only one human. Minutes passed, then one of The Little Ones finally reached a decision for the rest of them. All humans are interesting, he told The Elder, so they would simply experiment with the first human they could catch.

The Elder nodded again, and glowed proudly. Oh, how she loved their youthful enthusiasm.

CHAPTER FIFTEEN

Lisa was sitting under a pine tree when she saw him. She wanted to be where it was cool, away from the thick heat and sun. The cottage was too claustrophobic, and the tension inside there, with everyone staring blankly with huge, fearful eyes, was just too unbearable. Out here, out of sight of the silver cylinder, she found herself able to forget for a little while, to calm herself a bit. She was lying on a bed of pine needles, looking up at the green canopy above and enjoying the faint coolness, when she heard and saw movements in a nearby tree.

Her first reaction was alarm. She bolted upright to a sitting position, then she heard the rustling of leaves again and saw that it was only Mr. Hunter. He was high up in an oak tree, doing something strange. She frowned, wondering what it was he was doing, but she didn't move from her spot nor call out to him.

He climbed higher, gingerly testing each branch as he rose. At one point he almost fell, teetering for a horrible moment before regaining his balance. Lisa's hand shot to her mouth to stifle a gasp. She did not cry out because she was afraid she'd startle him and cause him to fall, and she also was curious to see what he'd do next. So with her hand still against her lips, she watched in rapt silence.

Keith held on to the trunk of the tree with one arm, while he reached out at empty air with the other. He seemed to be groping for something, as though he were a blind man. He leaned forward and extended his free arm as far as possible. He swept the air with splayed fingers. When it was certain he'd not find what he was searching for, he withdrew his hand and ascended to the next sturdy branch. He was shirtless, and his shoulders and chest were shiny with sweat.

Lisa stared at his body. His chest was hairy, dark and matted, and his arms were thick. So powerful and sexy, she thought. No boys she had ever made love to looked like this—so manly. She wondered how those arms would feel encircling her, or how his chest would feel crushing hers.

He's a married man, for God's sake! she

reminded herself. He's your best friend's father.

But this did not stop her from looking. There was no harm in admiring a man's anatomy, she told herself.

Keith's chest muscle rippled as he groped the air above him. She watched his bicep pull as he stretched, then was disappointed when he rose yet again to a higher branch and disappeared behind a cluster of leaves.

All man, she sighed wistfully.

She lay back down on the bed of needles and closed her eyes. She hadn't come to this spot to think about men, she told herself. She had come to escape the tension, to be alone.

Toni had wanted to join her, but Lisa told her she wanted a moment of privacy. Toni was the last person she wanted to be with, for terror was constant in her friend's eyes, and it was too infectious. It was from Toni, more than the others, that Lisa needed to get away.

Now as she closed her eyes and willed her mind to be blank, she heard rustling in another direction. Her eyes opened, and her head turned to the sound. Instinctively she tensed, but this time did not sit up. The creatures are coming! she thought. Then she remembered they didn't come out during the day, or was this an erroneous assumption?

Was she wrong to think she was safe, merely because it was daytime?

Maybe she should have never left the

cottage. There was safety in numbers, wasn't there?

Lisa contemplated running. Then she heard Maggie's voice, and the tension melted with an audible sigh.

"What on earth are you doing?" the woman said, but the question was directed to Keith in the tree, rather than Lisa. Because of the surrounding pines, Lisa escaped notice.

Keith ceased groping the air and looked down at his wife. "I'm looking for an opening in the shield," he explained. "Maybe somewhere there's a gap wide enough to escape through."

"You could fall and hurt yourself."

"I'm being careful," he assured her. "How high is the shield here?"

Keith shrugged, not certain. He looked upward, then shrugged again. "Completely invisible from where I'm standing. Can't feel it. Maybe if I climb a little higher—"

"No!"

He looked down at her, surprised that she had spoken so loudly and forcefully. "No?" he challenged, resenting the command.

"You're going to get hurt, Keith. Please come down."

"But I might find something up here. A way out for all of us."

"What good would that do way up there?"

"We could slide down the other side."

"We'd kill ourselves if we did that."

"I don't think so. Break a few bones,

maybe, but that's better than staying here."

"I still think you should come down," Maggie insisted. "It's too dangerous. The branches look too thin. They might break."

"Hey, I'm not a little kid. I know what I'm doing."

Maggie fell silent, realizing it was pointless to argue. Nervously, she watched.

"Why don't you go back into the house," he said irritably.

"I'm too afraid you're going to fall."

"I will if you keep gawking at me."

Maggie hesitated, then forced herself to turn away from the tree. After a few steps, she stopped and looked back.

"I'm not a little boy," he repeated. "I don't need you to look after me."

She nodded, reluctantly relenting. "Please be careful," she said, then turned away and headed back toward the cottage.

Lisa waited until she was certain Maggie was gone before she sat up again. She watched Keith, and this time was able to understand Maggie's apprehension. Keith was near the top of the oak, and the tree itself was swaying as though on the verge of snapping. Yet this was not deterring him, for his arm was stretched to the limit, groping for the shield.

Such a brave man, Lisa thought, a real man.

When she stood up, he spotted her immediately. He withdrew his arm, and for a moment he and the tree were motionless.

"Hello, Mr. Hunter," she said as cheerfully as she could.

"I thought I told you my name's Keith."

Lisa smiled. "Oops, sorry—Keith." She loved how friendly he was to her.

"Can't find the damn thing up here," he said in a voice that was only mildly angry and frustrated. "Can you see the shield from down there?"

Lisa tilted her head to one side, then to the other, but could not discern the shape of the translucent shield. It was only at certain angles and certain light that the barrier could be seen. "No, I can't," she said at length.

"Might as well come down. Nothing's here and I can't go much higher." He began his careful discent.

She watched him as the muscles in his shoulders bunched and rippled. No boys, she reflected, had muscles like that, not even the jocks at school. Keith's muscles were somehow more mature, not from pumping iron or injecting steroids, but from something natural. Keith's body was something real, not something that had been forced into shape. It was not a boy's body trying to be a man's.

Yes, Mr. Keith Hunter was a natural, real man.

With this thought, she moved toward the trees and waited for him to touch ground.

He skipped some of the lower branches and landed with a soft, yet heavy thud, almost losing his balance and falling to his knees. He quickly straightened, throwing his shoulders back, and slapped dirt and grainy pieces of bark from his palms. Now that he was only several feet away from Lisa, he gave her a smile that was somewhat sad as well as awkward—sad because he knew he had failed, and awkward because Lisa's womanly form was clad only in snug denim shorts and a skimpy halter top. She wore no bra, so her breasts and nipples were clearly defined beneath the thin fabric.

Lisa was aware of the effect she had on men and was proud of it. Men were always uncomfortable with her at first, but it never lasted long.

"I'm sorry," he said after a long silence.

The contrition surprised her. "About what?"

"This whole mess. You wouldn't be in it if it weren't for me and my wife."

"Oh." She didn't want to talk about this, didn't even want to think about it.

Unlike Keith's timid gaze, she let her own eyes be audacious and sweep across the man's hairy chest and thick shoulders. She marveled at the size of his arms, then her gaze rose to his face. It was not handsome, but it was rugged, filled with character, and the eyes were dark brown, filled with sensitivity and intelligence.

"Hold me," she commanded, her tone soft but urgent.

Keith blinked in surprise. Lisa took a small

step forward, not to be closer to him but to encourage him. "I'm scared, Keith," she explained. "I need someone to hold me."

He did not say anything nor make a move. It was clear that he was engaged in a mental tug-of-war. He was definitely attracted to her—she could see it in his face—but he needed more prompting.

"When I was a little girl my daddy would hold me whenever I was afraid," she said. She took another step forward. "I used to be afraid of everything—the dark, my closet at night, thunderstorms. Everything."

He still made no move. She thought of his marital status. She knew she should leave him alone, but something inside would not let her. Something was urging her onward.

"Please hold me."

This time Keith took a step closer, narrowing the space that separated them, yet he still could not open his arms for her.

"We're going to die, aren't we?" she said.

Saying nothing, he studied her face. He seemed to find something in it that encouraged him to comfort her, for after a long pause he moved closer and lifted his arms.

She closed the gap, stepping into the arms. He held her, hesitantly at first, then securely. He smelled of sweat, but she did not mind.

"We're not going to die," he assured her.

She pressed her face against his chest, for he was much taller than she.

"Hold me tighter," she now said to Keith,

her voice muffled against the matted hair on his chest.

He complied. "Don't be afraid," he told her. "I won't let anything happen to you. I'll get us out of here yet."

"I hope so." She could see the stubble of his day-old beard as she looked up at him. Or was it two days? She was so close she could almost count each black dot that freckled his jaw and lower part of his cheeks.

"Do you really think so?" she whispered.

"What?" He was surprised to find her studying him. His face colored, and she smiled inwardly at the blush.

She said, "Do you really think nothing will happen to us?"

"Oh. Yes, nothing will happen."

"I hope you're right. God, I hope you are." She pressed her face against his chest again, and this time added her breasts and thighs to his body. She pressed gently, half-expecting him to resist. To her relief and delight, he didn't.

"Hold me tighter," she reiterated. "Please."

Once more he complied, although he said, "We shouldn't be doing this."

"Doing what? Holding each other? There's nothing wrong in what we're doing. Daddy used to always comfort me whenever I was afraid, and I'm afraid now."

"I don't know. If Maggie saw us—"

"She won't see us. Trees are all around us.

We would hear her come through the bushes."

"I don't know," he said, shaking his head. But she noted his arms were still around her, his body was eager against hers. Just a little more encouragement, she told herself.

She kissed him.

He stiffened, but the response was brief. As she kept her lips over his, he relaxed and soon returned the kiss. It was easier than she had thought it'd be.

Her knees were suddenly tired and weak. No longer wanting to stand, she descended to the ground, urging Keith to drop with her. He resisted only slightly. It was so easy.

They made love. At first they tried to be patient and gentle, but the excitement and passion were too strong to bridle. Almost as quickly as it had begun it was finished.

"I didn't meant to lose control," Keith said in a broken, barely audible voice. "I'm sorry."

"I'm not." Lisa gave him a smile, hoping he'd believe her. Actually, she was disappointed. She had thought all men were patient and gentle. Then she reminded herself it was always this way the first time because of eagerness and the thrill of something new. The second time would be better.

Keith, however, didn't seem to be interested in a second time. "I better get back to the house," he said. Before she could protest, he was gone.

Lisa felt a numbness as she sat alone on the bed of pine needles. She was neither happy nor content, and she was not sad or disappointed either. She felt a surge of guilt. When it quickly passed she felt empty again, except for something twitching dimly inside her, something on the edge of her consciousness that she didn't want to think about.

Suddenly she realized what it was that was numbing her, robbing her of other feelings. It was fear—cold, heavy fear.

She forced herself to zip up her denim shorts, then she stood up. This was when she noticed she wasn't alone, that someone was behind a nearby pine tree.

It was Toni, and she had seen everything.

CHAPTER SIXTEEN

Toni could not believe what she had seen. Her own father! Her best friend! Hot tears welled up in her eyes, but anger kept them from spilling down her cheeks. Her hands clenched into tight fists at her sides. She just couldn't believe it!

When she first saw them she thought they were strangers, and she had quickly hid behind a tree. But as she did this she remembered there were no strangers, save the creatures within the transparent shield. Then she heard and recognized Lisa's voice, and still she could not believe what she'd stumbled across.

It did not make sense. They weren't lovers. What Toni was seeing had to be an illusion or something. Maybe the creatures were doing this to her, making her see things that weren't real. They had done something like that to her grandmother, hadn't they?

But Toni could not forget what Lisa had said earlier. She had admitted that she was attracted to men, especially to Toni's father.

But Daddy would never do this! Toni cried inwardly. Her father loved her mother, didn't he?

Toni had contemplated running, but she could not move away from the horrible, ugly scene before her. She felt a wave of disgust, a wave so intense she momentarily closed her eyes and grimaced. Yet, when her eyes were closed, she could still see the image of their squirming bodies.

She reopened her eyes, hoping the scene would vanish like a dream, but her father and friend were still at it. Their breathing grew heavier as their bodies moved faster. Toni wanted to throw up, to disgorge the horrible feeling inside her, but she couldn't. The feeling only grew and grew.

When they were done and her father had walked unknowingly past her toward the cottage, the tears finally spilled from her eyes.

Now she and Lisa were staring at each other. Lisa's mouth opened to speak, then closed in silence. Of course there was nothing she could say to explain what Toni had witnessed. The reason was obvious. Lisa was a slut!

Toni wanted to shout this last word at her,

but her voice could not be found. The two girls continued to stare at each other. The only sound around them was the faint slapping of water against the shield, a sound that seemed to be deliberately reminding them they were trapped. At length Toni broke away and ran back to the cottage.

At the porch she stopped, angrily wiped away her tears from her cheeks, then looked back over her shoulder. Lisa was coming, although she was walking slowly, as though dreading the confrontation that was inevitable. Toni looked away. What was she to do now? Tell her mother everything she saw?

She immediately knew she could not do this. Her mother would be crushed if she knew Daddy had cheated on her. No, Toni could not do this. So what to do? Act as if nothing at all had happened?

Lisa's footsteps sounded on the wooden porch floor. Toni stiffened. She thought of fleeing into the house, but everyone was in there and she wasn't certain if she could mask her feelings. She needed time to compose herself.

Lisa's hand touched her shoulder. "Toni."

"Get away from me!" Toni hissed.

"Toni, you gotta listen to me."

"I said get away."

"It just happened, Toni. I didn't mean for it to happen, it just did."

More tears began to form. Toni quickly wiped them away with the back of her hand before they could stream down her face. "I just don't believe you," she said when she felt her voice was strong enough not to crack. "I thought you were my best friend."

"I am."

"No, you're not!" she shouted, then lowered her voice, not wanting the others inside the house to hear. "You're not my friend. You're a slut, Lisa Fairbank!"

"Come on," Lisa urged gently, "please try to understand."

Toni gawked incredulously at her. "Understand? How the hell do you expect me to understand why you . . . fucked my father?"

"I want you to understand that it was, you know, an accident."

"Accident?" How dumb did Lisa think she was?

"Well, yeah, sort of. I told you, I didn't mean for it to happen. We were just talking when . . . well, when it happened. It was something that was stronger than both of us."

"Stronger than both of you?" Toni mocked contemptuously. How many times had she heard that clichéd excuse? Every horny lover in every steamy soap opera had used the line. It was not a reason. It was crap! "Bullshit!" she said.

"Please, Toni, let's be cool about this. What happened has happened, and I'm sorry. I really am. But, like you already know, the past can't be changed. You gotta try to forget, go forward and—"

"I hate you, Lisa." The words were uttered quietly, although they could not have been more intense if she had shouted them.

Lisa sighed, aware that it was hopeless. "I'll talk to you later," she said and started toward the front door.

Toni seized her arm, stilling her. "Oh, no you don't!"

"Don't what?"

"Go in the house. I don't want you anywhere near my father—or me."

"Are you serious?"

Toni glared at her, not needing to answer.

Lisa shook her head as though with dazed amazement. "You're overreacting, Toni. Look, if it'd make you feel any better, I won't let your father touch me ever again. Okay?"

Toni fought a powerful urge to slap her. Didn't the bitch understand what she'd done? Mom and Dad had been a perfect couple. Lisa had just destroyed something special. Why couldn't she understand that?

This time the tears flooded Toni's cheeks in a sudden, uncontrollable rush. Lisa looked at her in surprise, as though seeing the tears for the first time.

"Hey, take it easy," Lisa said. "It's not as bad as it seems. Really, it's not. I'm going to stay away from your dad, I swear. I didn't think you'd take it so badly. I really didn't."

"Shut up." The tears would not stop. She kept wiping them away, but they kept forming.

"Hey, it wasn't only me, you know. It takes two to . . . well, you know."

"I said shut up."

"But I don't want you to hate me. I told you I have a weakness for men. I couldn't help it. And, well, your dad wasn't exactly an unwilling partner. He seemed to want it just as much as—"

"Shut up!"

Lisa recoiled, at last silenced. A few seconds later Maggie was on the porch.

"What's going on?" she demanded.

Toni felt the anger depart, as though it had been booted violently out of her. Now she felt a wave of sadness and sympathy toward her mother. Mustn't let her know, she thought. It would kill her. "Nothing," Toni mumbled.

"Well, I heard you hollering," Maggie insisted, "so I'm sure something is going on."

Toni found herself unable to look at her. She was never good at lying, but she had to lie this time. She just couldn't bring herself to speak the truth.

Aware of this, Lisa came to the rescue. "We were just having a little argument, Mrs. Hunter. It was no big deal, really." She smiled, as though to prove this. "We were talking about a boy we both know. I told her I thought he was, you know, gay, but Toni doesn't believe me. That's why she was telling me to shut up."

Toni glared at her, and Maggie already seemed to have lost interest. Her eyes became cloudy, her mind now filled with other thoughts.

"Oh," she said faintly, then retreated into the house.

Toni waited until the screen door banged shut, then she spun toward Lisa. "I want you out of here, bitch!" she whispered.

"You're forgetting the shield. I can't go anywhere."

"You can stay outside. I don't want you in the same house with me."

Lisa gave a short, uncertain laugh, as though unable to believe this was happening. When she saw that Toni was adamant, that there would be no changing her mind, fear flickered in her green eyes and her crooked smile faltered. "I've got to be inside the house tonight," she said.

"No." Toni's voice was quiet and cold.

"But the creatures," Lisa reminded her.

"I don't care."

"They'll come after me."

"I said I don't care."

"Oh, come on, Toni,"

Toni went into the house. As the screen door banged shut after her, she caught a glimpse of Lisa's pale face.

Then she stepped back, closed the wooden door and, after only a small pause, locked it.

Reluctantly, Lisa walked away from the cottage. She nervously looked up at the sky, searching for the sun which had momentarily hid behind the clouds. As she feared, the sun was low, ready to sink behind the trees. Shadows were long. It was already late afternoon, and soon it would be dusk.

And soon the cylinder would open and disgorge the creatures.

Lisa stopped at the horrible thought and turned her body toward the cottage, but she did not go back. There was still plenty of time, she told herself. She could wait an hour or so, then she'd return to the house. That should give her friend enough time to cool off.

She forced herself to look away from the house. Her gaze swept the trees and the water, carefully avoiding the silver cylinder that was lying quietly on the ground like a sleeping monster. Maybe if she ignored it, it'd go away.

She walked toward the trees, where she and Keith had made love. There was a sense of security and isolation there, for the trees were thick and the ground was soft with pine needles. My little corner, she thought as she sat on the ground and pulled her knees toward her chin. She closed her eyes and willed herself to think of something that would make her forget about her predicament.

But it did not work. She could not forget. The cylinder was only a few hundred feet away, and the shield was all around her, and night was falling. She felt as though she were inside a cage with a bomb.

"Oh Jesus," she moaned, pulling her legs closer. Never had she been so scared.

She looked up at the sky through the network of branches. It was turning gray and the sun was gone. How long had she been sitting here? Night was coming too fast.

Leaping to her feet, as if something had pinched her, she started toward the cottage. En route she glanced at the metallic object. The surrounding trees and the deepening twilight darkened it, but as far as she could see no door was opening. She was still safe. There was still time.

Heart racing, breath tightening, Lisa forced herself to walk, not run, toward her destination. Toni will let her in this time, she told herself confidently. If not Toni, then the others certainly will. Actually, it had been silly to throw her out of the house. Where was she to go? The only reason she hadn't protested too vigorously was so that Toni could have more time to calm down.

She opened the screen door, then turned the knob on the wooden door. It was locked. Lisa emitted a short laugh and shook her head. The kid always did overreact, she thought, yet she still felt a rush of panic.

She knocked on the door. She did this softly, determined to keep her composure. When no one answered, she looked uneasily over her shoulder, half-expecting to see flickering lights bolting toward her and mouths with myriad, pointed teeth open in readiness to attack.

But all she saw was that the sky was even darker. Light was fading at an alarming rate.

She turned back to the door and knocked louder.

No one answered.

Why wasn't anyone answering? She could understand why Toni wasn't responding, but why not the others? Had Toni actually succeeded in turning them all against her?

"Come on, open up!" she cried, her voice now shrill and loud. This wasn't fair! She could die out here. Night was coming fast.

She looked behind her again. There were no creatures, no gaping mouths. Not yet.

When she looked back at the door she was surprised to find it open. Maggie was now in front of her, startled and confused by Lisa's frenetic behavior.

Fist in midair, ready to knock again, Lisa stared stupidly at the woman. Her face colored as she realized how scared and foolish she'd been. She'd been impatient and not given anyone enough time to answer the door. She had overreacted needlessly. Slowly, she dropped her hand.

"The door was locked," she explained in a low, embarrassed voice.

"Who locked it?" Maggie asked, surprised.

"I don't know," Lisa lied, not wanting to tell the truth. It would be a long, ugly story. She moved past Maggie into the house.

Toni was on the couch, ignoring her. Lisa wanted to say something, to make an apology of some kind, but there was simply nothing she could say that wouldn't arouse curiosity or suspicion from the others in the room.

Brice was at the other end of the couch, pale and silent. Vivian was at the kitchen table, staring vacuously at a cold cup of tea in front of her, and Keith was in one of the bedrooms, asleep.

"We were wondering where you were," Maggie said, closing the door behind her. Her voice was tight with reproach. "I was just ready to go looking for you. It's almost nighttime, you know."

Yeah, tell me about it, Lisa thought. Aloud, she murmured, "I'm sorry, Mrs. Hunter. I just wanted to be alone for a while."

Maggie seemed to believe her, for she tenderly touched her shoulder and gave her a small compassionate smile. "I understand," she said softly, then dropped her hand and moved toward the rocking chair near the couch. En route she picked up the iron poker from the fireplace and placed it across her lap as she sat down. Then she began to rock in the chair, as though to tranquilize herself.

Guilt plagued Lisa again. She tried to ignore it, but it was too heavy this time. Looking around her, she searched for a place to sit. At length she selected a chair at the kitchen table, across from Vivian.

For a long while she watched Maggie rock in her chair, then she looked over at the others in the big room. Nobody looked at her or at each other. Everyone was silent. Everyone was waiting.

Lisa's gaze slid back to Maggie and the

rocking chair. Her eyes focused on the poker on the woman's lap. She watched it move back and forth. Rock . . . rock . . .

It's going to be a long night, she thought. Rock . . . rock . . .

I gotta stay awake, she told herself. I gotta be on guard.

Rock . . . rock . . .

Slowly, she fell asleep.

CHAPTER SEVENTEEN

Maggie glanced at her watch; it was almost 11:00, and still the creatures from the cylindrical object hadn't appeared. What were they waiting for? For her to fall asleep? Well, it wasn't going to happen this time, she vowed. She had taken a nap, and she was not going to sleep again until the sun was blazing in the sky. She was prepared for them this time.

She was not tired, but the silence and stillness was numbing her, clouding her mind. She wished she had someone to talk to, but everyone else in the cottage was sleeping. So she continued to sit in the rocking chair and wait, iron poker across her lap, one hand over it in readiness.

Through the open bedroom door she could

vaguely make out her husband on the bed, but this was only whenever he stirred. The fireplace was lit tonight, and the light was feeble and pale. The fire, feeding on the branches she and Keith had collected earlier, danced weakly, but at least, with the oil lamp, it added more light to the room and helped Maggie discern the dark shape of her husband in one bedroom and her mother in the other.

Keith's behavior this afternoon puzzled her. He had been quiet, avoiding her. After climbing the trees, he came back inside and went straight to bed. He told her to wake him up for the night, and she had tried several times already, but he had waved her off each time and fallen back to sleep. Maybe it was frustration and a sense of failure that was making him withdrawn. She could always wake him up later.

Her eyes swept toward the window that was half-concealed by the propped bookcase. She stared for a moment, waiting to see if the incandescent bellies of the hideous beings could be seen, then looked away. Staring at one thing for too long made her drowsy.

She glanced into Vivian's room. The older woman had wanted to close the door, but Maggie insisted that it be open so she could keep an eye on her mother.

"But I am not a child!" Vivian had pouted. "I fail to see why I can't have my privacy."

"The situation is different here, Ma," Maggie had reminded her. "We should stay together, not separate ourselves with doors."

Vivian fell silent for a moment as she finished the tea she was drinking at the kitchen table, then she looked up at Maggie with doleful eyes. "But Henry might not come back if I'm not alone," she said.

"Ma, Dad is—"

"Yes, I know, he's dead, but he still might come back."

"Don't you realize what you're saying?"

The older woman quickly looked away, her chin quivering. "I don't know. I'm so confused. Yes, I know your father is dead, but it was not a dream I had of him. It was real, and . . . oh, Maggie, it was so wonderful having him back with me. You can't imagine how wonderful. It was like having a second chance."

"I can imagine, but it's not—"

"Not what? Not good?"

"Not healthy."

"But why isn't it?" she demanded.

Maggie had wanted to shout, "Because Dad is dead! D-E-A-D. Dead!" But instead, she spoke quietly and firmly, "The door is to stay open, Ma. I'm sorry."

Vivian had stared at her, resentment evident in her eyes, then she struggled to her feet. She had almost stumbled because of her age and weariness, and Maggie had quickly reached out to steady her. Vivian had shrugged her off, walking stiffly to her room, hesitated at the door, then started to close it. But halfway she had stopped and looked over at Maggie. "I'll compromise," she had muttered at length and left the door ajar.

Now she was sleeping. Maggie got up from the chair to check on her. She held the poker in one hand, not wanting to leave it behind. There was no telling when the creatures would return. She stood by her mother's bed and looked down. She could not see her face, but she could make out the shape of her head. She studied the dark form, feeling waves of sadness and love wash over her. Since her father died her mother hadn't been happy. She wished there was something she could do.

She kissed her mother's forehead, letting her lips linger on the woman's warm, dry skin. "I love you, Ma," she whispered. "You're just going to have to let time do the healing." Then, quietly, she went back out into the other room.

She looked out the window again and saw the dark cylinder in the night. For a long moment she stared at it, then returned to her chair.

She looked at her son in his sleeping bag. Losing his dog had crushed him. She promised him a puppy as soon as they were out of here. He had told her he didn't want a puppy. Nobody can take Commander's place, he had cried. But Maggie hoped he'd change his mind after seeing a new puppy.

Maggie then looked over at her daughter, who was curled up at one end of the couch, asleep. Lisa was at the other end. As though sensing she was being watched, Toni opened her eyes.

"Anything happened yet?" Toni whispered, rubbing sleep from her eyes and sitting up.

Maggie shook her head.

"What time is it?"

"Almost eleven."

Toni looked around her. She saw that everyone except Maggie and herself was sleeping. "Is that thing still out there?" she asked.

Maggie nodded.

Fear, which sleep had kept at bay, returned to Toni's pretty face, paling it. Maggie's heart reached out to her, filled with a mixture of love and guilt.

All my fault, Maggie thought again. It's all my fault that we're in this miserable mess.

"Mom?"

"Yes, sweetheart?"

"Can I . . ." The girl stopped, changing her mind.

"Can you what?" Maggie prompted.

Toni shook her head. "Never mind."

Maggie could tell her daughter wanted something very much but for some reason was embarrassed to say what it was. "I insist you tell me," she said in what she hoped was a firm as well as encouraging tone.

"I'm not a baby anymore," Toni said, as though this should explain it all.

"I never said you were, but what has this to do with anything? What were you going to ask me?"

Again Toni hesitated. She looked away, looked back, then at length blurted out, "Can I sit with you, Mom?"

The request surprised her to the point of sudden, unexpected tears. Of course you can sit with me, you silly girl, she thought.

She moved aside in the chair, patting the seat beside her. It would be a tight squeeze, but there was enough room.

Toni hesitated for only a moment, then she joined her. No words were spoken. Except for Keith, who had just begun to snore in the other room, there was complete silence. When Toni leaned her head against Maggie's shoulder, Maggie began to stroke her hair. It was a peaceful moment.

When was the last time she and her daughter felt such closeness and love? Once again Maggie experienced a twinge of guilt as she realized it actually had been a long, long time. She had been too busy with her job for her family.

But things will change, she vowed.

"We will survive this," she said positively. Toni said nothing, but together they held the poker across their laps and rocked synchronously in the chair.

At 11:35 Maggie saw the first flicker. She happened to glance out the window when she spotted it. She was still in the rocking chair with Toni beside her.

Maggie tensed, but did not rise to her feet. She waited for the spark to recur. Toni, sensing that something was happening, looked at her, then followed her gaze to the window. Only darkness stared back.

"What, Mom?"

Maggie did not bother to answer, certain that another flicker of light would appear. Tensing, Toni waited along with her.

The night seemed darker than usual. Keith's snoring grew louder. Maggie felt Toni grope for her hand.

Blue, bulbous light flared then vanished.

"It's them," Toni whispered, her voice unusually high.

Maggie swallowed, then nodded. "I'm going to wake up your father now," she said.

As she started to rise from the chair Toni's grip on her hand tightened, holding her back. Gently, Maggie pulled herself free, then patted the girl's cheek, mutely telling her not to worry.

Toni sat back, ramrod stiff, while she stared at the window. The blue light flashed on again, much closer this time. A second later a green flash was seen, several feet behind the blue one. Then a purple spark appeared.

Maggie, clutching the poker with both hands, rushed toward Keith in the bedroom. "Keith, wake up! Wake up!" Although she was determined to be calm, her voice was loud and edged with panic.

Keith stirred groggily, then bolted upright as though suddenly remembering where he was.

"They're on their way over here," Maggie said.

Keith leaped from the bed and ran past her to the window in the other room. From the chair, immobile like a mannequin, Toni watched. Brice and Lisa, hearing the commotion, began to awaken.

"Gimme the poker," Keith demanded, turning to Maggie. Lights, like monstrous eyes, were now shining and winking at frequent intervals near the house. "C'mon, I said! Gimme the poker!"

Maggie gave it to him, her hand shaking. She had meant to give him the instrument right away, but fear had made her slow to respond.

"Put more wood in the fire," he ordered, "and get your mother in here. I want us all together."

Maggie quickly threw the remaining twigs into the weak fire, then rushed into the bedroom where her mother was sleeping. As she shook the woman awake she heard Keith shout to someone in the other room, "Is the door locked?"

Maggie heard no response. It doesn't matter if it's locked, she thought. The creatures could break through the windows.

"What's wrong?" Vivian asked, awakening from a deep sleep. Maggie couldn't see her because of the darkness, but she could vividly envision the panicked terror on the woman's face.

She forced calmness into her voice. "We

should all be togther in the other room, Ma. Come on."

"But I'm all right here."

This is no time to argue, dammit! Maggie's mind screamed. In a controlled, tight voice, she repeated, "Come on." She groped, found her mother's arm and gently but firmly pulled her to a sitting position, then to her feet.

"My slippers," Vivian said, pulling back, feeling around in the dark.

"Not now." Maggie tightened her grip and inexorably led her to the other room. Keith was at the window. Brice had joined Lisa on the couch, and Toni was still frozen in the rocking chair.

Maggie glanced out the window. The creatures had reached the house. They flew past the glass, their forms vague shadows until they pulsed with light. One of the creatures pressed against the window, endeavoring to squeeze through, but the bookcase covering most of the window made the passage too narrow. The creature then began to push in an attempt to knock over the bookcase. Keith threw his weight against it. After a small struggle, the creature finally flew away to join its companions.

They circled the cottage. Near the dark cylinder, white light glowed. Maggie watched it wax to an almost blinding brilliance, then wane into darkness. She knew it was the mother.

"Don't stare at them, for Christ's sake!" she heard Keith shout. It took her a moment to realize he was speaking to her.

She looked at him blankly.

"They can hypnotize, us, remember?" he said.

She had forgotten about this. Quickly, she turned her back to the window, at the same instant wrapping a protective arm around her mother. Together they sat on the couch, close to Brice.

The creatures continued to circle the cottage. The wings could be heard flapping. Now and then there was a faint screech, sounding somewhat like the raucous caw of a crow. Maggie cringed, feeling her flesh grow cold and tingly. The creatures were searching for a way into the house. She was certain they were going to break one of the bedroom windows.

This had already occurred to Keith. He began to close the doors, only to find them all without locks. There was no choice but to stay in the center of the main room and watch and wait, poker solidly in hand.

Toni still did not move. Never had Maggie seen the girl so rigid and inert. She contemplated rejoining her in the rocking chair, but was reluctant to leave her mother's side, afraid the woman would flee to the bedroom. Vivian did not fear the creatures. To her they held the secret to something she desperately coveted—the return of her deceased husband.

"You okay?" Maggie asked Toni.

The girl did not seem to hear her. She appeared to be in some kind of trance, staring straight ahead.

Maggie felt her heart race as she sensed something was wrong. Swiftly, she followed her daughter's gaze and saw that she was looking at the mother creature outside the window. Almost instantly Maggie felt the magnetic sensation. Before it could take strong hold she pulled away and looked back toward the rocking chair.

Toni was no longer in it. She was walking toward the front door.

"Toni, where are you going?" Keith shouted.

The girl ignored him. She moved trance-like, her hand reaching for the doorknob.

"Hey!" Keith shouted.

"No, don't!" Maggie cried.

It was too late. Toni had opened the door. Keith started to run toward her, to slam and lock the door, but again was too late. With astonishing rapidity, Toni was seized and pulled through the screen of the second door.

"Toniieee!" Maggie screamed.

She and Keith raced after their daughter. They ran into the night, each in turn stumbling over branches and tree roots, but the two creatures, gripping Toni's arms with their teeth, were too fast. As these creatures flew, frenetically pulsing light, they pulled the girl along, letting her feet scrape the ground. There was no struggle, for the girl was completely under their hypnotic power.

"No, nooooo!" Maggie shouted at them. "Let go of her!"

Keith leaped forward when he felt he was close enough to seize Toni's trailing legs. His hand touched a heel, but was not quick enough to grip it. As Toni slipped away, he lost valuable time jumping back up off the ground where he had thrown himself.

Now ahead of him but still behind Toni, Maggie struggled to gain more speed. No, God! Please, no! If only her legs could move faster. It seemed the more she ran, the more the distance between her and her daughter grew.

The creatures were taking the girl to the cylinder.

The mother was waiting. There was a spectral, swelling sphere of brightness, then darkness.

"Leave my baby alone!"

They whisked her inside the cylinder, then the mother followed.

"No!" Maggie screamed, louder than she'd ever screamed in her entire life. "Don't take away my baby! Don't take her away!"

The entrance to the cylinder closed the instant she and Keith reached it.

CHAPTER EIGHTEEN

Toni felt as though she were swimming underwater. The only difference was that she could breathe normally. Her vision was wavery; everything around her was murky and in slow motion. There was something at each arm that pulsed light. She could feel pain in her arms, near her wrists, and she knew these things were biting her. Yet, for some reason, she didn't care. All that mattered was the wonderful sensation, the floating euphoria she was experiencing. They could eat her alive, and she would not stop them.

Air brushed against her face. She knew she was moving fast, toward a certain destination, but again she was filled with indifference. She could be heading toward Hell and she wouldn't care, just as long as the heady feeling inside her did not go away.

She heard shouts, and after a few moments it occurred to her she was hearing her parents, hearing her own name over and over. Of course, it did not matter.

She saw something large looming ahead of her. Beside it something glowed white, then faded. These were familiar, things she was certain she'd seen before. Gradually, as she sped forward, it came to her. The cylinder and the mother. These were the things that once had petrified her, but not now.

Once inside the cylinder she had never experienced such darkness. She heard a soft whoosh behind her, and without looking back she knew the entrance had just slid shut. Then she ceased to move. She heard the fluttering of leathery wings as the two creatures held her upright by her arms. Their teeth clamped tighter, sharpening the pain, and for a fleeting instant it actually mattered.

"What are you . . . going to do?" she asked, her voice thick and slow.

The sound of flapping wings increased. Toni felt as if she were in a cave filled with bats. She knew she should be petrified, but she wasn't. She still felt strangely detached, and she began to combat this feeling. This isn't right, she told herself. I should be scared. I should be helping myself.

She knew the instinct to survive is a person's strongest instinct—a teacher had told her this once—so why wasn't she responding? Did these creatures know how to curb the instinct?

She was powerless, at their mercy, and yet the fear was mild.

She began to feel herself move again, but this time the creatures pulled her slowly. The air stirred as wings flapped all around her. Without any resistance, she let these creatures take her to wherever they wished.

They took her to a room that was dimly illuminated with small, numerous red lights along the arched ceiling and the floor where the walls met. At one end of this room was a table, also outlined with red, bulbous lights, resembling an airport landing strip at night. The surface of the table itself was lost in darkness.

The creatures lifted and lowered her onto this table. More creatures surged forward, fanning her face with their wings and warm, sour breath. They pushed her back until she was flat on the hard, metallic surface. Instantly, clamps sprung up and snapped in place around her legs, arms and waist, binding her.

Toni felt a stirring of panic, but she did not let it mushroom. Somehow it didn't seem worth the effort.

Turning her head to one side while her body remained confined by clamps, she saw that white glow again. It was a small distance away in a dark corner of the room. She watched it brighten and fade, felt it mysteriously control her. She smiled, experiencing a fresh wave of that wonderful euphoric sensation, then looked away.

Nothing mattered but this wonderful feeling!

The Little Ones babbled excitedly among themselves. It had been so easy to abduct the human female. Of course, The Elder was responsible for most of it, for she was the one who could ensnare the human with her mind. But if the female's mind hadn't been so accessible, like an entrance left wide open, it would not have been so simple. All The Elder, with her wisdom and skill, had had to do was merely step into the human and find and work the controls.

The Elder emitted a harsh cry. It was a warning to be silent. She told them they were being too confident of themselves, and that could be dangerous. Then she glided foward to the table while the others moved back to clear the way.

Except for the flapping of wings that kept the creatures aloft, the interior of the cylinder was silent. The Elder had flown toward the table, but now stood before it and quietly examined the human female at great length. The female was young, at the beginning of sexual maturity, and her name, judging from what the older humans had shouted as they pursued her, was Toni.

That would help The Elder open more doors. "Toni" would be the key. With some effort she let the name form in her throat, practicing until she produced the same sound she had heard the other humans use.

"Toni," she said, slowly and clearly.

Immediately the room came alive with chatter from The Little Ones. The Elder screeched for silence again, and again they obeyed promptly.

The Elder, satisfied, returned her attention to the table. She understood The Little Ones' enthusiasm. It certainly must have seemed strange and surprising to hear her utter something humanlike, but she needed the silence to work. If they wanted to find out about the mind of these species that inhabited and ruled this world, they would have to let her concentrate.

When there were no more distractions, she said, "Toni . . . Toni . . . Toni . . ."

The red, diminutive orbs outlining the table and following the contours of the chamber were enough for her to see the female in clear detail. Her eyes could see better in darkness with the aid of dim lights than in glaring brightness.

She leaned forward and this time repeated the name easily. "Toni . . . Toni . . ."

The human looked up at her. The Elder detected a faint trace of panic and quickly eradicated it.

The Elder slipped through that first doorway in the human's mind. At first it was a whirling mass, thick and vague as her own mind penetrated the other, then as the two merged, it ceased to swirl and became thin and clear. It was like gliding through a fog that was separating two worlds. Now she had crossed over, and the adventure was ready to begin.

The gate to the human's mind was so flimsy, so incredibly easy to open.

The Elder could sense disturbing emotions coming from the human and was astonished that there were so many. Certainly there was a lot to learn from this subject. She stepped back, leaving the human's mind open, and gestured for The Little Ones to come forward and have a look.

Eagerly they complied, crowding around the subject at the table. Their cries of glee and beating of wings grew louder as their excitement intensified. The Elder had opened the first entrance—the most difficult—for them and now they could explore to their young hearts' content. It was like having access to a palace with countless rooms. Some of these rooms were locked, and only someone like The Elder could unlock them, but many were not.

The Little Ones concentrated together and slipped through the fog that separated the minds. Mentally, they held claws and began their journey, one room at a time. Soon they, too, were astonished at the myriad of bad emotions that filled their subject.

One emotion at this time seemed stronger than any of the others. It was an emotion that The Little Ones could not seem to grasp. They concentrated, wanting so much to understand, to learn.

The human female desired to be loved; this, The Little Ones were able to understand. But to be loved, especially by the human male, the female felt she would have to be sexually active, something she clearly did not want to be. It was the reason for her reluctancy, however, that perplexed The Little Ones. There was an emotion that was stopping her. It was an emotion that she labeled guilt.

Guilt. What was that? She could be loved by many men if she were not afraid of the guilt that would haunt her later.

The Little Ones turned to The Elder, urging her to explain this baffling discovery.

The Elder took a long time to answer, for she herself was not certain. Guilt, she told them at length, was a bad feeling that humans have whenever they felt they had done something wrong. As to why they let themselves have these feelings, she did not know. Perhaps this was something learned, not inherited.

The Little Ones pointed out that the human female could be happy if she removed this foolish guilt.

The Elder was aware of this, but for some strange reason the female wouldn't or couldn't rid herself of the crippling emotion. Any more questions?

No more, The Little Ones informed her. Together they returned to the table. Concentrating once more, they resumed their exploration. Now that they were aware of the baffling emotion, they began to find it everywhere. At age nine she had spotted a five dollar bill on the kitchen table at her home. She had glanced about to see if anyone was watching, then snatched the money from the table and stuffed it into her jeans pocket. Now she had reason to be happy—she was a little richer—but that weird emotion intervened again. Guilt. Two days later she gave the money to her mother.

It did not make sense.

The Little Ones turned to The Elder again. Nothing about the humans, she patiently informed them, made much sense.

Toni felt the onset of panic again, but it was weak, like a bird with a broken wing trying to take flight. She could move her head and look with dazed bewilderment at the creatures surrounding her, but she could not move her body because of the clamps binding her to the table. What were they doing? What did they want?

She still felt heady with euphoria and now and then smiled at the creatures. She didn't care what they were doing, not really. She was curious, but not worried.

She knew they were doing something to her head. Not only were they giving her the wonderful, happy feelings, they were causing some pressure, some dizziness. Sometimes her mind would feel like a washing machine going into a wild cycle, spinning thoughts around and around until they ceased to be thoughts and were a foggy blur.

Not that it mattered.

They could do anything they damn well pleased with her, as long as they didn't take away the good, pleasant feelings.

The Little Ones continued to explore, searching for their subject's feelings. They no longer were interested in the feeling called guilt, but were eager to find something else that was equally strange and puzzling. They sensed waves of hate, resentment, and anger as they delved deeper into the human's mind, into the past. They also sensed love, joy, and euphoria. Then they came to a barrier that they could not penetrate. They turned to The Elder, knowing she would help them.

This was the entrance to a past experience, she told them. Most life forms, as they already knew, had this. Some were easy to open, freely merging with present existence, but some, as in this case, were solidly blocked. To The Elder this was nothing more than a rusty door that was stuck. Perseverance was all that would be needed here.

She concentrated while The Little Ones gave her the silence she needed. "Toni . . . Toni . . ." She paused each time she uttered the name. "Toni . . . Toni . . ."

She gave a final mental push and at last the barrier gave way. There was a sharp pain in her head, but with ease she willed it away. Then she stepped back and The Little Ones rushed forward, as though she had just opened a box of toys.

The human female, The Little Ones quickly found, was now different. Gone were the thoughts of wanting to be desired by many men. Now the subject cared about only one male, someone whom she called Lawrence. He had fought and died in a war—a second world war—and, although the subject lived many Earth years after this Lawrence had died, she continued to desire him, just like the other human female that was now inside the cottage. Both females loved a deceased male.

It did not make sense, as usual.

The Little Ones continued the exploration. The subject had lived a long life for a human, although a miserable one. Even moments before her death, before her passing, her thoughts were of Lawrence. That name dominated the mind. Lawrence.

The Little Ones found themselves relieved when they came to another barrier. Without any verbal communication they moved back to let The Elder through to help them. With perseverance, she again pushed open a door that separated the subject's lives.

And again The Little Ones surged forward with impatient hunger for knowledge. This time they found the female concerned about another war, a war about white and black people of the North and South, a strange, angry war. The human female was angry, too, but it was not because of this war, but because of a woman who she believed was lovelier than she. Because of a sister.

The human, The Little Ones soon learned, despised her sister, who not only was lovelier but younger. She did not believe it was fair that her sister should attract so many more men than she. Also, it was not fair that her sister should become their father's favorite. The human female was older, therefore she should be first in everything.

But it seemed she was second, always behind her sister. At one point she made an attempt to mar the other's beauty. Feigning clumsiness, she swept a lantern in the direction of her sister's face, as the two of them were hurrying in the night toward a barn to check on a sickly horse. But the sister had ducked in time.

The Little Ones detected that strange emotion again. Guilt. This time it was ephemeral and not as intense. There was mostly indignation and contempt now. The subject had fought violently with her sister many times and had frequently dug her nails into the other's flawless face, but the damage had always been temporary.

The human female desperately wanted to do something to destroy her sister's beauty forever. She had thought of a plan. She would splash kerosene on the other's face and then set fire to it—under the guise of an accident, of course. The sister would not die, for she would be saved in time, but her face . . .

The human female came close to executing this plan, but lacked courage. So she spent the remaining time of this life miserable with jealousy. When her sister died at 16 from pneumonia, she found herself not filled with grief but with relief, something that was difficult to mask. Everyone, it seemed, could not stop mourning her sister. No one could forget her beauty. Even when the human female died in a boating accident seven years later, no one had forgotten her sister.

The Little Ones came to yet another barrier, but this time they did not step aside to let The Elder penetrate it. They were tired now, ready to stop. One by one they moved away from the table and joined The Elder at the other end of the room, where she had been quietly watching them.

The happy feeling was fading. Toni fought to retain it, but it continued to slip away from her. Now she felt as though she were awakening from a dream in the middle of the night, for darkness was all around her.

She saw the red lights on the ceiling and along the floor and knew she was not in her bed or on the couch in the cottage. Because of these small, bulbous lights she could discern the shape of the ceiling and the size of the room.

Suddenly she knew she was inside the cylinder.

She turned her head and saw pulsating lights, the size and roundness of melons. The creatures were clustered in a group, and in the center of this gathering was the mother, radiating ghostly light. Intuitively, Toni knew they were watching and discussing her.

The panic that had been writhing weakly inside her began to thrash, but she was still too groggy to find her voice and scream aloud.

The Little Ones told The Elder they were tired, and was it time to go to sleep? The Elder informed them that it was, that the night was over. Were there any questions? she asked them in her own tongue.

There were so many things they did not understand, they told her. Humans, it seemed, went to great lengths to be unhappy. They seemed to want to suffer and be miserable. Why do they let themselves miss things or people that no longer existed? Why did they let this feeling called guilt keep them from being happy? Why did they let jealousy make them miserable? And why did they let love from another human make them sad? Love was supposed to make one merry, was it not?

The Elder spread her wings, then drew them together, a signal that commanded silence and attention. She told them that these were questions she could not answer, but they were definitely questions to think about.

Why could not humans control the bad emotions? one of The Little Ones asked. Was it really because they wished to be unhappy?

The Elder told him that she did not know why. Maybe the humans have not yet learned to control these feelings.

The Little Ones found this difficult to understand. They argued that emotions were very simple to control. Only excitement and eagerness were sometimes difficult to bridle, but not bad emotions that got in the way of good feelings. This did not make sense.

But then, The Elder patiently pointed out once more, there were many, many things about the humans that did not make sense.

CHAPTER NINETEEN

Maggie scarcely noticed that the night was fading and the clouds along the horizon were tinted orange and pink, signaling sunrise. Maggie, also, scarcely noticed that Keith had stayed with her throughout the night, pacing back and forth, throwing rocks at trees, water and the shield in frustration. She was oblivious to everything, except the cylinder looming monstrously above her as she sat on the ground, directly below the spot where the entrance had been. She had made a vow not to move until her daughter was back out, back in her arms.

Keith had pummeled his fists as well as thrown rocks at the cylinder repeatedly throughout the night, but this only succeeded in increasing his frustration and rage. At one point he had plopped down next to Maggie and wept. "Not fair, not fair," he had mumbled, and she had cradled his head against her breasts.

"She'll come back out," she had assured him, although she herself was filled with trepidation. "She'll come back out safely."

She had spilled tears and moaned when Toni had disappeared inside the cylinder, but for most of the night she sat in stunned, hopeful prayer. Now she was tired, her body aching to lie down and sleep, but she was determined to remain awake until her daughter was safely in her arms. When her eyelids drooped, she forced them to open wider. She would not go to sleep, she vowed.

A sound jolted her to full awareness, as though cold water had been thrown at her face. She rose slowly to her feet, hope soaring as her eyes stared at the spot where she had heard the faint sliding noise. The door of the cylinder had started to open!

Keith had stopped pacing behind Maggie, and together they gawked at the slowly opening entrance. The interior of the cylinder revealed only darkness.

"Oh God, please," Maggie whispered.

Toni appeared. At first she was only a dark form, but as she moved forward trancelike, she grew clearer. She paused at the edge of the entrance, blinking at Maggie, then at Keith.

"Mom? Dad?" She held an arm over her eyes to shield the glaring morning light, which was in harsh contrast to the darkness that had surrounded her for so many hours.

"Sweetheart!" Maggie cried, breaking into a run toward the girl.

"Thank God," Keith sighed with relief.

"Mom? . . . Dad?" Toni repeated uncertainly. She seemed to find it difficult to believe she was free, that she was actually seeing her parents.

Maggie hugged her, unwittingly squeezing her until the girl gasped in pain. "Oh, sweetheart, my baby, are you all right? Did they hurt you in there?" she gushed.

"I-I'm all right," Toni said slowly, as though still in a daze. "It really happened, didn't it? It wasn't just a dream?"

"What was?"

Before the girl could explain, Keith pulled her away from Maggie and into his arms. "Christ, you had us worried. Are you really okay, baby? What happened in there?"

"In there?" Toni echoed, then paused a moment. "It wasn't a dream, but it felt like one. They were all around me. They . . . they . . ."

"They what, baby?" Keith urged gently.

Toni looked at him for a moment in silence, then gradually remembered something, something that she found distasteful. She pushed away from him and returned to Maggie's arms.

Keith stared at her, stunned. "What, baby? What's wrong?"

Toni shook her head, turning her face

away from him. Clearly, she did not want to talk about it.

"What did they do to you in there?" he demanded.

Maggie stroked the girl's hair, endeavoring to soothe her. Softly, she said, "They didn't hurt you in any way, did they? Please tell us if they did."

"I don't think so, Mom, but they did do something."

Alarm shot through Maggie as she immediately suspected the worst. She willed herself to be calm. "What did they do?"

"I'm not sure. They made me feel funny. It was awfully dark in there, and everything was unreal like a crazy dream. I kept having weird thoughts, thoughts about . . ."

"Yes?" Maggie prompted. In the periphery of her vision she saw Vivian, Lisa, and Brice hurry toward them from the cottage.

"Thoughts about feelings," Toni went on. "It was as if these creatures were inside my head, Mom. I knew they could tell what I was thinking and feeling. They seemed so deep inside me that I could tell what they were thinking and feeling, too. Weird, huh?"

Maggie did not think so. Nothing was weird or too strange anymore. Vivian and Lisa stopped several feet away to listen, as though fearing their presence might interrupt and silence Toni. Brice stood beside his father.

"There seemed to be no language barrier," Toni went on. "I could understand them.

There were no words, really, just . . . feelings, you know. They were surprised that I have so many bad emotions, Mom, and they were surprised that I don't have control."

"Bad emotions?" Maggie echoed uncertainly.

"Yeah. Envy, Guilt. Those kinds."

"But they didn't hurt you?" Maggie repeated, to be certain.

"No, I don't think so. They just made my head feel funny, that's all. It really felt like they went inside it, like they were digging deep, but I didn't mind. It hurt at times, but I still didn't mind. It was really weird, Mom."

"This bad emotion stuff," Keith said, stepping closer, "can you tell us more about it?"

Toni looked at him, and to everyone's surprise her eyes grew hard. "Bad emotions," she uttered slowly and venomously, "like the feelings I have for you right now."

Keith backed up and frowned uncertainly. "What're you talking about, baby?"

"Don't call me that!" she hissed.

"Hey, what the hell did they do to you in there?"

"Nothing that has to do with this." She glared at him with open contempt.

"Then what is *this*?" Keith demanded, his frown deepening.

The glare intensified, like a flame brightening with a fierce light, then Toni looked away. "I'm tired," she suddenly said. "I want to go to bed."

"Of course," Maggie escorted her to the cottage and glanced back at Keith, wondering what had just happened.

Inside the cottage she sat with Toni for a while, holding the girl's hand as she lay on one of the beds. For a long moment nothing was said. Toni's eyes were closed, but that did not hide the fear, for it was evident in the pallor of the girl's skin and in the tightness of her mouth. Maggie stroked her cheek, desperately wishing she could make everything right. She wished she could start over again.

"My baby," she whispered. It was funny how fear and terror had brought mother and daughter together again, she mused. No, on second thought, it wasn't funny at all.

"Mom." Toni opened her eyes.

"Yes, sweetheart?"

"I just remembered something."

"Yes?"

"The creatures seemed to light up mostly when they're excited or confused."

"Oh?"

"Yeah. I remember lying on a table looking up at them. I remember them being confused about some feeling they'd found in me. They were blinking like crazy, Mom. And the big creature, it stayed real calm throughout the whole thing. They're weird creatures, all right." She fell silent, closed her eyes, then added with a tired sigh, "Really weird."

Soon she was asleep. Maggie kissed her forehead, whispering, "As long as you're all right. That's the important thing." Then, quietly, she retreated from the room.

Vivian was waiting for her near the door. "Will she be all right?" she asked.

"I think so, Ma." Maggie managed a smile, although it was small and weak. "I certainly hope so."

"What did she say about that thing out there?"

"Not really much," Maggie said, deciding against telling her that the creatures had probed the girl's mind. This would serve no purpose except to worry and frighten her mother more. "She said it was all like a dream."

"Yes, they can do that—make things dreamlike," Vivian whispered, as though speaking thoughtfully to herself. "They made Henry come back like a dream—a lovely, lovely dream."

"Then you admit that's all it was, a dream?"

Vivian stared pensively at her. "Oh, Maggie, I'm not sure. I admit only that it was confusing but so lovely." She paused, then asked, "Did Toni mention anything about Henry?"

"Why would she, Ma?"

"Well, she would if . . . if she'd seen him inside that thing."

"Why would she have seen him?"

"Because he could have been in there somewhere."

"Ma, he wasn't in there," Maggie said slowly and emphatically. "He was only a dream. He wasn't real. When are you going to understand that? He was only a dream!"

"Please don't shout at me."

"I'm not—"

"That's all you've been doing to me lately, Maggie—shouting at me, shouting as if I were a little girl. I'm your mother, Maggie. I hate it so when you shout."

Aware that Vivian was losing control, Maggie pulled her into her arms. "I'm sorry, Ma," she said softly. "We're all tense. We're all scared. That's why we're doing things we don't mean to do. I'm sorry."

For a moment Vivian wept quietly against Maggie, then she extricated herself, as though suddenly embarrassed that she'd betrayed a weak side. Stiffly, she turned her face away from Maggie and wiped her eyes with a crooked finger. "I'm tired," she declared. "I'm going to lie down awhile. I didn't get much sleep, worrying about Toni all night."

Nodding, Maggie understood. She reached for Vivian's hand and gave it a squeeze, hoping this would console her somewhat, but Vivian's countenance betrayed nothing.

After watching Vivian disappear into her bedroom, Maggie went outside. She found her husband and Lisa under a tree, the former glaring at the silver cylinder a few

feet away, and the latter idly doodling something in the dirt with a twig. They were
silent, close together yet seemingly far apart.
Lisa shot to her feet when Maggie came near.

Jumpy, Maggie thought dully, but then,
who could blame the girl? Everybody was
jumpy.

Lisa gave her a quick smile, then hurried
past her toward the cottage. Keith never
looked away from the huge vessel before
him.

Maggie leaned against the tree near her
husband and hugged herself. Although it was
warm and the shield prevented any wind, she
was cold. God, would this ever end?

She heard soft splashing sounds and
looked over at the lake. Brice was sitting on
the wharf, his shoulders slumped forward
and his feet in the water, listlessly making
ripples. When he grew bored with this, he
stood up, taking his sneakers he'd left on the
wharf, and headed for the cottage.

"There's not much food left," Maggie said,
turning back to Keith.

"We'll make it stretch."

"How?"

"I don't know, dammit!" he snapped.
"We'll just have to make do the best we can,
okay?"

Maggie hugged herself tighter. She wished
Keith would be nicer to her. She knew she
was responsible for most of this mess they
were all in, but still she wished he'd be nicer.
It would help her be less afraid.

"I think I can find a way to remove the fucking shield," he suddenly declared. "Did you know the door to this thing was open all the while the creatures were inside the house?"

Maggie shook her head.

"Well, the next time it's open and they're all busy inside the house, I'm going to sneak inside that thing somehow and find out how they'd put up the barrier. I'm sure there's something in there that'll remove it."

"That could be dangerous."

"Yeah, well, somebody's gotta do it."

"Maybe they'll go away. Maybe they'll get sick of us and move on."

"Maybe."

They both stared at the metallic object. It seemed to stare back, silently and defiantly.

At length Keith rose and started toward the cottage. "Might as well get some sleep," he said. "Might have another long night ahead of us."

Maggie lingered a bit longer, then pulled herself away from the tree and followed him. Intuitively, she knew he was right. Another long, long night would be waiting for them.

CHAPTER TWENTY

They awoke one by one and saw, as always, that The Elder was already up and waiting for them. Quickly, they licked themselves clean, ate tasteless synthetic food that a machine spat out for them, then in a flock flew to the main chamber, The Elder leading the way.

Once they were inside the main chamber they began to make plans for the approaching night. The human female that they had abducted and released the previous night had been interesting, indeed, and so had the older female with the deceased mate before that. But they now wanted something different. They had grown tired of probing the humans' minds.

The Elder asked if they wished to study a

lesser life form again, like the dog, but The Little Ones told her that they did not. They still wished to examine the humans, but no longer wished to explore their minds or emotions.

Then what is it you wish to study? The Elder wanted to know.

They told her they wanted to see what the humans looked like inside, to see what kind of internal organs they possessed.

They wanted to dissect a human.

This admission generated excitement, and The Little Ones began to squeal and flicker furiously in the dark chamber. The Elder spread her wings, demanding silence. When she at last had it, she held on to it for a long moment. Then she bowed her head and gave them the permission they sought.

You may dissect the human of your choice, she told them.

Once more the chamber came alive with their unbridled enthusiasm. The Little Ones could scarcely wait for the night to begin.

PART THREE

PART THREE

CHAPTER TWENTY-ONE

The bedroom was shadowy when Vivian awoke. She lay on the bed for a long while, doing nothing but staring at the ceiling, which was made of pine boards like the walls and the floor. This made her feel as though she were inside a wooden box, rather than a room. She listened for sounds, but heard only the soft, rhythmic creaking of the rocking chair from the other room and knew Maggie was keeping vigil.

The door was ajar, but all Vivian could see was golden light from the oil lamp in the other room and a small part of the couch. She thought of getting up and joining the others, then changed her mind. She did not want to be with them, not really. She did not belong. Maggie had Keith and her children.

Lisa was with Toni. Vivian had no place with them.

She looked away from the door and returned her gaze to the wooden ceiling. She knew she was feeling sorry for herself, but she couldn't help it. She missed Henry so much, and seeing him the other night—dream or no—made it all the worse. She was reminded of how wonderful it had been to be a twosome, to share life with someone. Now she was alone. Of course she knew she had a lovely daughter and grandchildren who were willing to help and take care of her, but this was not the same. It was not help she wanted, nor occasional companionship. She wanted an equal. Henry had been a part of her.

"Damn you, Henry!" she cursed under her breath. "It wasn't fair to leave me like this."

Feeling tears coming on, she abruptly looked away from the ceiling and turned her head toward the other side of the bed, away from the door. She blinked until her eyes were dry, then stared at the old bureau that Keith had moved to block a window. Although it was a large bureau with five drawers, Vivian was certain she herself could move it.

Although, why on earth would she wish to do that? She suddenly wondered.

Because she wanted to look out the window behind it, an inner voice replied. She wanted to see if the creatures were out of their vessel—to see if Henry was with them.

Vivian turned away from the bureau. I'm being silly, she told herself. She didn't want to see Henry again. It would only make everything worse and make her miss him all the more.

Slowly, her gaze returned to the bureau.

She pulled herself up to a sitting position. She looked down at her watch on her wrist, a dainty Waltham that Henry had given her on their last anniversary. The time was 8:20. Outside, it would not be dark yet, but because the windows were partly blocked, the interior of the cottage was already gloomy.

She looked back at the bureau. It wouldn't be easy, but she was still certain she could move it. Besides, she would only have to push it slightly to one side, just to give herself enough room to open the window and poke her head through. She knew the cylinder was at the far right of this window.

Leaving the bed, she paused before the old piece of furniture. Its walnut finish was dull, worn and grayish at the edges. As she stared at this, she was once again filled with doubt about her actions.

She began to push at the bureau. It moved with some strain, but as the legs began to scrape loudly against the floor, she stopped. She feared the others would hear the noise from the other room. They would demand an explanation, and what would she tell them? That she wanted to say good-bye to Henry? That she wanted to see him just this one last time? No, they would never understand. They would stop her.

Discouraged, Vivian returned to the bed. She was ready to forget this foolishness, for foolishness was certainly what it was, when her eyes fell on the small, braided rug between the bureau and the bed. An idea occurred to her. There was a way she could move the bureau quietly.

Lowering herself to her knees, she pushed the rug close to the bureau, then she lifted one corner of the bureau up, pulled forward, then lowered the leg onto the rug. Already breathing heavily, she waited a few minutes, then proceeded with the other leg of the bureau. Once she had two legs on the rug she was ready to push again. The side that was on the rug moved easily and silently, while she kept the oppposite side slightly above the floor. She could only do this in spurts, inches at a time, but eventually she succeeded in moving the bureau away from the window.

Then she sat on the bed to catch her breath. When she felt strong enough, she returned to the window and looked out. The view was only of trees and shadows. The lake was on the other side of the house, and the metallic object was out of sight here. But if she opened the window . . .

The sash was difficult to slide up at first. She pushed, feeling her face burn as she strained, but she did not give up, for she could feel the window begin to slide. It was only a little swollen. She kept at it until it finally gave with a grating, scraping sound.

Vivian felt her heart hammer furiously, and for a horrible moment she was certain she'd have a heart attack. She clutched her chest and closed her eyes, praying and willing the vital organ to slow down. At length it obeyed, and she felt better.

That was close, she thought.

She opened her eyes and found herself looking out the window. There was no breeze. The outside air didn't seem to be any cooler than the interior of the room. It was so warm, so stagnant. Vivian poked her head through the window and looked toward the right. A portion of the cylinder was visible, but most of it extended out of view, beyond the other side of the cottage. She waited and watched, hoping to catch a glimpse of the creatures and, of course, Henry. Soon her neck began to ache.

Pulling her head back inside, she contemplated putting a stop to this nonsense. Also, she contemplated something else. She could crawl out the window and be closer to the cylinder. A part of her, however, swiftly rejected this absurdity. After all, she was no teenager. Sneaking out of a house via a window at her age was simply ridiculous.

But her body ignored her mind. Taking a long breath, mainly to keep her heart tranquil, she climbed out the window.

Five minutes later she was standing before the silver hull. Again her hand was over her chest, her heart racing at an alarming rate.

She waited, and to her relief the frenetic beating began to slow. Then with her other hand she reached for the metallic surface of the cylinder and knocked softly.

"Henry," she whispered. "If you're in there, please come out."

She was not afraid of the batlike creatures that she knew were inside. Why should she be? They had given her back her Henry, so that meant they were compassionate beings, didn't it?

"Henry?" She spoke louder, then knocked louder. "I just want to see you one more time, that's all. Then I won't ask again." There was no response. "Oh, please, Henry, just one more time. I want to say good-bye. Please."

The last time Henry had appeared she had been surprised and startled. This time she'd be ready. She'd take full advantage of the moment. Maybe she'd even enjoy his lovemaking.

"Please, Henry, another chance, then I won't ask to see you anymore. Please."

The door slowly opened. Vivian experienced a spark of fear, but mostly excitement and relief. She had been heard! She would be given another chance to see her husband!

Drawing her hands together and holding them close to her lips in anticipation, she moved closer to the vessel. A smile grew on her face as she waited for someone to appear at the entrance.

After what seemed an interminably long
time, the motherlike being emerged. She
stood in the round entrance in silence,
glowing so brilliantly that Vivian was forced
to avert her face. Then the light dimmed until
all that could be discerned was a dark bulk
with wings. In the brief moment that this
creature had pulsed light, Vivian had sensed
its annoyance at being disturbed.

Vivian took a step back. Perhaps she'd
made a mistake coming here.

She hadn't been afraid of this creature
until now because she thought it had done
her a favor. She had thought Henry had been
something of a gift—a kind, friendly gesture.

Now she realized she'd been wrong. The
hostility the creature was emanating was
unmistakable. Dropping her hands and
wringing them, Vivian took another
backward step. "Henry," she said, in a
desperate attempt to explain. "I thought he'd
be in there."

The creature did not move. It was obvious
that it was waiting and expecting Vivian to
leave it and the others alone, but Vivian
could not bring herself to go away, not until
she had some answers about her late
husband.

"Was it a dream?" she asked. "Was that
all it was?"

Two smaller creatures joined the larger
one, now filling the entranceway. They
watched Vivian in silence, as though in mild
curiosity, but they stayed at the mother's side,

never moving forward.

"Was it?" Vivian demanded.

The larger creature momentarily blinded her with white light. Vivian could actually feel the heat of the glare. Also, she could sense the creature's thoughts. It seemed to be telling her to go away. It—they—were no longer interested in her.

"But was Henry only a dream?" Vivian reiterated with determination. "Or did you really bring him back?"

The creature's light faded, then grew bright again. *We found the man in your mind. He had been so strong, so vivid. We knew you wanted him back.*

"Then you actually brought him back!" Vivian exclaimed to the voice that seemed to be inside her head.

It was a creation from your own mind. We only let you think you saw him.

"But it seemed so real. I could feel him, smell him."

It was simple to do. There is so much that a mind can do. Humans have not yet learned everything about this. There is so much that is inside you that you do not yet know. There is so much you need to learn. There is so much you can do but you do not have the knowledge.

The light faded.

"Are you saying that Henry was just a figment of my imagination? That my mind recreated him?"

There was a pause, then the light returned.

The man was not recreated. It was your image of him that we let you see as you looked and touched one of us. It was only in your mind that he existed. Only in your mind.

"So I only thought I saw him," Vivian said incredulously.

The creature's light waned. It did not brighten again to reply, but it did not need to, for Vivian knew the darkness and silence meant "Yes." Henry had never returned at all. It had only been her mental image of him, with the creature's help, that had made it all seem so incredibly real.

Then she remembered the horrible love-making. Why had that happened? Why had the feel of Henry been repugnant at the end? As soon as these questions came to her, she knew the answer. It was not Henry she had touched; it was one of the creatures. These creatures had skillfully played with her mind; they had made her see only Henry while she touched a creature and kissed it.

"Oh, my God," she murmured sickly. "You made me think it was Henry while I . . ." She couldn't finish.

The entrance to the cylinder began to slide shut.

"Why did you do this?" Vivian cried.

The door stopped. There was a pause, then the larger creature's light brightened once more in reply. *The Little Ones were curious. They wanted to learn why you would torment yourselves over someone that was nonexistent. You had intrigued a Little One into conducting an experiment.*

"I'm not a guinea pig!" Vivian flared.

But so much can be learned from guinea pigs, the creature replied.

The statement lingered in Vivian's mind, then the creature's light ebbed for a final time. The door slid shut, leaving Vivian to stare at the smooth, metallic surface for a long, stunned moment.

She would not see her husband tonight. She would not ever see him again. The creatures had only been interested in an experiment and were now probably bored with her. They hadn't allowed her to see Henry because of a favor or friendly gift, as she had first believed and hoped. They had been merely interested, like a cat moment-arily fascinated with a piece of yarn.

"We're not guinea pigs!" she cried again, this time at the hard, blank surface of the vessel. She knew her words were lost to those inside, but maybe God was with her and was listening. Maybe He would intervene and end this horror. God, of course, knew humans were not guinea pigs. He knew they shouldn't be treated like laboratory animals, didn't He?

"Of course He does!" Vivian declared out loud, then crossed herself. "Help us, almighty Lord. Please," she implored, then turned toward the cottage.

Halfway, she met Keith, who had seen her from the house.

"What the hell are you doing out here?"

he demanded. "Have you lost your mind?"

Vivian walked on past him. She did not have to explain anything to him, not that he would understand anyway. To her knowledge he had never lost anyone that was so dear to him, as Henry was to her. No, he would never understand.

Keith turned around and followed her back to the house. "Answer me, Mom."

"I want to be alone," she said, never breaking her stride. She tried to hurry, so much wanting to gain distance from him, but her heart was pounding fiercely again. Soon she was forced to stop and catch her breath.

"What happened, Mom? Why did you go over there? You saw what they did to Toni, didn't you? Were you trying to get inside that thing? Was that what you were trying to do?"

"No," she finally answered. Her voice sounded so old and weary to her ears. "I wanted to see Henry again, but I don't think I want to anymore, at least not through them."

"Them?"

"Never mind. Just leave me alone, please."

This time he relented. He stood back and watched her in puzzlement as she started once more for the house. When she was inside she headed straight for her room. Toni was still asleep, but the others were up.

"Ma, what—" Maggie began. Vivian shook her head, silencing her. Not now, her gesture pleaded. Please, not now.

Inside the bedroom she closed the door, this time completely. She needed to be alone, at least for a little while. She had been so hopeful that she'd see Henry.

She felt as though he had died all over again, and, all over again, she would have to suffer the pain of losing him. But after this, with God's help and a little bit of time, she would eventually learn to accept her husband's death. She would have to; there was no choice. She knew now that she definitely could not—would not—count on the creatures out there in the cylinder.

They were evil.

CHAPTER TWENTY-TWO

Keith stopped following Vivian to the cottage and looked over his shoulder at the silver cylinder. The night was deepening and the metallic exterior was darkening, beginning to disappear in the shadows of the surrounding trees. Its presence, however, was still felt. Keith knew it was going to be around for another night.

"Go away!" he hissed at it, as though it were a pesty bee.

Of course there was no response. The cylinder stared inanimately back at him. Like a bomb, he thought. There was no telling when it would explode.

Christ!

Of all the places in this fucking world, why did these monsters pick this one? Was it because it was so isolated here? The nearest neighbor was probably a half mile away, if not more. Did that have something to do with it?

Abruptly, Keith looked away, hoping the less he saw of that thing sitting there the less he'd think about it. It scared him, and for some reason he was certain something bad was going to happen tonight—something really horrible.

He walked quickly into the house. Maggie, Brice, and Lisa looked up at him the moment he entered, but Toni avoided him. He wondered, for the hundredth time since she had emerged from the cylinder, why she seemed so contemptuous toward him. What had those creatures done to her?

"You okay, baby?" he asked gently.

Toni gave him a brief glance, nodded curtly, but said nothing.

Keith wanted to hold her, as her mother had held her, but he knew she'd push him away again. Maybe in time she'd come around, he told himself. Maybe she was still too shook up about her awful experience, and it was only natural for her to want her mother. Yeah, that was all it was. She'd come around.

He walked over to Maggie, who was in the rocking chair, and took the iron poker from her lap. "I'm on watch tonight," he said. "You look tired."

"But I'm not," she protested.

"You were on watch last night."

"That's okay. I don't mind."

"You didn't do such a hot job," he reminded her. He knew he was obliquely blaming her for Toni's abduction, but it was partly true. If she had awakened him a little earlier, maybe he could have prevented the whole nightmare, and the girl wouldn't be acting so strangely toward him now. "Yeah, I'll take over now," he said firmly.

Maggie's lips tightened, but she remained silent.

This was going against her grain, Keith knew. Maggie did not like to play the passive role; she was one who wanted control, but Jesus, so did he. Maybe that was why their marriage wasn't so terrific anymore. They both wanted to be the stronger half, but he was the man of the family; it was only natural for him to have the controlling hand. If only she would accept this, then their marriage would be healthier. God knew that he still loved her very much.

Clutching the poker firmly in his hand, Keith stood by the window behind the bookcase. He would protect the family tonight, and he would make damn sure no one was abducted. As he made this vow, however, he was filled with doubt. Something terrible was going to happen.

The hours passed slowly. The silence and the waiting made him drowsy, but determination kept him awake. Vivian was asleep in the bedroom, Toni was asleep on the couch, Brice in his sleeping bag, and

Maggie in the rocking chair. Only Lisa was
up with him, and she was glancing
frequently over at him. First, he responded
with an awkward smile, then a nod, and
finally a brief but riveting stare.

He averted his head, feeling a warm rush
of blood fill his face. Not again, he told
himself. Once with the kid had been a
mistake, and he was not about to make
another. But she kept looking at him, and he
could feel her eyes explore his body.

How the hell could she be thinking about
sex at a time like this? he thought. Didn't she
know there was a bomb sitting outside?

But what he found even more disconcerting was that her sweeping gaze was actually
giving him an erection. Jesus Christ, what
was the matter with him? Why was he horny
when he was scared enough to piss in his
pants?

As he asked himself this, he knew the
answer. Danger and fear fueled fire, making
it rage and soar, rather than extinguishing it.

"Why do they always make us wait like
this, Keith?" the girl asked, her voice a soft
whisper.

It took Keith a moment to realize she was
referring to the creatures outside. "I don't
know. Maybe they know we're watching for
them, so they wait until we're tired. They
wait until our guards are down a little."

"Are you tired?"

"No." He looked at her, and again their
eyes locked.

"But you will be later, won't you?"

"Not tonight." This time he couldn't pull away from her gaze. He had never seen such green eyes. They were bright and shiny, like light burning through green glass. "I'm ready for them."

A moment passed, then Lisa said, "Are you sorry?"

"About what?"

"You know . . ." Her eyes fell away, then returned to his face. "About yesterday?"

Keith looked nervously at his wife in the chair. They shouldn't be talking about this, he thought. What if Maggie wasn't really asleep? "Let's forget about it," he replied at length in a low, almost inaudible whisper. "Okay?"

"I was scared, Keith," she went on anyway. "That's why I wanted you to . . . well, hold me."

"I said let's forget about it."

Another silent moment passed. "I just wanted to tell you I'm sorry. What happened yesterday was mostly my fault."

"It wasn't all your fault, Lisa. A lot of it was mine, too."

More silence ensued. Keith returned his attention to the window.

"Is anything happening out there?" Lisa asked.

Keith shook his head. The bomb was sitting there. He could almost hear it ticking away in his head. When will it explode? In the next hour? Next minute?

What a fucking mess Maggie had got everyone into!

"I'm still scared," he heard Lisa say. There was a girlish sob in her voice, and he found himself wanting to soothe her. At the same time he would be soothing himself.

He was scared, too—probably as scared as she was—and what's more, he was still horny with an erection.

He looked back at her on the couch, then he glanced at the others in the room; all were sleeping. He told himself he shouldn't even be considering having another round with Lisa. He was a family man, for Christ's sake! But like Lisa, he needed something comforting, something that would momentarily warm him from the chilling fear.

"Daddy used to hold me—" Lisa started to say, then stopped when Keith held a finger to his lips. He had already heard this. There was no need to explain, and besides, she was talking too loudly. They would have to go where no one would hear them.

Keith immediately thought of the bathroom, then as quickly dismissed this. Too cheap. Then he considered the bedroom and again decided against it. It was too close and would arouse suspicion if Maggie or the others saw them entering the room together. So that left only the porch for privacy. They could innocently step outside and just as innocently come back in.

Of course they'd be taking a big risk; they would not have much protection against the creatures on the open porch. But then, the creatures hadn't been silent and inconspicuous in their previous attacks. Chances were good that they'd signal their approach with their usual raucous cries and frenetic blinking. They would give Keith and Lisa ample time to hurry back inside the house.

And besides, the thought of this risk was already proving to be a powerful aphrodisiac. He couldn't remember ever wanting anyone this much before.

"Come on," he said, nodding toward the main door. "The porch."

"But—"

"We'll be safe."

He looked at his family, and when he was confident everyone was deeply asleep he extended his hand to Lisa. "It's the only place we'll have privacy," he whispered. "We'll stay near the door."

The girl mulled this over for a moment, then she got off the couch, careful not to disturb Toni at the other end, and joined Keith at the door. Together they stepped outside into the warm stagnant night.

"I shouldn't be doing this," Lisa said when Keith turned to face her. "Toni is my best friend. She was furious with me when—"

"Was?" Keith frowned. "What do you mean?"

"Uh, did I say was? I-I meant *will*," she stammered.

Keith's frown deepened. He could tell she

was holding something back from him, but as he searched her youthful and incredibly sexy face in the dim light of a half-moon he decided to question this later. They did not have much time now, for there was no telling when the creatures would appear.

He kissed her.

"I'm gonna hate myself later," he heard her murmur as she pressed her shapely body against the hardness of his.

He pulled her even tighter against him. "Think about now. The hell with tomorrow." His tongue pried the girl's lips apart and probed the interior of her mouth—wet and sweet and so young. Maggie's face flashed before him, but with determined force he pushed it out.

He pushed his body brutally against Lisa's, pushing until she was pressing flatly against the side of the cottage. Once he had her pinned he began to unbutton and unzip her denim shorts. With equal fervor and haste she worked on his trousers. They both knew there was no time for foreplay.

"I shouldn't be doing this . . . I shouldn't be doing this," Lisa repeated over and over in a faint whimpering voice. As she said this, her hands continued to undress him.

Keith pushed her shorts down, pulling her scanty underwear along with them, until they were low enough for her to step out of and kick aside. When his own trousers and underwear were low around his thighs he thrust himself against her.

"I think I love you," Lisa moaned dreamily.

Keith grunted in reply. He suddenly remembered they were outside and vulnerable to the creatures. He quickened his pace, at the same time listening for approaching sounds.

But what he heard were not caws or flappings of leathery wings. It was a gasp at the front door beside them. He looked over and saw his daughter, Toni, was gawking at them.

He pulled away from Lisa, who, still moaning, was unaware of a third person on the porch. Then he hastily turned away from the shadowy form of his daughter and pulled up his trousers and underwear. When he was decently covered, he turned back. Now Lisa, at last aware of Toni's presence, rushed for her shorts and briefs and donned them.

"Baby," Keith began, then fell silent, his mind blank.

"How could you, Daddy!" Her voice was loud in the quiet night. The moonlight did not reach her face, but Keith knew it was filled with disgust and contempt.

"Baby," he tried again. "I-I . . ."

Lisa made an attempt to slip back into the cottage, but Toni quickly moved closer to the center of the doorway, intercepting her.

"Slut!" she screamed.

Lisa recoiled, retreating back onto the porch. She stood near Keith, and Keith knew she wanted him to hold her, protect her from Toni's wrath, but he couldn't. Instead, he stepped away, as though to prove to Toni that the girl truly meant nothing to him.

"Why?" Toni demanded, her voice louder still. Her hands were tight fists at her sides. "Why, Daddy, why?"

Keith held his palms out in a desperate attempt to pacify her. "Don't yell. You'll wake up the others."

"Why are you doing this?" she shouted.

"You're overreacting, baby. Take it easy and I'll try to explain—"

"Don't call me baby!"

"All right, all right, I won't. But I can explain."

"I bet!"

"What you saw . . . it wasn't . . . I mean . . ."

Aware that he was having difficulty, Lisa lifted her chin and said defiantly, "We don't have to explain anything, Toni."

"Shut up!" Toni yelled. Again Lisa recoiled, her chin dropping quickly.

"Look," Keith said, "let's talk when we're all calmer, all right? I swear it's not as bad as it looks." He knew this was a lie, that it was exactly as it looked, but he felt he had to say something to placate her.

"How could you do this to Mom?" she wailed. "I thought you loved her, Daddy!"

"I do, ba— I really do. I love your mother more than anything in the world."

"Then why?"

Keith moved forward, arms extended, beseeching forgiveness. How could he make her understand, especially when he himself didn't? All he knew now was that he was sorry he had hurt Toni.

"Don't touch me, Daddy! Don't you dare touch me!"

With a doleful sigh, he let his hands drop. "And I love you more than anything in the world, too," he said softly. "I never wanted to hurt you. You just don't understand my needs." He knew he was sounding like something from a crappy soap opera, but it was the truth. He meant every word he said.

Toni stared in silence. He still could not see her face, but he could sense the contempt, and he knew he had failed to soften it. She hated him now. It couldn't have been more obvious if she had shouted it out loud.

A long moment passed as Toni continued to glare in the darkness at Keith, who was partly visible in the moonlight, then in an explosion of disgust, she spun on her heel to go back into the house. She collided into Maggie who was just emerging.

Another frozen moment ensued. Maggie had come to investigate the commotion, and the instant she saw her husband and Lisa on the porch, she knew.

With a sob, Toni ran past her mother into the cottage. Maggie took Toni's place and glowered at the guilty couple. Keith expected her to shout with outrage also, but she only stared in silence. And for some reason he found this to be much, much worse.

Lisa cleared her throat, then said, "Toni's overreacting, Mrs. Hunter. You see, your husband and I were just stepping out for a breath of air."

Maggie's eyes dropped to the girl's tight shorts. The zipper was undone. Keith groaned inwardly. The dumb kid had brought attention to herself and confirmed his wife's conviction. There was no fucking way out of this one.

Maggie's gaze slowly returned to Keith. "Again," she said simply. It was not a question; it was a statement betraying quiet incredulity.

The air thickened and grew chilly in spite of the stagnant night.

"I'm sorry," Keith said, putting as much feeling into the word as he could.

Maggie took a step back from him, as though repulsed. "Once was horrible," she said in a controlled, yet icy voice. "But twice? My God, Keith, you are despicable."

"Maggie, please—"

She began to interrupt him, maybe at last snapping out of that cold, contemptuous state and exploding into a rage, but her mouth froze. Something had distracted her. And the instant Keith realized this, he heard a noise behind him.

Flapping wings!

Simultaneously, he and Lisa spun around. Lisa let out a scream. Keith stood frozen in

horror, thinking: Where's the iron poker?
What did I do with the fucking poker?

The creatures were coming toward him—
and he had never seen them fly so damn fast!

CHAPTER TWENTY-THREE

Aware that Keith was not moving, but only staring at the winged beings rushing toward them, Maggie seized the back of his shirt and screamed, "Get in here!"

This prompted a response. He spun around and ran into the cottage, slamming and locking the door after him. Almost the instant he did this the creatures were heard slapping and thudding against the door.

Maggie cringed at the sound. The rapidity of it suggested an aggression that was savage and frightening. Toni, also cringing, moved closer to her mother and buried her face in her mother's chest. Maggie wrapped an arm around her, holding her closer.

Keith looked over at Maggie, and their eyes held for a brief moment. "Thank you," he told her tacitly, and she looked away, thinking that maybe she should have let the bastard stay outside with those demons.

Keith began to search for the poker and soon found it on the couch, where Lisa had been.

The noise at the door grew louder and more frantic.

"I'm going to bash your heads in!" he shouted at them as he gripped the iron rod with both hands, swinging it in readiness. "Come on, come on!"

It seemed certain that the door would burst open at any moment, for the creatures were repeatedly slamming themselves against it, acting like a battering ram. But suddenly the noise stopped and there was silence. Everyone in the room glanced quizzically at each other. Vivian had emerged from her own room and joined the others, and Brice had left his sleeping bag to be closer to his mother and sister.

"They're evil," Vivian whispered. "They can't be trusted."

Maggie looked at the front door, then at the ceiling, as though expecting to hear the creatures flying above the house. She heard nothing. The silence was somehow much worse than the frenetic noise that had preceded it.

"Think they went back?" Toni asked.

Maggie said nothing, but she didn't think so. She had an uneasy feeling that the creatures were still close to the house, that their silence meant they were up to something.

"I-I'm afraid, Mom," Brice said.

Maggie pulled him closer and kissed the top of his head.

Keith paced from window to window, poker now shifting from hand to hand. Lisa's eyes followed him from the couch, where she sat trembling against a corner with her feet tucked under her. It was evident that she needed someone to hold her, for she was petrified, but neither Maggie nor Toni could bring herself to go even near her.

"What are they doing?" Vivian asked.

"I don't know," Maggie said.

"Come on, bastards!" Keith suddenly boomed at the door, startling everyone. "I'm ready for ya!"

More silence ensued, thicker because of the loudness of Keith's voice before it, then a distinct smell began to permeate the room. It was a faint, acrid smell—the stench of burning wood.

"Look!" Lisa cried, pointing to the bottom of the door. Gray smoke was seeping into the room.

"Jesus!" Keith bolted toward the door.

"No!" Maggie shouted. "Don't go out there!"

"They're trying to smoke us out, dammit! Got to stop them before—" He flung open the door, and to everyone's horrified surprise exposed a flaming porch. Charcoal-gray smoke curtained the doorway, but through

this thick haze orange flames flickered along
the railings and post, outlining the porch
with angry, ragged light.

"Get water and blankets!" Keith ordered
as he ran outside to stamp out what he could
of the fire.

Simultaneously, the others burst into
action. Vivian and Lisa ran into the bedroom
and yanked blankets off the beds. Maggie,
Toni and Brice pulled out bowls and
saucepans from the kitchen cabinets and
filled them with water. When the group
reached the door, Keith had already
extinguished most of the fire.

Coughing and holding a forearm over the
lower half of his face, he seized a pan from
Maggie and threw the water against a
burning railing. Then he turned back for
another pan and then another. When all the
pans and bowls were used, he yelled for
more. As his wife and children fled back
inside with empty vessels, he snatched a
blanket from Vivian and violently slapped it
against a post, smothering the flames while
Lisa did likewise on another post. When the
others returned with more water, the fire
was out.

But their problems were not over.

Almost as soon as everyone was able to
catch his or her breath, the creatures began
to rush forward. They had been hiding
behind a row of pines. Lisa screamed and ran
back into the house. Vivian remained frozen
until Toni and Maggie grabbed her and

hustled her inside with them, Brice at their heels. Keith followed, but as he turned to slam the door shut he found that he was too late. Many of the flying beings had sped past him into the house, the larger one leading them.

Lisa screamed again, ran into the master bedroom and closed the door. Keith frantically looked around him, cursing himself for losing the damn poker again. Quickly he found it near the front door where he had dropped it. Grabbing the instrument and swinging it wildly, he yelled, "Come on, come on, come on!"

Maggie hugged her daughter while Vivian hugged her grandson. Fearfully, they watched the creatures fly and frenetically pulse lights around them. There was a sickening *thunk* as Keith whacked one of the creatures with the heavy poker. The animal emitted a startled shriek, blinked furiously, then fell to the floor, where it squirmed as it continued to pulse light. For a long moment it blinked slowly and intermittently, each spark weaker than the last, each beat longer. Then it ceased altogether.

Keith struck another creature and succeeded in killing this one also. This prompted a piercing cry from the large motherlike creature who was in a corner of the room as a spectator, apart from the others. She began to pulse rapidly, her pure light no longer a calm glow but a frantic beacon. She flew over to the first dead creature, then to the second, and back to the first.

She emitted another piercing cry, and it seemed as though she was endeavoring to get the other creatures' attention, but the others were rapidly circling Keith, like hornets in a frenzy. Maggie broke away from her daughter and ran into the kitchen area for a chair. She could see Keith was in horrible danger. The creatures were seizing him by the arms, legs and hair, gripping him with their teeth. Below him the mother continued to move back and forth between the two lifeless beings, as though in a desperate attempt to revive them.

Maggie lifted the chair by its back and swung at a creature, but missed. It was moving too damn fast; it was like trying to swat a housefly. She tried again, and this time managed to hit one. The creature did not even pause in flight. It was as though she hadn't hit it at all. She tried attacking another creature and again was unsuccessful. The creatures were in too much of a frenzy to be aware of her or the chair, or of the mother crying out to them on the floor.

They began to pull Keith out of the house. He screamed, shouting at them to let him go. The poker dropped to the floor as a creature sank its teeth into his wrist and hung on.

Lisa leaped off the couch and grabbed the iron instrument. Joining Maggie, she swung at the beings. She hit one, but did not kill it. Only Keith, it seemed, was strong enough to deliver lethal blows.

"They're taking him away!" she screamed.

Maggie threw herself against the closed door. In horror she saw the creatures rush toward her, pulling Keith with them. They were blinking furiously, their wings fanning violently at her face, but Maggie fought the powerful instinct to flee from their path. She swung the chair wildly, yet her speed was no match for them. The creatures were able to dodge the chair and bite her hands and arms until she was forced to let go.

She threw her arms up to protect her face. Teeth dug into her forearms, and she tried to fling the creature aside, but they dug deeper, filling her with hot, intense pain. She could feel her skin tearing as she shook her arms to dislodge the teeth.

"Off! Off!"

Blood flew from her arms and sprayed her face. Even in her frantic attempt to protect herself she could feel the warmth and wetness of the red liquid on her cheeks and forehead. She could feel it well up in her arms where the teeth continued to dig, forming deep, slippery pools. My God, she thought, they're making hamburger out of me!

She felt teeth pulling at her hair. Crying out in agony, she swung at the assailant, but no matter how violently she hit it, it would not let go. It kept pulling, and to prevent the pain from heightening she began to move along with the creature rather than away from it. She moved until she was no longer in front of the door.

In an instant, a creature bolted for the doorknob and, with its mouth, turned it. The door opened, and the creatures, pulling Keith with them, flew out.

"No!" Maggie cried. The creatures that had clung to her arms and hair released her to rejoin the others. Maggie ran outside after them, Lisa and Toni quickly following, but it was impossible to run fast enough.

Maggie couldn't believe this was happening all over again. First it was Toni they had whisked away. Now it was Keith. As she ran, she could see the dark cylinder ahead of her, see that the entrance to it was open, and she could see that she'd never, never reach it before it closed—with her husband inside.

It was all so hopeless, all so horrible.

When the door to the cylinder slid shut, just as she touched it, she dropped to the ground in frustration and despair. Hands cupping her face, she began to sob.

The tears would not stop. Her body racked convulsively, even when she felt a hand on her shoulder. She just could not stop. She didn't know how long she wept, but when she finally lifted her face she was surprised to find that the hand on her shoulder was Lisa's. Angrily, she shook it off and jumped to her feet.

"Mrs. Hunter, he'll be all right," the girl said, also leaping to her feet.

Don't talk to me! Maggie mentally shouted at her. Don't you *dare* talk to me!

"Remember, Toni came back out all right. So I'm sure your husband—"

Abruptly, Maggie headed back for the cottage, leaving the girl behind. Before she could reach her destination, Toni came rushing toward her.

You're bleeding, Mom!"

Maggie looked down at her arms. Blood had stained both of them, including her hands, reminding her of rust-colored paint. Funny, she thought dully, they don't hurt anymore.

Toni wrapped her arm around her and quickly walked her into the house. Once inside, she fetched a sheet, ripped off strips and bandaged Maggie's arms. "You're gonna be okay, Mom," she assured her. The bleeding had already begun to stop.

In a burst of love and gratitude, Maggie stroked the girl's cheek. In return, Toni hugged her. They remained in a tight embrace for a long moment. Once more tears began to burn Maggie's eyes, but this time she willed them away.

Somewhat reluctantly, she disengaged herself from Toni and appraised the room. Keith's blood had made a dotted trail across the wooden floor, reminding her of the violence and struggle that had occurred between her husband and the creatures. He had fought them so vigorously, but there had been too many of them, and they had been too fast. In the horrible struggle, only two of the creatures had perished.

As she remembered this, she noticed that only one of the creatures was in the room. She quickly looked around for the other one. "Where is—"

"She took it," Vivian said, aware of what she was looking for.

Maggie looked at her. The poor woman was standing in the center of the room, hugging herself, her body trembling as though she had Parkinson's disease. Her face was ashen. "Who took it?" Maggie asked.

"The mother. At least I think it's the mother. She took it back to her place out there. She did it while the others took Keith. She was right behind them. She tried to carry both of them but couldn't. Too heavy, I imagine. I guess she's going to come back later to get this one."

As though controlled by one mind, everyone moved tentatively toward the inert being on the floor. Forming a semicircle, they stared down at it in silence. Toni and Maggie winced at the small body while the others studied it with awe.

In the glow of the oil lamp the creature was unmistakably ugly. It was on its back, leathery wings spread out behind it, mothlike. It was dark brown, almost black, which was why it could easily become invisible in the night. Its belly was large, bulbous and soft-looking. Maggie was certain it would burst open like a swollen, pus-filled boil or blister if pressure was applied. She could almost envision the viscous greenish liquid squirting from it, and she shivered with repugnance.

The being's sole eye was a pale, yellowish green and was open, staring vacuously at the ceiling. Also open was its mouth, much too large for its head—a hideous black hole fringed with tiny, pointed teeth that glinted like gilded needles in the amber light.

Two reptilian slits were above the mouth, and something was leaking from them, something watery and reddish brown. Blood from the nostrils? Mucous discharge? Maggie held her stomach tighter, certain she'd soon vomit. She averted her head for a moment, waited for the nausea to pass, then looked back when she felt she had some control.

There seemed to be no ears, and she wondered if these creatures had something else in lieu of hearing—some kind of mental telepathy.

The two feet protruded from short, thin legs that were no more than six inches in length. Without knees, there was no doubt that these birdlike extremities were used mostly for perching and alighting than for walking. The tips of their toes, three on each foot, were long and hooked, resembling talons. At the end of each wing were larger talons. Maggie cringed at the thought of being slashed by one of these vicious claws.

"Wow!" she heard Brice exclaim.

"Where do you think this thing came from?" Toni asked in a stunned, fearful voice.

"Hell," Vivian replied confidently.

"Space," Lisa said, disagreeing.

Maggie looked away again, this time keeping her back to the horrendous being. She didn't want to look at it anymore. Not only was it ugly, she was certain it was evil. She had to agree with her mother that it, indeed, did look like something that had flown in from Hell.

She moved toward the window and looked out at the huge cylinder sitting among the trees. That thing had come from the sky, she remembered, so actually Lisa was probably correct. That object was a spacecraft, and the creatures were aliens—vicious, violent aliens—not at all like that friendly creature in the Spielberg film, *ET*.

Maggie looked up at the black sky. It was a clear night with countless stars dotting the heavens. Which star system did these despicable monsters come from? Why did they come?

She returned her gaze to the cylindrical craft. What were they doing inside there now? What were they doing to Keith? She told herself that he was not worth worrying about. He was an unfaithful bastard. She had already caught him twice, and Lord only knew how many other times he'd cheated on her. She should have nothing to do with the louse.

Yet, no matter how she tried to convince herself of this, she couldn't stop worrying about him.

Toni stood beside her. Sensing what Maggie was thinking, she said, "Maybe they won't hurt him, Mom. They didn't hurt me, and in the end they let me go."

"You think so?"

"Sure. They're probably doing to him right now what they'd done to me."

"And exactly what was that?"

"Well, I'm not too sure. They made me sense weird stuff. They went inside my head, I think. But," she pointedly reminded her, "they didn't hurt me."

Maggie gave her a small smile to show her that she felt a little better, but the smile was fake; she didn't feel better at all. There was an uneasy feeling in her stomach that would not go away. Somehow she was certain that Keith would not be as fortunate as Toni.

She was confident that the aliens, at this very moment, were doing something ghastly to her husband.

CHAPTER TWENTY-FOUR

The Elder fought for control. Usually this was simple to do. Emotions were easy to turn on and off, but right now she could not seem to do it. Perhaps it was being in an alien world that was making it all so frightening, and perhaps it was because The Little Ones themselves were uncontrollable with excitement.

Control. Control.

There simply was none.

Inside the craft The Little Ones hovered around the man. He was strapped to the table, making loud, grating sounds with his mouth. He, too, was out of control with emotions, but then, humans always were, it seemed.

The Elder flew restlessly from one end of

the vessel to the other. She cried out to The Little Ones, demanding attention and cooperation, but they paid no heed. They were too eager to begin their experiment with the man. She tried to tell them that two of their companions were already dead, and that one was still inside the humans' house, but they did not care. This was her problem—hers alone. She would have to get the remaining Little One back inside the vessel. It was her responsibility.

She contemplated returning to the humans' house and dragging the body back, as she had done with the first one, but she had succeeded that time only because the confusion and excitement prevented anyone from noticing, let alone stopping her. Now the five humans inside the house would be waiting for her, and they would kill her if she returned alone.

Still no one paid her any heed. She entered one of The Little Ones' mind in desperation, and still she was ignored. Yes, they were definitely out of control.

And she was out of control, too. She had really thought no harm would come to The Little Ones when they came here. She had been so confident they would be safe. Oh, how careless she'd been! How neglectful!

For the first time in her adult life she threw her head back and wailed.

CHAPTER TWENTY-FIVE

Keith swung wildly and ineffectually. His fists continued to miss the nimble creatures, and his body could not shake vigorously enough to dislodge them. They held on with their teeth, and they pushed and pulled him toward the silver cylinder. They were surprisingly strong, and they outnumbered him. He knew he didn't have a chance, yet he continued to fight them.

Their screeches and cries were deafening. First they reminded him of frantic crows, then of ecstatic children screaming shrilly with delight. These creatures were definitely excited about capturing him, and they couldn't seem to get him inside the cylinder quickly enough.

Keith yelled at them to let him go, hoping

his booming voice would scare some of them and weaken their hold on him. He succeeded only in exciting them further. They pulsed light more rapidly and brilliantly, their cries grew shriller.

He shouted for Maggie and heard her yelling somewhere behind him. Remotely, he found this surprising. Why should she be running after him, trying to save him? He had betrayed her again. He did not deserve to be saved, yet he clearly heard her call out his name.

"Help me, Maggie!" he cried. He dragged his feet on the ground, endeavoring to make himself heavier, but the little monsters pulled him onward without even a pause. He felt his pants rip at the knee as it scraped against a rock. Never had he felt so damn helplesss, and this angered as well as frightened him.

They reached the entrance, a black mouth ready and hungry to devour him. Keith twisted and kicked. Then in a burst of energy, the creatures pulled him up off the ground and into the vessel. The entrance slid shut behind him.

Keith continued to struggle, although he knew it was over now. There was no way he could escape from the cylinder. He looked frantically around him as he thrashed. Darkness was everywhere, except for the red bulbous lights outlining the floor, the curved ceiling, and something rectangular at one end. It was the latter that he found himself rushing towards.

It was a table.

"What the fuck—"

They dropped him on it. With sharp, quick clicks, clamps fastened him to the hard surface. Now he found himself unable to move, let alone kick or swing. The clamps were tight around his arms and thighs, digging into his flesh. He grunted, tried to push against these clamps, but they were as strong as steel.

"What do you want?" he bellowed at a creature who was only inches away from his face. In return, the creature let out a squeal and blinded him with yellow light. Keith turned his head aside, thankful that he could at least move this.

"Get away from me!" he shouted. "All of you! Get the fuck away from me!"

He heard a cackling sound, like an explosion of sparks one would hear in a fireplace, only much louder. Soon he felt sharp, hot pain in his arm. He tried to look but could see nothing, only a blinding electric flash. Then he experienced another pain, this time excruciating and relentless. He screamed again, rocking his head from side to side. A strange sound filled his ears, further intensifying the agony. It was a whirring, strident buzz that seemed to rise to a grating, unbearable crescendo. It was a piercing sound that was not unlike an electric saw severing wood—or bone.

Now too filled with pain to scream, he gritted his teeth as he rocked his head.

When the strident buzz ceased, Keith reopened his eyes, although the pain was still intense. He saw the beam shrink back toward the ceiling, toward darkness. There was a wave of relief, then horror rushed back as he noticed the hovering creatures were passing something around with their mouths. In midair they would inspect this curious object for a quick moment, then give it to the next creature. Keith could only see this object whenever light pulsed from a creature's belly and illuminated it in a confusion of color and brilliance. This object, Keith eventually realized, was a human hand.

Keith craned his neck to see if this was his own hand these monsters were passing around. To his frustration he could not see well, partly because the lighting was poor, and partly because his vision was beginning to blur. Still gritting his teeth against the pain, which was now a violent throb, he waited until more light pulsed in the direction of the hand. He felt something wet and warm under him, soaking his pants. Had he pissed in them? A part of him knew this wasn't what had happened. He knew he was lying in a puddle of his own blood. And when at last enough light from the creatures illuminated his arm, his fear was confirmed.

There was nothing beyond his wrist.

His hand was in the air, going from one creature to the other.

Keith gawked with disbelief. This couldn't be happening! He would be unconscious by now, wouldn't he? But as he thought this, his vision grew even blurrier. Yes, he was slipping now, and the puddle of blood under him seemed thicker and warmer.

He watched a creature sniff his hand, lick it experimentally, then pass it on to another creature who did the same. Dimly, Keith was reminded of a time when he was a kid in school, and a fossil of an insect was passed around the classroom. He had done the same, had sniffed and licked the rocklike substance. The teacher had chided him for doing the latter. "You could catch something dreadful," she had warned in a harsh, nasal voice. Now, in a groggy state, Keith wanted to mimic that teacher's voice and say the same thing to the creatures. Don't lick! You'll be sick!

But he was too weak; he could only stare and watch his hand go by.

Then the blue beam of light appeared out of the darkness again. Looking at it, he numbly saw it grow longer and longer. This time it was aimed at one of his legs.

No please, he protested wearily, not my legs. No, not my . . .

There was a second explosion of pain, and it immediately revived in him the stark horror. The grating sawlike sound filled his head, causing him to grit his teeth once more. When the agonizing pain subsided to an aching throb, and his mind began to spin lazily, he saw a shoe go back and forth among the creatures. He blinked, straining to see clearer. Something was dripping from the shoe, something dark.

It was blood, his own blood, and it was not just a bloody shoe these bastards were sniffing and tasting, either. His foot was inside it. Keith knew this without looking down at his leg. He knew not because of the pain that the blue beam had caused him, but because the table under him was now incredibly slippery and wet. If it weren't for the clamps, he'd definitely slide off.

He closed his eyes. He was so damn tired and weak now. In a few seconds he was going to slip away. He wanted to hold on somehow, to keep from drifting, but he was too weary.

Behind his lids he saw blue light. It was brilliant, almost blinding, even with his eyes closed. He quickly opened them and gasped in surprise and shock. The beam was now directly above him, and this time it was aimed at—

Oh, Christ, no!

Now they were after his head.

Maggie spent another night kneeling before the metallic craft, waiting and praying. This time she was inwardly certain her prayer would not be answered. Keith would not return safely. Beside her was Toni, and behind both of them at a slight distance was Lisa. They did not want her near them, and the girl sensed this. She stood against a tree and waited in silence. Inside the cottage Vivian and Brice watched from a window. It was a long, interminable night.

The dead creature was now in the closet in the master bedroom. Maggie had wanted it out of sight, but she did not want to dispose of it, for she was confident that the mother would want to reclaim her child before the night was over.

Repeatedly, she told herself to forget about what had happened between Keith and Lisa on the porch earlier this evening. This was not the time to think about it, but it kept paining her. Had he actually stopped loving her? Was this something that was beyond fixing?

Whatever the reason, this was not the time to think about it, she reminded herself.

But the hours moved slowly, and her mind kept whirling. She could not stop thinking about it. Keith had no right to cheat on her like this—practically right under her nose! How little he must have thought of her! She shouldn't have to put up with this. She *wouldn't* put up with this!

Now, however, was not the time.

She concentrated on a prayer. Father, who art in heaven, please help my husband . . .

Was God punishing Keith because he had committed adultery? Swiftly, she swept the question from her mind. She was being silly. God had nothing to do with what was happening now. He did not punish sinners. He forgave them, didn't He?

And besides, she was a sinner, too. It was partly her fault that Keith had strayed. She had spent too many hours away from him. Yet, on the other hand, she'd been with him these past few days, and still he cheated.

She heard a faint scream—or had she only imagined it?

She waited. A minute later she heard it again, and this time there was no doubt. It was Keith.

They were killing him in there.

The door to the craft slid open. Toni and Lisa had returned to the cottage, but Maggie was still on the ground, waiting. She was shrouded in darkness, about to nod off when she noticed the white spectral glow of the motherlike creature. The light filled the entrance and illuminated Maggie's face, then it ebbed as it stepped forward. The door behind the creature slid shut.

Hesitantly, Maggie rose to her feet. She took a step back, then willed herself to stop. She wanted to confront this thing, for she could see that her husband had not come out with it.

"Where is he?" she demanded.

The creature did not answer. It flew slowly toward Maggie, and Maggie had to use all her willpower not to run from this monstrosity.

"You've got my husband in there. I want him back," Maggie said in a firmer, louder voice.

The creature stared at her with its sole eye, and almost instantly Maggie felt its effect. Quickly, she averted her face. This was no time to be hypnotized, she reminded herself. She must keep her mind closed and form a protective shield against it.

The creature flew past her toward the cottage.

"No!" Maggie cried, running after it. Now she knew what it wanted—the dead child—but she was not going to let it have it, at least not before she had Keith back.

Gaining as much speed as she could, Maggie ran past the creature and reached the cottage first. She flung open the door, rushed through the large main room and slammed the door to the master bedroom shut, startling everyone. Then she dragged the rocking chair to this door and pushed it against the doorknob, blocking it. She hoped this would hinder the larger creature from retrieving the smaller one on the other side.

Vivian, Brice and the two girls looked questioningly at her from different parts of the room, then simultaneously their gaze swung toward the glowing creature as it emerged through the front door.

"It wants its child," Maggie explained hurriedly, panting from the strenuous run, "but I'm not letting her have it, not until she gives me back Keith." She frantically looked around her. "Where's that goddamned poker?"

Toni spotted it first and made a grab for it. She gave it to her mother.

"All right, where is he?" Maggie demanded, hefting the iron rod as she faced the creature. She made sure her eyes were not fully on the creature's face and that the shield in her mind was firmly in place.

The creature alighted on the floor and stood motionless for a long moment. It seemed to be deciding what move to make next. It took a step forward, only to retreat when Maggie swung wildly in a threatening gesture.

"Go get my husband!" she shouted at it. "Bring him back."

Angling its head toward the ceiling, the creature sniffed the air, apparently seeking the smaller creature's scent. It found it instantly and turned toward the bedroom door.

"No!" Maggie screamed. She swung the poker again, and for the second time the creature retreated. It stared at Maggie with a gleaming, belligerent eye.

"I . . . want . . . my . . . husband!" Maggie enunciated each word.

The creature appeared to understand but

was not willing to cooperate. It openly appraised Maggie, then turned its attention to the others in the room. The silence was heavy. Maggie kept the poker in motion as a reminder not to make any sudden moves.

The creature looked at Brice, at the two girls, then rested its gaze on Vivian. Almost belatedly, Maggie realized that her mother was holding the gaze, that the creature was succeeding in entrancing her.

"No, Ma!" Maggie yelled, hoping her voice would be loud and piercing enough to shatter the contact that was developing between the two, but Vivian responded without looking away.

"Yes, dear?"

"Don't look at it," Maggie ordered. "It's trying to hypnotize you!"

"It wants a Little One," Vivian said in a thick, sedated voice. She was still staring at the creature. "It needs The Little One, Maggie."

"Stop looking at it!" Maggie shouted at her, then turned to the creature. "Stop it!"

But the two continued to gaze at each other.

"It can't understand why we won't let it near The Little One," Vivian said. "I explained this was because Keith hasn't returned. I told it we want him back."

"Ma, stop looking at it! Look away! Look at me!"

"Maggie, it's communicating with me.

Can't you see that?"

"Look at me, I said!"

Vivian hesitated, then with visible force she averted her head away from the creature. "It's desperate," she told Maggie. "It knows that the other creature is dead in the bedroom, but it still wants it."

"And I want Keith—just as desperately."

"It knows that, but—"

"But what?"

"It doesn't seem to care."

"Get away from that thing!" Maggie commanded, her voice hard with contempt. Swinging the poker more vigorously, she took a menacing step toward the creature. "If you don't give me back my husband, I'll kill you!" she hissed.

The creature looked at her, then quickly away. It actually seemed afraid, but also determined. It made an attempt at the bedroom door, pushing the rocking chair aside. Its mouth managed to reach and twist the knob, but Maggie rushed forward and slammed the poker down on its head. The creature shrieked and flew away from the door, its swollen abdomen pumping white light like a furious heartbeat.

"I want my husband back!" Maggie reiterated. "Then, and only then, can you have what you want."

The creature seemed confused. It looked over at Vivian, apparently wanting to communicate with her again, but the woman would not look back at it. At length the creature returned its attention to Maggie, who this time let the shield in her mind drop. Shouting demands, Maggie realized, would not get her anywhere. She would have to make the creature understand with thoughts, but she'd also have to be careful not to fall into a trance and come under the creature's power.

Maggie said to the others in the room, "Whatever happens to me, don't let this bitch go into the bedroom." Then she turned to the creature, now ready.

The effect was almost instantaneous, like a dam bursting. Maggie felt a cold numbness in her mind, then a gradual floating sensation. But all the while she experienced the intrusion she reminded herself not to lose control. Soon thoughts flashed, thoughts that were not her own.

The creature wanted The Little One that was in the bedroom. It wanted it now.

Maggie refused. She wanted her husband back now, too.

That was not possible, the creature informed her. The Little Ones were still busy with the man.

Busy doing what? Maggie demanded.

Studying the specimen, the creature responded, then repeated the demand for The Little One.

Maggie felt her control slipping. She felt as though she were in space, weightless while holding onto something like the rungs of the ladder to a spaceship. But now she was growing weary, and her fingers were slipping away from the rung. Soon she would be drifting in space.

Maggie shook her head faintly. Far away she heard a metallic clang and dimly realized that the poker in her hand had fallen to the floor. She thought of retrieving it, but her body would not move. She had only one finger on the rung now, and that was quickly losing hold.

The creature made its demand once again.

Maggie drifted. She felt herself move away from the door she was blocking. Whether she did this herself or the creature nudged her out of the way, she wasn't sure—and she didn't care. She simply continued to drift.

She felt as though she were on the verge of sleep when a piercing scream jolted her to full awareness. It took her a moment to realize what was happening. Toni had rushed forward with the oil lamp and was shining it in the creature's ugly face, and Lisa had the poker in her hand and was attacking the creature with it. In response, the creature was flying frantically around the room, cawing and shrieking in a mixture of fury and agony. At length it bolted out the already open front door and sped into the night toward the dark bulk of the craft.

Still groggy and unsteady on her feet, Maggie pursued the girls and the creature.

"Don't kill it," she cried. If they did this, she feared they'd never see Keith alive again. The smaller creatures might retaliate by killing him. "No, don't kill it!"

The girls stopped running, and Maggie caught up to them. Together, they watched the blinking creature reach the cylinder. It paused at the closed entrance, hovering while glancing frequently back at them. It could have been so easy to club it to death as it waited for the door to open. Maggie was reminded of a housefly batting against a window, straining frantically to get to the other side.

How was it going to open the entrance? Maggie wondered. Seconds passed and still the door did not open. Obviously a creature from inside had to be alerted, but the mother was not making any noise; it was only staring at the door, waiting.

When the door finally opened, it occurred to Maggie what the creature had done. It had communicated mentally with those inside the craft, as it had communicated earlier with Maggie. Now the creature was safely inside, the entrance once again closed and invisible.

"Bitch!" Lisa spat at it. Maggie and Toni hugged each other, as though to steady the other's trembling. When Lisa saw that she was not to be included, she walked back into the house.

Maggie watched her and for a moment was

actually tempted to call her name and include her in the embrace—but she just couldn't.

With Toni, she sat on the ground and waited. The night was not over yet.

CHAPTER TWENTY-SIX

The Elder never had experienced such a lack of control. Not only was she panicking, she was losing control of The Little Ones. They were overflowing with curiosity and enthusiasm, like beasts who had been deprived of food for days. They were too hungry to pay attention to her. It was actually miraculous that one had heeded her command and broken away from the group to let her in the vessel. She would have kept the entrance opened if she hadn't feared leaving The Little Ones exposed and vulnerable while she was away. Now she realized she never should have gone out alone at all, but she had been so desperate to retrieve The Little One from the humans. She had been afraid to lose it and be forced to return home without it. She had tried to persuade a few of The Little Ones to join her, but she hadn't been able to get their attention, let alone their cooperation.

But now she will demand obedience!

Concentrating harder than she'd ever done in her life, she screamed silently and relentlessly as she entered each and every Little One's brain. It was strenuous and tiring, as she knew it would be, but eventually she succeeded in controlling the group.

She paused to regain her strength, then told The Little Ones of her predicament. She must have The Little One's body that was inside the humans' house. She could not go home without it. But before she could have it, she would have to relinquish the man.

The Little Ones protested. They wanted to bring the man back home with them, to study him some more, to divide the pieces among themselves and keep as a remembrance.

The Elder told them this could not be done. The man would be needed to get The Little One's body back. Then she instructed the group to gather the pieces of the man and deposit them into a bag.

There was still enough time before daybreak to deliver the bundle.

CHAPTER TWENTY-SEVEN

Maggie struggled to stay awake, but after an hour had passed she found herself asleep on the ground before the cylinder. Tony was nudging her.

Groggily, she looked over at her daughter.

"Something's happening," the girl whispered.

In unison, she and Toni rose to their feet, clasping each other's hand.

The mother creature emerged first. She walked rather than flew forward, her steps small and jerky. Close behind her were two Little Ones, also on foot. Together they dragged something between them, a bag that was larger than they were.

The mother moved to the side and the two smaller creatures pulled the bag forward.

They deposited it before Maggie and Toni, then quickly retreated to the mother's side.

A cloud passed and the moon shined through, illuminating the large, lumpy bag. There were dark stains on it, but before she or Toni could examine it closely, the moon slipped behind another cloud.

Maggie could not bring herself to touch the bundle at her feet. There was a horrible, uneasy feeling in her stomach. She looked over at the mother creature. "What is this?"

The creature glowed pale light in response. It seemed much calmer now, Maggie noted. She wished she could say the same for herself, but the uneasy feeling kept growing inside her.

As Maggie stared at the mother, demanding an answer, she began to feel pressure against her mind. Instinctively, she developed a shield, refusing to let the creature enter. As she did this, she realized there was no other way they could communicate. If she wanted answers, she would simply have to open her mind and let the creature in.

Reluctantly, she released the mental barrier.

Once more she asked about the bag. The creature informed her that it was her husband. Then it demanded the body of The Little One that was in the house.

But Maggie had pushed the creature out of her head the instant she was told what was in the bag. Her husband? The bundle was too small, too lumpy.

The moon came out again.

Once more she saw the dark stains. They looked wet. She touched one of the stains, then drew her hand away quickly. It was wet—and sticky. It was—blood.

This can't be Keith, she thought. It can't be!

She felt pressure against her mind again. For a fleeting instant she let the creature enter and repeat its demand for The Little One, then she violently pushed it out.

She stared at the bag for a long moment, unable to decide whether or not to open it. When she finally made a decision to look inside the bag, she found it difficult to summon enough courage. At length she knelt before the bundle and began to loosen the cord that fastened it. Toni helped her.

The bag was of a smooth, silver fabric that was cool to the touch. The cord that she and Toni were pulling loose was thin and silky, yet incredibly tenacious. When they finally had the bag opened, a stench filled their nostrils. It was a sweet, warm smell—the smell of meat.

Maggie drew back, hesitating to go any further. Toni opened the neck of the bag wider and peered inside. It was too dark to see anything. She looked over at Maggie, clearly not wanting to put her hand into something that could not be seen.

Maggie swallowed, mustering more courage, then began to lower her hand inside the bag, but the moment she touched something, something that was cool and wet, she yanked the hand back.

She couldn't do it.

The moon came out again.

The bag shined silvery. Once more Maggie swallowed, garnering courage. She looked into the bag.

The moonlight illuminated some of its contents. Most of what was inside was still hidden in shadow, but what she did see was enough to cause her to become nauseated. It was a face, looking up at her with wide, terror-filled eyes. The mouth was a gaping cavity, frozen moments after a scream had been unleashed. It was Keith's face. It was his unattached head. It was just sitting there on top of a hairy, blood-matted chest, just sitting there and looking back at her.

Maggie fainted.

When she came to, the bag was gone, as well as the creatures. Toni rushed to her side, dropping to the ground and reaching for one of her hands.

"What happened?" She looked at the cylinder in front of her and saw that the entrance was gone. How long had she been unconscious?

The image of Keith's horrified face flashed in her mind. She shuddered, then emitted a sigh, clutching her hand over her mouth. "Oh, my God."

"I went to get you some cold water, Mom," she heard Toni say. There was a wet towel in her other hand. "I've been trying to wake you up." She began to pat the cool cloth on Maggie's forehead and cheek, but Maggie pulled herself upright.

"I-I'm all right," she said, but she wasn't right at all. She doubted if she'd ever be right again, not after seeing that face in the bag.

She felt a sudden urge to vomit.

"Let's go back into the house," Toni suggested.

Maggie nodded and, with Toni's help, rose to her feet. "Where's the . . ." She couldn't finish the question.

"They brought it back inside."

"What about the dead creature? Did they take it?"

"No. They tried. They all came out to get it, but we put up a big fight with the poker and the lamp. Not one of them was able to get through that bedroom door."

"Lamp?"

"I think it blinds them."

"Oh." Of course. She should have known that. That was probably why they came out only at night and had sabotaged all the electricity in the house. They were evil; they hated the light. They were creatures of darkness.

Inside the cottage, near the oil lamp,

Maggie could see that Toni had been crying. On the couch, Brice was scarcely moving, staring at his feet. He sniffed and wiped his eyes and nose with his arm, then was still again. Maggie knew the tears were for his father.

"Did anyone get hurt?" Maggie asked, looking around the large room. Vivian, in the rocking chair, wearily shook her head, and Lisa, next to Brice on the couch, did likewise. Maggie then returned her attention to Toni, who also shook her head.

"We were ready for them, Mom," she told her. "We're bigger and stronger than those things are."

But not as fast, Maggie thought. She sat at one end of the couch, then quickly rose to pace the room. A minute later she went into the master bedroom to look at the dead creature inside the closet. There was not much light for her to see clearly, but she could make out its small, squat body. She just wanted to stare at it for a while to be sure it wasn't moving, to be certain it was dead. When she was confident of this, she returned to the main room, sat on the couch again, then once more got up to pace.

She felt as though she was losing her mind. There were so many powerful emotions surging through her—grief, anger, contempt and above all—unrelenting terror. When was it going to end?

Now that Keith was gone, she knew she both loved him and hated him. She had forgiven him the first time he cheated and had tried to understand him, but the second time was different. She could not do it. She was human, not divine.

Yet she loved him just the same, and the thought he'd been so gruesomely killed stunned and pained her. He was a bastard, true, but he did not deserve to die the way he had.

"Maggie."

"Yes, Ma?"

"Is it true? Did they really kill Keith?"

Unable to respond at first, Maggie finally nodded, not trusting her voice.

Vivian looked down at her hands that were twitching unconsciously in her lap. "I couldn't believe that I once thought those monsters were good," she said. "I thought they were holy or something like that because they'd brought back your father. Now I can see they're not that at all. They're evil, Maggie. Devils. That's what they are—devils."

Maggie said nothing, for there was nothing to say.

"Maggie?"

"Yes, Ma?"

"I'm sorry. I know I always criticized Keith before. I always told you I didn't like him, but now I feel terrible that he's gone. I really am sorry, dear. I wish we could start over. I would be so much nicer to him."

"Ma, please don't torment yourself like this."

Vivian reached for Maggie's hand and squeezed it. "Sorry," she whispered again, then, after a final pat with the other hand, let go. Maggie resumed her pacing.

She was still pacing when the sun came up.

At noon Maggie fell asleep and dreamed of Keith, when she had first met him. He had her in his arms and was kissing her. So much love poured out of him, leaving her with no doubt that she was first in his life, and when he broke the kiss and looked at her with those dark, sensitive eyes, she felt the flood of adoration and love once more. No, there was no doubt at all.

Then he dropped his arms and picked up a briefcase that was sitting on the floor between them. She thought it was his briefcase, but he gave it to her. Feeling a surge of excitement and euphoria, she gratefully kissed him, then hurried on her way, her new briefcase swinging at her side. When she looked back, wanting to blow him a last kiss, she found him embracing a young woman in a scant bikini.

She stood staring in disbelief, then rage seized her and she flung the briefcase toward him. But the briefcase sailed through the air in slow motion, as though it were nothing but a sheet of paper. When at last it reached its destination, Keith and the young woman were gone.

Maggie woke up with a start, surprised to find herself so furious. Sitting upright in bed, she held her head in her hands and tried to calm down.

She fought back tears. No more, dammit! she told herself. She had certainly cried enough. With this renewed resolve, she slid out of bed and went outside.

Vivian, Brice, and Lisa were on the porch, and Toni was sitting on the wharf. It was another warm, humid day.

"Wonder what today will bring," muttered Toni as Maggie joined her.

I wonder what *tonight* will bring, Maggie mused.

They sat on the wharf, their feet in the tepid, motionless water, and waited in silence.

It was a long, hot afternoon.

CHAPTER TWENTY-EIGHT

Slowly, the sky darkened. The outlines of the trees were motionless inside the shield, but outside they swayed silently in the breeze. Tonight the moon was visible and the stars plentiful.

Toni and Maggie were still on the wharf, occasionally splashing the water with their feet, just to break the silence and stillness that would grow too oppressive. They hadn't eaten all day, but they weren't hungry, their stomachs too unsettled by fear. They were still waiting, each glancing now and then to their right, where the large craft sat beneath the pines and hemlocks.

Maggie spent most of the afternoon contemplating ways to escape from their prison. She felt as though she were a fish in a tank. And how do fish escape from their tanks? she wondered. Occasionally they would leap out, but usually there would be nothing they could do, except swim. Were she and the others here this helpless? There must be something they could do.

But the shield seemed complete and impenetrable. There was nothing to do except release it somehow, and that would mean going inside the cylinder. There must be some kind of device in there that had produced the shield, and it seemed likely that this same device would remove it as well.

Somehow she would have to get inside the craft and find it.

Suddenly the cylinder was opening. Her heart pounding violently in her chest, she nudged Toni. "Look."

The moon enabled them to see almost clearly. They stared, not moving, at the entrance. There was a man, naked, his penis and testicles in shadow.

It was Keith.

Mother and daughter still could not move. What they were seeing did not seem possible.

"Mom, I think that's . . . " Toni could not finish. She seemed so uncertain of her eyes. She frowned, began to smile with relief, then frowned again; her father's nakedness was embarrassing, but mostly frightening.

Maggie found herself reacting the same way. She wanted to cry out with joy and run to this man in the entranceway. She wanted to shout, "You're alive! You're alive! Thank

God, you're alive!" But the image of Keith's terror-stricken face in that hideous bag kept flashing in her mind. Keith was dead. There had been no doubt about that.

So what in God's name was this man before them?

An illusion! Maggie suddenly thought, remembering that Vivian had seen Henry, although he had been dead for several months.

Keith, or the image of Keith, had been looking toward the cottage and now was looking in their direction. Spotting them, he spread his arms to welcome the twosome. His skin was dull, almost colorless in the bleached moonlight.

"Mom, I'm not sure . . ." Again Toni couldn't finish. She took a step back.

But Maggie was more curious than afraid. She waited for her husband to make another move.

"Maggie," he said, moving forward and keeping his arms open, as though in desperation to have someone fill them.

"Keith?" Maggie moved closer, absently pulling Toni along with her.

Keith nodded in confirmation. His head moved slowly, dreamlike, convincing Maggie that this was, indeed, an illusion.

"You're not real," she declared, stopping, "so go away!" Dimly, she felt Toni close behind her, pressing against her back with trepidation.

Keith made another move forward, leaving

the cylinder behind him. His gait, also, was in slow motion. Yes, Maggie told herself again, an illusion.

Somehow, deep inside, she did not believe this. She had an uneasy feeling this was actually someone who had returned from the dead.

"Maggie," he repeated, his voice thick and sluggish. "I'm . . . so . . . glad to see . . . you."

Maggie could not bring herself to move forward and meet him, but she did not turn away either. She stood still with Toni behind her, and waited.

"You're afraid of . . . me," Keith said as he walked with what seemed like a great effort toward her. "Please . . . don't be . . . afraid."

"You're not real," Maggie finally blurted out.

"Of course I'm . . . real." He seemed to have difficulty in finding the right words.

"But you were dead," Maggie told him. "You *are* dead."

"No." He shook his head in that slow, unnatural way again. Then he stopped, as though stillness was the only way he could concentrate and say what he wanted to say. "They put me . . . together . . . again."

Illusion! Maggie's mind vehemently insisted.

"I'm almost . . . like . . . brand new, now . . . Maggie." His arms were still open for her, and he was now only a few feet away.

"Mom . . ." she heard Toni's small voice

behind her " . . . I'm scared."

"It's your father. He won't hurt you."

He reached them and kept his arms extended, but when he gradually realized they would remain empty, he let them drop. His face, dim in the moonlight, was filled with sorrow. It was apparent that he wanted his family to smother him with love, and they couldn't.

"I wish . . . we could . . . start over," he said. "Oh, God . . . how I . . . wish that."

He tilted his head upward as he spoke, and Maggie noted there was something like a wire around his neck. It threaded in and out of his flesh as it circled the neck—as if his head had been sewn back on.

Maggie's hand shot to her mouth. This was no image of her husband. This was him in the flesh—flesh that had been put back together again, piece by piece.

This time Maggie recoiled, stepping back until she bumped into Toni behind her.

"I love you . . . Maggie," Keith said. To Maggie's relief he stopped moving closer. "I've always loved you . . . Maggie . . . It's just that . . . I'm weak . . . sometimes."

"You're dead," Maggie said.

"But they gave me . . . new life."

"You're not the same, Keith."

"I'm . . . not?"

"No." She shook her head, then licked her lips which were suddenly dry. "No," she said again, her voice cracking. "You're different."

"I won't hurt you," he went on. "I promise

. . . not to hurt you . . . anymore." He lifted one arm, hand splayed. He wanted to touch her, but Maggie cringed, eluding his grasp.

You're a monster now, she thought.

"Don't you . . . love me . . . anymore?" he asked.

She almost blurted out that she didn't, but caught herself in time. She did not know how he'd react. "How . . . how did they do this to you?"

"Do what . . . Maggie? Kill me? . . . Put me back . . . together?"

Maggie nodded to both questions.

Keith dropped his hand and fell silent as he concentrated on the answers. His dark eyes were flat, no longer sensitive and intelligent as they used to be.

At length he said, "They dissected me . . . like a frog . . . Maggie." He lapsed into another pensive silence, then continued, "They had me in . . . something like . . . an oven . . . It was warm in there . . . Maggie. . . Hot beams kept spearing me . . . Maggie . . . They woke me up and . . . and still the beams kept . . . hitting me . . . The beams made funny sounds . . . sizzling sounds . . . I thought they . . . were cooking me."

He paused and raised both hands to his head. "But they didn't . . . cook me," he continued. "They brought me . . . back . . . and sewed me back up . . . Maggie . . . and they said they . . . did it for . . . you."

"Me?"

"Yes. You have something . . . they want

... and they had something ... you wanted."

But they were wrong, Maggie thought. This was not what she wanted. She did not want a naked man who had returned from the dead.

"Mom!" Toni shouted from behind her. She saw her daughter's hand point at the creatures flying toward the cottage. There were about five or six of them, and leading them was the larger creature, pulsing its ghostly light.

"They might hurt Brice and Grandma!" Toni said in alarm, breaking into a run toward the house.

Maggie did likewise, and behind her Keith followed. He ran slowly at first, then developed surprising momentum. "I'll kill ... them," he vowed as he ran. "I'll kill them ... like they killed me ... Maggie."

He was like a machine that had suddenly shifted into another gear. The more he pumped his legs, the faster he moved. Yes, a machine, Maggie thought. That's exactly what he was now—not a monster but a machine.

He reached the house before she did. As he disappeared inside, something occurred to Maggie, causing her to come to an abrupt halt. When she had looked over at the cylinder, she had seen that the entrance was open. This could be her chance to release the shield!

She peeked inside the cottage, saw that Lisa and Vivian were holding the fireplace poker and lamp respectively. They were guarding the door to the master bedroom. Maggie almost shouted at them to let the creatures have the body in the closet since it didn't matter anymore, but changed her mind. First she would remove the shield. This was definitely the time to do it.

She spun around and made a dash for the cylinder.

Vivian gasped when she saw the creatures fly into the room and gasped again when she saw Keith. She was certain she'd have a heart attack, but there was no time to clutch her chest or will herself to be calm. She ran for the oil lamp the moment Lisa recovered from the sight of the ghostly, naked man and made a dash for the poker. Vivian then rushed toward the door to the master bedroom to slam it shut. Maggie, she remembered, had said not to give up the dead alien in the closet until Keith was back, but she and Lisa did not reach the door before three of creatures had slipped into the bedroom.

Lisa slammed the door shut, trapping the creatures inside, then she leaned against it and brandished the poker at the other creatures hovering about.

"Come on, you fuckers!" she challenged. "Let's see you get by me."

With trembling hand, Vivian thrust the lamp toward the creatures, knowing it would blind and perhaps disorient them. She could see two or three of the creatures and the mother fluttering about the room.

The instant she glimpsed the larger creature, she experienced the familiar pressure develop inside her head. The mother, she knew, was pushing its way into her mind.

"Go away," Vivian said, determined to reject it. "Go away."

Keith suddenly snatched the poker from Lisa's hand and began attacking the creatures. From under the kitchen table, Brice watched his father in disbelief and horror.

The room came alive with strident shrieks and frantic fluttering of wings. Keith was like a madman pursuing these winged monstrosities. He swung the poker, missed, and slammed the iron instrument violently against the fireplace, shattering loose chunks of stone. Then he spun around and ran after the creature that had escaped. He swung, missed again, and splinted the rocking chair.

Never had he moved with such blinding force, and never had he moved so stiffly. Like a robot, Vivian thought.

"I'll get you . . . you son of a . . . bitch," he said, his tone flat yet hard with resolve. "I'll get . . . you."

He struck a creature and sent it hurtling across the room like a baseball. It cried out, shrieking in panic and agony until it crashed violently against a wall.

"Son of . . . a bitch," Keith repeated tonelessly.

The creature slid down the wall, smearing it with dark, watery blood. It jerked spasmodically, then expelled its last breath, shuddered and collapsed in permanent silence.

The mother creature cawed in horror and flew toward the smaller creature, but Keith moved between them, clutching the poker in readiness.

"Bitch," he said, "come . . . on."

He swung the poker back and forth, widening the arc with each swing. The mother stopped, hovered for a brief moment, then flew away.

Keith turned toward another creature and swung.

Maggie ran until she reached the entrance to the cylinder, then hesitated and looked back at the cottage. No one, as far as she could see, was following her, but, of course, this did not mean no one or nothing was waiting for her inside the craft. She knew she was taking a risk, but she also knew she had to. The only way to escape this ungodly horror would be to remove the shield.

Steeling herself, she entered the dark interior of the cylinder. It took several minutes for her eyes to adjust to the gloom, which was broken only by the feeble, red bulbs of light along the ceiling and floor.

She stopped for a minute, not sure which way to go. She waited an additional minute to see clearer in the darkness. The red lights outlined a rectangular object at one end, but at the other end there was nothing. She shuddered as she realized that someone or something could easily be hidden. If that someone or something could see well in the dark, it could be watching her.

Tentatively, she continued onward, deciding to go in the direction of the rectangular object. As she reached this object, she saw it was a table. In spite of the red lights along the edge, she could not see the surface clearly. Hesitantly, she touched it, then drew back her hand. The surface was wet and sticky. She quickly rubbed her hand against her thighs. What had she touched? Blood?

Repulsed, she moved away from the table. She groped her way onward into the seemingly endless gloom. At length she came to a wall, followed it, then found what felt like a door. It slid open the instant she touched it, and another dark room faced her.

Haltingly, she entered it. There were no lights at all in here. The air was warmer than in the other room, prompting Maggie to realize that the winged aliens came from a world that not only was dark, but warm as well. She wondered where this world was. Was it in this solar system, or was it many, many light years away?

How many other worlds were there that similar vicious creatures inhabited?

In the sea of blackness, Maggie vaguely

discerned darker objects scattered here and there. They were egg-shaped, and there were about eight of them. Gingerly, she touched one of these objects and found it to be of smooth metal and warm. To her surprise it opened, as the entrance to this room had done, the moment her hand had made contact with it. Startled, she gasped and recoiled, then curiously waited.

The egglike object apparently had hatched, but nothing emerged from it. She wished she had a flashlight, even a candle, so that she could peek inside it. She thought of poking the interior, which was only about two feet high and three wide, but could not summon the courage. What if one of the winged creatures were inside there?

As she thought of this, she realized the oval object was about the correct size to accommodate one of the creatures. Then it occurred to her that there were about the same number of these objects as there were of the creatures. Perhaps these were their beds, and this room was their sleeping chamber.

She found another room as her hand automatically opened a sliding door. This room was equally dark, but was smaller. Another egg-shaped object was in here. This one was larger than those in the other room. The mother creature's sleeping chamber? Maggie wondered.

Groping ahead of her, Maggie crossed this small room until, once more, a wall impeded her. She followed this wall, touching the metallic surface until she found another entrance.

Unlike the sleeping chambers, the room that now faced her was erratically dotted with the red, bulbous lights. This is it, Maggie thought intuitively. At last, she had reached her destination. This was the control room. In here she'd be able to release the shield.

But how?

Vivian cowered in a corner while her son-in-law attacked the creatures in nonstop, machinelike fashion. The shrill caws and shrieks were deafening.

Brice, still transfixed with horror, watched from under the table. Lisa stood staunchly in front of the door to the master bedroom while Toni shivered and hugged herself in a corner of the room. Vivian shouted at her and Brice to come close to the lamp, but her voice was too weak to be heard over the creatures' frantic outcries. She looked for Maggie.

Where was she? Had Maggie gone out? Was she . . . ?

Oh, please. God, no.

Rigid with terror, Vivian turned her attention to Keith.

He hit a creature and sent it speeding toward the fireplace, where it smashed against the stone surface. Then Keith hit it repeatedly, emitting low grunts as he swung the poker. The creature shrieked, struggling to get away. Another creature attacked Keith's back, tearing at the flesh with its teeth. Keith ignored it as though it were only an innocuous, pesty moth. He continued to assail the creature in front of him, swinging at it in rapid succession until its belly split and erupted dark, greenish fluid and organs.

One of the girls screamed.

Keith now slammed the poker downward, mashing the being that had dropped to the floor. He attacked maniacally until the creature was unrecognizable, then he returned to the creature clinging to his back.

He slid the poker in between his back and the creature and, with surprising strength, popped it off. A patch of skin and muscle ripped loose from Keith's back in the violent release, yet he did not flinch in pain.

No feelings, Vivian thought. He is a machine.

Keith swung the poker as the creature tried to dodge and attack him. This time the mother creature had joined the battle, but Keith, immune to pain, was able to fight aggressively and relentlessly.

He killed the creature that had ripped his back, puncturing its belly as he had done the other one, then he turned to the larger creature. Grunting, eyes narrowing with concentration, he readied himself for the ultimate kill. But the mother creature cried out in a mixture of rage and anguish, fled through the torn screen door, and flew away from the cottage.

Keith ceased swinging the poker, looked over at Lisa, his two children and Vivian. Slowly, a smile spread across his otherwise blank face. It was as though he'd just realized what he had done. Clearly, he was proud of himself.

Vivian was reminded of a dog who had just protected his master and was now wagging its tail. Suppressing a shudder, she looked away from her son-in-law's smiling face.

Maggie swung around the instant she heard the noise. She had just begun to enter what she was certain was the control room in the dark craft. Now she could hear the flapping of wings coming directly toward her.

Then she saw a white light blinking frenetically, growing brighter as it came closer. It was the mother creature, and Maggie knew it had spotted her.

Frantically, she groped for the entrance that would lead to the next chamber, but she could not seem to find it. Behind her, the mother blinked, occasionally letting out a cry that sounded like a strident wail, but it did not come after her as she had thought it would. It just stayed close behind her.

Maggie groped until she finally found the entrance, then she broke into a run, speeding through the darkness until she tripped over an oval object. She let out a cry, scrambled to her feet and bolted forward.

The mother emitted a second wail, and this time pursued Maggie.

"No!" Maggie screamed, falling yet again. The mother dived toward her. Maggie fought it, waving her hands wildly to ward it off. "Go away! Go away!" she screamed. As teeth sank into her shoulder, she whacked the creature as hard as she could. Then she jumped to her feet, ran, and crashed into a wall.

The mother clamped its jaw on her back, but she swung around and slammed her back and the creature against the metal wall. The creature shrieked, then released its grip on Maggie and flew back a short distance. It seemed certain it would charge forward and strike again, but to Maggie's relief it hovered, its belly pulsing light at a rapid, convulsive pace.

Maggie resumed groping for the exit, keeping her back to the wall as she followed the length of it. The mother followed, keeping a distance. Its light, Maggie noted, was no longer winking fiercely; it was slowing down, becoming a waxing and waning glow. It seemed to be regaining control.

It watched her for a long, silent moment, as though trying to decide something.

"Please release the shield," Maggie implored as she continued to grope the wall behind her. "Why are you keeping us trapped like this? What on earth do you want from us?"

The creature did not try to communicate with her. It just hovered, watching, wings flapping and fanning the air.

"What do you want?" Maggie screamed.

In reply, the creature brightened, then faded. If it were not for the sound of fluttering wings receding in the darkness, Maggie would have not known it had left her. Sobbing now with relief as well as frustration, she turned toward the wall and continued for the exit.

When she finally found her way out of the cylinder, she ran toward the cottage.

CHAPTER TWENTY-NINE

The Elder fought down panic, knowing it would only impair her thinking. She would have to stay calm and somehow make the best of this.

Fury had exploded when she saw the human female. The Elder hadn't been able to restrain herself from attacking it, for the human female had been alone and vulnerable, and it had been a way to retaliate for what the human male had done to The Little Ones. But all the while The Elder had assailed the human female she repeatedly reminded herself to gain control. At length she had succeeded.

Control was the only way her species was superior to humans.

But now it was so hard. Perhaps it was

because she was so far from her home that
made her lose control. She felt out of her
element on this planet.

Earth was not at all like her home planet.
Intelligent life forms survived on the surface
of this world, whereas it was beneath the
surface of hers. She was used to darkness
and warmth. Here it was sometimes too
bright, and when it was not, it was too cold.

Yes, she was out of her element. It was no
wonder that maintaining control was so very
difficult at times.

The Elder flew restlessly around her
sleeping chamber. She wondered what she
should do. She now regretted ever agreeing
to this task. She'd never dreamed it would
lead to this. How could she have been so
careless and neglectful? How foolish she'd
been to assume the humans were slow and
harmless. She had made the terrible mistake
of letting her confidence dominate caution.

Other teachers who had taken their pupils
out to educate them on the life forms in the
universe had never run into any problems
like this. But then, they had not been so sure
of themselves as she had. They had been
cautious.

Now what was she going to tell her
superiors, and worst of all, the dead pupils'
parents? They would literally have her head!

The Elder flew faster around the chamber.

Control! Control! she reminded herself
again.

She contemplated taking off in the craft and disappearing in the universe somewhere, but she knew The Superiors would locate her and magnetically pull her homeward. With their advanced knowledge and technology they could do this before she got too far. She could actually envision herself awakening hundreds of years later from her frozen slumber and looking up at The Superiors' and parents' angry faces. They would still be alive, she knew, for they did not age as quickly as humans did. Humans grew older in one decade than her kind did in a century.

And besides, cowardice was something she, herself, did not tolerate. No, there was no alternative except to appear before The Superiors and report the deaths.

Of course she could revive the dead pupils, but she knew this would not be the same. This method was not acceptable on her world. Once one was dead, he or she was forgotten. And if one caused a death, intentional or accidental, he or she must die also—and be forgotten.

She knew there was one thing she must do. Three Little Ones were still inside the humans' house, and as far as she knew, they were still alive. She would have to get them back on the craft. Three were better than none.

She knew she would still be destroyed, but at least the three Little Ones would be saved. It was her duty as a teacher to get those pupils, as well as the dead ones, back home. Yes, she would do this.

Otherwise, what kind of teacher would she be if she left all her pupils behind?

CHAPTER THIRTY

"**W**here were you?" Maggie heard her daughter say as soon as she was inside the cottage.

Brice threw his arms around her waist before she could answer and buried his face in her breasts. She hugged him tightly, catching her breath, then explained to everyone in the room that she'd been inside the spacecraft and that the alien had attacked her.

Then she noticed the cottage around her.

Under the soft glow of the oil lamp the blood on the wooden floor, pine walls and stone fireplace glistened darkly. There were three substances at different parts of the room that were unrecognizable and formless, clumps of dark, wet matter in puddles of watery blood.

"Beat 'em . . . to a . . . bloody pulp," Keith said.

Maggie looked over at him and was surprised to see a strange smile on his face. She quickly averted her eyes away from him, finding the smile and his animalistic nudity disturbing. The fireplace poker was still in his hand, but the tip was resting against the floor, dripping and forming a pool with the aliens' blackish blood.

She looked away from this. She saw a wing that had been severed. Sticky with blood, it had adhered to a wall like a bizarre ornament. She turned away from this also and saw something small and bulbous. It was shiny and yellow, and when she realized what it was she quickly covered her mouth with her hand, certain she'd vomit. The yellow ball was an eye.

Maggie squeezed her own eyes shut, not wanting to see any more of the horror. This was when she heard shrieks and flapping of wings coming from the master bedroom. She opened her eyes and looked over at the closed door. Now the sounds seemed louder.

"I'll get 'em . . . Maggie," Keith said, raising the poker until it was resting against his shoulder, then he headed toward the bedroom, moving with slow, mindless determination. When he reached the door he had to stop, as though trying to remember how to open it. He touched the knob, paused again to think, then turned it. When he was finally inside the other room he mechanically began to swing at the three creatures in there.

A part of Maggie wanted to rush into the bedroom to help Keith, while another part wanted to put an end to the horrible killings. But before she could respond, Lisa seized the lamp that Vivian had set down on a table and ran into the bedroom.

In the sudden flood of light the creatures screamed louder. They tried to escape, but were temporarily blinded. They crashed into the walls, missing the door. Keith slammed the heavy rod into them repeatedly, even after it was certain that all three creatures were dead.

Unable to endure the violent sound of the poker hitting the soft bodies, Maggie shouted at him to stop.

Slowly, he obeyed. He looked over at her and smiled.

Maggie, suppressing a shudder, turned away from him. She clutched Brice closer to her and pressed her face against the top of his head. What's next? What is the mother creature going to do when she learns that all her children are dead? Oh God, what is going to happen next?

Maggie watched the sun come up as she sat on the wharf. This time she was alone, needing to think, although her mind was weary. She found herself wondering how much strength she had left to fight, to survive. It seemed like a long time ago since she and the family had first come to this godforsaken place.

So much had happened since she thought her world had fallen apart, when she had found Keith in bed with that woman. When will this all end? How will it end?

She found herself even too weary to weep, so she silently watched the sun rise higher and higher.

Keith, now clad in jeans and a shirt, wanted to join her at the wharf, but she told him to go away. He obeyed, like a good child. Fifteen minutes later he was back, though.

"I need to be alone," she told him.

"You don't love me . . . no more."

"Please leave me alone, Keith."

This time he would not leave. He stood firmly on the wharf, looking down at her. Maggie tried to ignore him, hoping he'd go away. Her husband had literally returned from the dead. Would she ever face that?

"Maggie . . . please forgive me."

She said nothing for a long while, then forced herself to look at him. Should she be honest, or lie to silence him?

"I don't know," she said at length, deciding to be truthful.

"But you . . . wanted me . . . back," he reminded her.

"You were dead," she replied. "I don't know if I can handle that."

"But I'm . . . alive now . . . Maggie."

"Yes, I know, but you're not the same."

Keith mulled this over, then said. "You wish . . . I was still . . . dead?"

"No, of course not." She looked back at him, then quickly away. The sight of him unnerved her. He was so pale, his lips dry and cracking like sun-baked earth, and the skin around his eyes were bluish black, making the eyes seem larger and darker than they really were.

"Yes, Maggie . . . you do wish I was . . . dead," he said flatly.

Once more Maggie debated whether or not to be candid. She sighed, then eventually conceded, "Perhaps in a way, Keith."

Silently, he turned to leave.

"Wait a minute!"

He stopped. "Yes . . . Maggie?"

"I do love you, Keith," she explained slowly. "I always did. It was you who seemed to have doubts. When I caught you the first time, I decided we both made a mistake. I thought we were both wrong, and that we should start fresh. That's why I wanted to come here. But when I caught you the second time, I realized that it didn't matter what I did anymore. You'd just stopped loving me. You didn't want to start fresh."

"But I never stopped loving you . . . Maggie."

"You cheated on me, Keith. You made a fool out of me," she said. She was surprised there was no pain or threat of tears as she spoke these words. There was only a weary dullness inside her. She sincerely wanted to be left alone, but felt she should at least explain her feelings to Keith. "A person wouldn't do this to someone he loves," she went on. "He wouldn't keep on hurting her."

"I said . . . I was sorry."

"The first time you said it I believed you. The second time—no. I can see you're not sorry at all."

"What I had done . . . to you . . . is not the only reason," she heard him say. "You can't accept that I . . . have been brought back . . . Why?"

Maggie found herself suppressing a wry laugh. Why? What a silly, silly question!

"Why?" he insisted.

"You know why," she said finally.

"I want you . . . to tell me . . . Maggie."

She kicked at the water in frustration and briefly watched the concentric ripples spread away from her bare feet, then she sighed. "You're not the same anymore. I'm not sure if you're even human. I'm sorry, Keith, but . . ." Her voice trailed off.

"But what?" he urged.

"You frighten me."

"Why can't you accept it that . . . I once was . . . dead?"

"Why can't I?" Maggie said incredulously. "Maybe it's because it is something unheard of."

"It is heard of now."

Maggie shook her head. "It is against the rules."

"Against science?"

"Yes. Against nature. The dead do not come back!"

"Maybe the rules are . . . different elsewhere . . . Maggie."

"What are you saying?"

"Maybe the rules are not . . . the same everywhere . . . in the universe."

"Maybe. But here on Earth the dead stay dead."

"Keith, I really need to be alone. Please."

He hesitated for a brief moment, then quietly left the wharf.

"Thank you," Maggie whispered without looking back at him. She kept her gaze focused on the water before her, thinking that nothing will ever be the same again.

What was she to do with Keith? Then, as though suddenly aware that this was not the important question right now, she pushed it from her mind and replaced it with another. What was she to do with the mother alien? Certainly it would come out again tonight.

Maggie pondered over the creature's weaknesses. Light seemed to confuse and disorient it, but what else? As she mulled this over, recalling incidents of past evenings with the winged creatures, she wondered why the mother usually pulsed light slowly while the smaller creatures pulsed rapidly. They seemed to pulse in almost the same way humans pump blood. The creatures pulsed faster whenever they were excited or agitated, but the mother, being older and more mature, had more control.

But this had not always been the case, Maggie remembered. The mother had been frantic last night. The creature had blinked so frequently that it was constantly visible at times. Could this be a weakness? Rage and panic would make the alien pulse more frequently, make it more visible in the dark, thus make it more vulnerable.

Maggie looked over at the gleaming spacecraft among the trees. She knew, with the same certainty that she knew the sun would eventually go down, the craft would open and the bitch would emerge, like a vampire from her coffin. But tonight would be the last night, Maggie vowed. Win or lose, it would be over.

CHAPTER THIRTY-ONE

Maggie made supper, using the last can of tuna, the rest of the bread and warm Pepsi. She made five sandwiches, excluding one for herself. Keith ate eagerly while the others nibbled. When the meal was over, everyone left the table, went to the other section of the room and waited.

The creatures' bodies had been moved to the master bedroom, the door to it closed. Maggie fleetingly wondered how long it would take before the corpses would begin to reek of decay.

The front door, however, was left open. There no longer was any sense in keeping out the mother creature. A confrontation was inescapable.

But there's nothing to fear, Maggie told

herself repeatedly. It is six against one now.

Yet she still felt uneasy. That creature had been so violent and savage that numbers did not matter.

As Maggie thought this, her gaze fell on Keith. The fireplace poker was in his hand, but he was not at the window or pacing as he'd done the previous night. He was standing erect in the center of the room, like a sentry—or rather, like a toy soldier, Maggie reflected. Wind him up and watch him kill.

Why had he been able to kill the creatures last night and not before? When the creatures had put him back together again did they realize they were creating an enemy? Unwittingly or not, they had made Keith stronger and more aggressive. How did they do this? Was Keith actually stronger, or did mindless determination to win a fight have something to do with it? Maggie suspected it was the latter. Before last night Keith had fought like a man. Last night he had fought like a machine. There was a difference.

Maggie looked away from him. God, what was she going to do with her husband? He wasn't human anymore.

She looked out the window. The night had deepened. The stars and moon were clear. The cylinder was brighter than usual, seemingly more silvery. A meteor fleetingly streaked across the black sky, then disappeared.

For a long, thoughtful moment Maggie

stared at the ebony heavens. She wondered how far it expanded. Was it without end? Did the universe continue on and on, or did it stop and another begin—a totally different kind of universe that was beyond man's craziest imagination? Were there many, many universes out there? Suddenly feeling small and insignifcant, even frighteningly vulnerable, Maggie turned her gaze away from the sky and looked once more at the cylinder.

She was stunned to find it open.

At the same time, she heard her son cry out, "Mom!"

She whirled and saw the mother creature on the other side of the screen door, almost invisible, its body dark against the night. Maggie expected it to glow, at least once, but it remained in darkness. She somehow knew it was staring at her—only her.

"I'll kill it . . . Maggie," Keith declared.

"No," Maggie said without turning to look at him. She didn't want to attack first. The creature was at a disadvantage now, so there was no need for violence—at least not yet.

She stared at the dark shape behind the screen door and waited for it to make a move. At the same time she lowered her guard, letting her mind open a little for the creature to enter and communicate. The instant she felt it control and dominate her she'd push it out.

Control!

The Elder had it now. So great was her control that she was able not to pulse any light. It was like holding a breath, willing calmness into one's body. It was quite easy, once you had a grip on it.

The Elder tried to penetrate the human female's mind. She wanted to tell it something, make a few demands, and then she would leave, but the human female had learned how to shield itself against The Elder. It knew that determination was a power, that the Elder could not enter by force.

The Elder could only enter a small portion of the human female's mind. State your business and leave, the human female seemed to be saying to her.

So The Elder stated her business. She wanted the rest of her pupils. Also, she wished to have the dead bodies as well. She could not go home without them.

Maggie pushed the creature out of her mind. The rest of its pupils? Was this thing a teacher of some kind? A teacher trying to gather its children so it could go back home?

Maggie had a sudden, strange urge to laugh, although she did not find anything humorous. Absurd, yes. Even bizarre. But nothing funny.

Maggie looked back at the creature. It glowed very faintly, but that was all. She knew it was fighting for control, waiting for her to reply.

But she could only stare at it and keep the gate in her mind firmly closed. She couldn't summon enough courage to impart the truth. She felt the pressure increase as the creature strained to enter, but she fought it. Eventually, the pressure ceased.

The creature glowed again, brighter this time.

The Elder could feel its control slipping away. She struggled to retain it, for she knew she would gain nothing if she did not. She was outnumbered; she could never force her way through the humans' house and survive. Where were the remaining Little Ones? Couldn't they sense her presence?

If they could, wouldn't they have cried out to her?

And why couldn't she sense their presence?

She told herself they were still alive. They could not all be dead. Not all of them.

Maggie took a deep breath, mustered all the courage she could, and let the creature communicate with her. She reasoned it would learn of the truth eventually, so actually there was no reason to procrastinate.

Hugging herself, Maggie slowly opened the door in her mind. With a surprising rush the creature entered. Maggie had to push against it a little to keep it from entering too deeply. When she felt it was in far enough, she took another deep breath, steeling herself for the worst.

Immediately she was asked of The Little Ones' whereabouts. The teacher informed her that three of them should still be alive and, also, it wanted the bodies of the others. Then, and only then, would it leave Maggie and the others alone.

"First, release the shield," Maggie demanded out loud. Dimly, she was aware that she must look like a lunatic to the others in the room, carrying on a one-sided conversation.

The teacher refused. It wanted proof that The Little Ones were still alive.

"They are alive," Maggie lied, hoping it could not see or sense the truth somehow.

The creature was silent, as though trying to decide whether or not to believe Maggie. It pushed, endeavoring to probe deeper, but Maggie stood firm. She threatened to push it from her mind entirely if it did not stop.

The creature relented, telling her it was more powerful, more superior than humans. Therefore, its demands should be respected. Superiority always ruled, it informed her.

Maggie countered that it was a matter of opinion as to who was superior and who was not. She told it that as far as she was concerned, *she* was far more superior.

The teacher snorted, then reminded Maggie that humans had yet to conquer space. Humans were still confined to a little world, whereas it and its kind had traveled the stars. Therefore, there was no argument as to who was the superior species.

"It's silly to argue," Maggie declared. "If you will not release the shield, then I won't give you what you want."

The creature informed her that it could resort to violence.

"And you call yourself superior?"

Humans are a violent species as well, the creature told her.

"Release the shield!" Maggie shouted. "Why can't you just let us go!"

As she said this, she felt the pressure in her mind ease. The creature had slipped out and, its body still at the door, began to look around, apparently for another mind to invade. It stared at Keith, then before Maggie could respond, it took flight and flew through the ripped screen, passing her.

"No!" Maggie screamed, not certain what the creature was doing. When she saw it circle Keith, she knew it would try to hypnotize him. "Don't look at it!" she shouted at her husband. "Close your mind to it!"

He stared at Maggie, confused.

"Don't look at it," she enunciated, as though he were deaf and could not understand.

To her relief, he obeyed, going to great lengths to avoid the creature, averting his head whenever the creature flew near it. He lifted the poker but the creature kept circling him, moving so much faster than the smaller creatures had done. Then, to everyone's surprise, the creature darted toward the door to the master bedroom, turned the knob with its teeth, and pushed against the wood. The door swung open, and the creature was inside the room before anyone could stop it.

The Elder flew into the bedroom. Without the glare of the oil lamp, she could see better in here. She circled the room until she spotted the door to the closet. She opened it and saw a Little One on the floor, bleeding profusely. Then she spotted the second one.

Below these two Little Ones were five more. They were in a heap that she had first thought were humans' garments. She alighted, rushed toward the bodies and sniffed. Death!

She screamed. All The Little Ones were dead. All of them! She screamed again and again, her cries long, piercing wails of anguish and rage. There was no more control.

She whirled, took flight, and attacked the first human she saw.

Maggie heard someone scream. At first she thought the creature's wail had changed pitch, then she realized it was Vivian she had heard. The creature, blinking furiously, was attacking the older woman.

"No!" Maggie shouted, running to help her mother.

With her frail hands, Vivian swung

frantically at her assailant. Most of the time she succeeded only in batting empty air, for the creature was too quick. Maggie, however, was a little faster. Able to see the creature clearly, for it was pulsing steadily, she seized it and endeavored to yank if off her mother's arm, where it had a firm hold with its teeth.

The feel of the creature in her hands made Maggie shudder. Her instinct was to let go in revulsion, but with resolve she held on. The body was repulsively soft to the touch. She could feel her fingers sink into the dry, leathery flesh. It seemed boneless, like clutching a bag of water. She was certain it would burst at any moment and squirt its liquid contents into her face. So certain was she of this, she actually braced herself and squeezed the body, using both hands, but she found the body stronger than she thought it would be, the dry flesh surprisingly supple.

The creature sank its myriad teeth deeper into Vivian's arm as Maggie continued to pound at it. Blood began to bubble around the creature's mouth, then spray outward as Vivian struggled. The creature released its hold and bit into her shoulder.

"God, please help me!" Vivian shrieked. Her legs buckled, and she would have collapsed in a faint, but the creature held her upright, its wings beating powerfully.

Maggie pummeled at the creature as hard as she could, but it seemed oblivious to her blows. In the periphery of her vision she saw her husband rush forward, the poker high in his hand as though it were a sword. Her first reaction was that of relief. Keith was going to save her mother. This, however, quickly turned to alarm. Keith, she was certain, would fight brutally, hurting not only the creature but Vivian as well.

"No!" Maggie screamed.

The poker was raised high over Keith's head, ready to crash down on the older woman.

"No!" Maggie shouted again, leaping upward to snatch the rod out of his hand.

Keith stopped, then blinked in puzzlement at her. In the middle of struggle and terror, he incongruously waited for an explanation.

"You'll kill her!" she said. Now that Keith was no longer a threat to her mother, she gave up trying to reach for the poker and resumed her attack on the creature. She hammered her fists into it, over and over.

Toni and Lisa joined her in the struggle, and dimly she wondered what on earth had taken them so long. She didn't seem to realize that only a few seconds had elapsed since her mother had been attacked. The girls' response had only seemed slow.

Together, they dislodged the creature's grip on Vivian. When the creature soared toward the ceiling, readying itself for another dive and another attack, Keith swung the poker at it and missed.

At least it kept the creature from gaining another hold on anyone.

"Ma, are you all right?" Maggie asked as

she saw blood staining her mother's sweater from the wounds in the shoulder and arm.

The woman nodded, although her face was alarmingly pale. Maggie wished there was time to stem the bleeding, but the creature was flying fast, diving and soaring like a violent hawk.

Gently, she took her mother's good arm and led her into the closet, where the heap of bodies were. "In here," she said, "you'll be safe."

Vivian recoiled at the sight of the bloody corpses, but Maggie pushed her forward. She then looked for Brice and also shoved him into the closet. "You'll both be safe in here," she said as she shut the door.

The creature swept down at her and pulled at her hair. Keith swung the poker at it and it let go, rushing toward the ceiling again, shrieking furiously as it went.

The shield! Maggie suddenly thought. This would be the perfect time to release it! While Keith kept the creature at bay, she could make a run for the cylinder and remove the shield.

She fled the house.

The instant the screen door banged shut the creature pursued her. Maggie tried to pump her legs faster than she had ever pumped them. Her speed, however, was no match to the alien's. With one of its horrible claws that protruded from a wing, it swooped down and slashed her back. She fell forward from the sudden force, feeling the back of her shirt tear. She experienced hot pain as the hooked talons tore her skin. Almost instantly she felt warm blood saturating and sticking her shirt to her back.

Maggie scrambled to her feet and once more ran headlong toward the cylinder. The creature attacked her again, and she realized there was no way it was going to let her enter the craft. At length she was forced to turn around and run back toward the cottage.

As she rushed back, arms flailing to ward off the creature, Keith darted forward with his poker and swung at the creature. This time it seemed ready for him. With its mouth it seized the instrument and yanked it from Keith's grip. The poker firm between its teeth, it flew toward the lake and dropped the rod into it.

Maggie watched helplessly, feeling as if it were hope itself plummeting into the water. Now they were defenseless. There was no weapon, no way to fight back.

The creature seemed aware of this, for it emitted a loud cry that sounded victorious. Then it bolted toward the group that had gathered on the open porch.

"Inside!" Maggie screamed. Everyone promptly obeyed, except Keith, who seemed lost without the poker. "Come on! Inside!" Maggie pulled at his arm until at last he responded.

Once everybody was in the cottage, Maggie slammed the wooden door shut, locking it. Then she frantically looked around for a new weapon. There must be something they could use. She ran into the kitchen and opened the utensil drawer, but only found one carving knife among the blunt silverware. She took the knife, then looked around for something else. There were three thin Teflon pans and an aluminum tea kettle. All were lightweight and would probably buckle at the first impact, but they were better than nothing.

"Maggie! Maggie!" She heard her mother whimper from the bedroom closet.

Maggie ran toward it and flung open the door. Vivian was standing at the far end of the closet, clutching Brice close to her. "Thank God, you're all right," the older woman said, her voice faint and shaky. "Is it over?"

Maggie embraced her mother and son, endeavoring to soothe them. Then she slowly shook her head. "No, Ma. Not yet."

Never had The Elder experienced such fury, and the fact that she had lost control to this fury seemed to enrage her even more. As she repeatedly attacked the humans a part of her mind questioned this loss of control. Was it because she was affronted that a lesser species had succeeded in destroying her own kind? Was that the reason? This was certainly something unprecedented.

Her kind was superior to any species on this planet as well as on her home world. Her kind ruled. A lower life form had never destroyed her species before, and her kind had taken great pride in this.

Yes, this was a first. It was no wonder she had lost control.

But she would not give up now, for she and her kind were fighters. They would destroy those who tried to destroy them. This was partly why they were superior.

She was too aggressive and too intelligent to be vanquished.

The Elder flew away from the cottage and entered her spacecraft. She went directly into the control room and, with her teeth, extracted from a metallic cabinet a delicate capsule, the size of a small egg. Careful not to puncture this dangerous capsule, for it certainly would terminate her in an instant, she flew back outside. She hovered over the cottage and waited until she was perfectly centered above it.

Then with cackling glee, she dropped the capsule.

CHAPTER THIRTY-TWO

They waited in silence, holding their breaths. With the front door locked, everyone was in the middle of the main room, each clutching something weaponlike in hand. Lisa, Toni, and Brice had cooking pans, Vivian held the aluminum tea kettle, Keith was ready with a carving knife, and Maggie gripped a heavy wooden cutting board. They were a pathetic army, Maggie knew, maybe even ludicrous, but they were ready. They were the majority.

The creature's gleeful cry sounded above them, and everyone looked at the ceiling. The cry had been different from the wrathful cries that had preceded it. It seemed to be a cry that was punctuating something.

A small, explosive pop was heard, then silence.

"What do you think hap—" Toni began, then stopped when she realized everyone was listening intently, searching for the answer to the question she had begun to ask.

Faintly, the flapping of wings could be heard circling the air above the cottage. Because there were no more enraged caws or shrieks, it was apparent the creature was waiting for them.

Waiting for what? Maggie wondered. For everyone to run out? Well, no one was going to do that, unless—

She smelled smoke.

Toni caught a whiff at the same time and yelled, "The house is on fire!"

The smell became stronger, then smoke appeared all around them, rapidly seeping through the surrounding walls and ceiling. At first Maggie thought it was some kind of poisonous gas, then she heard crackling sounds above her and knew flames were burning the roof.

"We've got to get out of here!" Maggie shouted as she began to push the others toward the front door. "Out before the ceiling falls!"

"But the creature—" Lisa reminded her.

"Out!"

Toni unlocked the door and ran out into the clear night. Lisa followed, then Maggie and Vivian, each grabbing Brice's arm, hurried out together. Only Keith remained behind, still staring at the ceiling.

"Keith!" Maggie screamed from the porch.

Out here she could see the orange flames consuming the roof. She didn't know how the creature had started this fire, but it was already incredibly full-blown and savage. "Keith!"

He finally heard her and looked through the open door. The smoke, now dark gray, coiled around him, almost obscuring him. He stared blankly at Maggie, oblivious to the surrounding smoke, until she shouted his name again. Then he moved hurriedly toward her.

As he stepped outside, the creature swooped down and slashed the back of his head with its claws. Belatedly, Keith tried to stab the creature with his knife, but the creature flew away, furiously flashing white light in the dark, fire-tinged air. The creature made a circle, then plunged toward Vivian, its maw opened wide. Maggie, seeing this, pushed her mother out of the way, causing the creature to miss its target and soar upward again.

Frantically, Maggie looked around her. She realized now it did not matter that they outnumbered the creature; they were still at a horrible disadvantage. They were vulnerable now, confined in a glasslike dome without shelter, whereas the creature could escape upwards out of reach from harm.

Although Maggie had felt trapped for days, the feeling was not quite as terrifying as it was now. At least the cottage had provided some protection.

Oh God, she prayed, please help us.

As if on cue, she spotted a metallic glint at the far end of the driveway. Of course, the car! That would protect them.

The creature attacked Lisa, who screamed as it bit her, at the same time swinging the frying pain at it, repeatedly missing.

"Come on, in the car!" Maggie ordered. She grabbed Brice's arm once more and ran.

Again with the exception of Keith, everyone rushed toward the Ford wagon. As they ran, the creature made another attempt at Keith's head.

"Keith, come on!" Maggie shouted.

Keith jabbed the air with his knife in a futile attempt to fight back. He was still standing in the same spot, his head tilted upward, watching the creature circle the air, when the others scrambled into the car.

"Keith! Please!"

The creature zoomed toward him from the sky. Maggie screamed his name again, and at last he obeyed. He started toward her and the car, but he did not run; it was as if he had forgotten that something was attacking him.

He can only think of one thing at a time, Maggie suddenly realized, and right now he is concentrating on obeying her command.

"Come on, Keith. Hurry," she urged, her voice still loud but more controlled. "Please, hurry."

He quickened his pace, frowning as he concentrated on the movements of his legs.

Maggie waited, keeping a car door open for him. The creature began to descend on him, then in midair changed course and shot toward Maggie and the open door.

Realizing this in time, Maggie slammed the door shut. The creature narrowly missed colliding into the car. It soared to the sky, but as it swooped down again Maggie had reopened the door, and Keith and she were already inside. Door closed, the creature slammed into the window.

Simultaneously, Toni and Vivian let out a gasp. Maggie tensed, holding her breath. The hard impact on the thick glass stunned the creature only briefly. It flew uncertainly for a moment, then soared again.

Won't it ever stop?

Deliberately, it crashed against the windshield. The impact stunned it again, but this time it recovered more quickly. Then, to everyone's amazement, it attacked the windshield a second time. Now it no longer needed time to recover, for it seemed to have developed an endurance to the hard blows against the glass. It seemed to toughen with each attack.

What kind of creature was this? Why was it so savage, so bent on attacking everybody? Nothing, it seemed, would stop it—certainly not the windshield.

As Maggie stared at the repeated attacks, recoiling each time the creature made violent contact with the glass, she thought about its home world. She was certain it was an intelligent planet, highly advanced in many ways. Their ability to travel through space left her without doubt about this. But also, she was confident the planet was an extremely violent one. She shuddered at the thought that such a creature could rule a world. It was a horrible, horrible thought.

The creature was attacking the car like a shark in a frenzy.

As she made this comparison, she was reminded of something she'd read somewhere, about the longevity of the shark. It was one of the longest-living species on Earth, and this was believed to be attributed to its ferocity. It had survived so long because of its savage aggressiveness.

Maggie shuddered again. Intuitively she was certain this creature assailing them had been in existence for a long, long time as well. She even had a strong feeling that it was perhaps the oldest species in the cosmos, all because of its intelligence and violent nature.

She knew now the creature would not stop until it broke into the car and killed them all.

They had to do something—now!

She looked over at Keith on the seat beside her. Climbing into the car after him, she had ended up behind the steering wheel. He was craning his neck to see above the car, where the creature had flown in one of its tireless ascents. He seemed awe-struck, almost boyish, and as he peered upward, Maggie noticed the cuts the creature had made on the back of his head. The wounds seemed

deep, yet blood was trickling slowly. Maggie
would have thought there'd be much more
blood than this. The bleeding seemed to be
synchronized with the rest of him—sluggish,
unnatural, half-alive.

She forced her eyes away from him and
concentrated on the crisis at hand. Suddenly
a solution came to her.

"The key!" she blurted. She looked back
at her husband, carefully avoiding the slow
leak matting the hair on the back of his
neck. "Do you have the car key, Keith?"

He pulled his gaze away from the window,
just as the creature crashed into it and flew
away. "What?" He frowned at Maggie.

"The car key. Where is it? Is it on you?"

He gave this some thought, then said,
"No."

Maggie struggled to keep her patience. "Do
you know where it is?"

"It's on the bureau . . . in the bedroom
. . . Maggie."

Hope crumbled, and Maggie hugged
herself, suddenly feeling very, very cold.
What were they going to do?

"I'll go . . . get it . . . Mag—"

"No, you stay here."

"But . . . you want the key . . . badly." His
face searched hers. "I can see . . . you want
it . . . badly."

"We'll think of something else."

The creature slammed into the window
and Maggie saw that the glass was
developing spider-web cracks. Soon it was

going to give.

Maggie closed her eyes and prayed.

Then she heard the door open, and Keith got out of the car, closed the door and started toward the burning cottage.

"Keith!"

Of course he could not hear her with the doors and windows shut. The creature charged after him. It slashed ineffectually at his head, then returned to clamp its teeth on his back, looking like a hideous hump between his shoulders. Keith continued forward in a steady gait, determined to reach his destination.

Maggie opened the door to run out after him. As she started forward, however, Toni pulled her back.

"No, Mom! Please, no!"

"But your father needs me."

"No!" Toni screamed again. "He doesn't deserve you!"

"Oh, Toni, this is no time—" The sentence trailed away as Keith disappeared into the flaming house.

She was too late.

The Elder held onto the man, sinking her teeth deeper into his back. She was surprised the human did not struggle to dislodge her. Then she remembered it was no longer capable of doing too many things simultaneously. At the moment it was concentrating on going inside the house.

The Elder tried not to look at the brilliant

flames, for they were hurting her eye. She bit harder into the man's flesh, determined to kill him before he got too near the blinding light. She tightened her jaw and twisted violently, endeavoring to work loose a sizable chunk, and she would have succeeded, if it were not for the agonizing brightness that was looming closer and closer.

Already she could no longer see anything. Everything was a disconcerting glare. She hated this blindness, for it disoriented her, triggering panic and terror. For centuries she had avoided bright lights, and she found she could not stop now—especially with the light that was rushing toward her. It was too intense. It seemed to be penetrating her, filling her with its horrible starkness. She began to whimper. It was too strong. It was too much.

She needed the comfort of darkness immediately, or else she feared she'd lose her mind.

With a piercing cry, she let go of the man, turned and bolted toward the car.

Maggie found herself holding her breath as she waited for Keith to emerge from the cottage that was mostly shrouded in flames and smoke. She saw the creature fly out from the burning structure, and her trepidation deepened. Keith, she realized, no longer had any sense of danger. He reacted mindlessly. He would perish in the fire because she had asked if he had the car key.

The creature was back, slamming itself against the windshield.

Behind her she heard Lisa sob with fear. Maggie was tempted to turn around and snap at her to stop. It was too late for tears now. It was too late for anything. It was over.

The fire would burn down the house, then it would spread, burning the trees and the car, and finally the car would explode.

Yes, it was definitely over.

Then she heard Brice yell, "Look, Mom!"

The boy was staring at the cottage. Among the angry flames Keith emerged, walking rapidly toward the car. Maggie sighed with relief.

The creature did not notice Keith until he had reached the car and was opening the door to get in. Pausing only briefly, the creature continued to batter the windshield, spreading the network of cracks in the glass.

Keith gave Maggie the key. "But I thought . . . we couldn't go . . . nowhere," he said. "I thought we were . . . inside a . . . shield."

"We are," Maggie replied without explaining. She had a plan, but she wasn't sure it would work.

"You can't penetrate . . . the shield," Keith went on, puzzled. "I think I remember trying it . . . Maggie . . . The shield is . . . too strong."

"I know, I know." Breaking through the shield wasn't part of the plan. She had something else in mind.

"Then how . . ."

The creature crashed into the windshield again, seemingly more violent now. Blood was beginning to smear the glass. The creature was definitely like a shark, Maggie realized with stunned horror. It would kill itself before it gave up its prey.

There was a hole in the windshield now, and Maggie began to doubt her plan. There was probably not enough time.

The creature attacked the car again. Maggie had started to insert the key into the ignition, but the impact on the windshield had claused her to drop it. With a trembling hand she groped for it on the floor beneath the seat.

No, there was not enough time.

At any minute the creature would break through, and when it did, she and the others might not be quick enough to flee.

Maggie finally slipped the key into the ignition, turned it and gunned the motor.

"Mom, what are you doing?" Toni asked from the back seat.

"I want you all to hold on," she said, ignoring the question. "Everyone put on their safety belt. Toni, hold on to your brother," she said as she pulled her own belt across herself. "You, too, Keith. Put on your belt."

"But what are—"

"Just put it on. Please hurry."

The creature was making a wider hole in the window. It would only take a couple more impacts to make the glass collapse.

"Hurry," she urged the others in the car. "Please, hurry." Glancing in the rearview mirror, she saw that Lisa and Toni were strapped in, Brice on Toni's lap. Vivian, between the girls, had no belt. "Hold onto the girls, Ma," she told her.

"Mom, what are you going to do, for God's sake?" Toni asked, her voice cracking.

Maggie looked over at Keith. It was taking him a long time, but at last he had his belt fastened. "I'm going to kill the bitch," she replied at length. Then she shot the car forward.

The creature had been in the air at the time. When it swooped down, aiming for the windshield, it was thrown back by the car in motion. Maggie stepped on the accelerator. She was about to run the alien over as it fell to the ground, but before she could reach it, it flew upward. Strong bitch! she thought. A survivor in every sense of the word. But then, she was a survivor, too!

She slowed down and waited for the creature to attack again.

The creature smashed into the glass, this time breaking through.

Maggie floored the accelerator. Where was that damn shield? She had backed up in the driveway to gain distance and speed, and now that she was racing forward, the shield seemed farther away than she had thought it'd be.

Come on, shield! Come on!

The creature was pushing against the glass. Any second now it would be inside the car.

Maggie glanced at the speedometer which was rising rapidly.

Come on, shield!

She braced herself.

Any second now.

The car slammed into the invisible shield. Maggie felt herself shoot forward and felt something slam into her abdomen with such violent force that she thought she'd literally break in two. Somewhere, seemingly far away, she heard grunts and cries.

After she had pitched forward, she fell back against the seat. The safety belt had saved her. Now she stared at the windshield in a daze and noticed nothing was behind it. The creature was gone.

"Mom, you hit—" Toni began, then stopped when Maggie already recovering from her numb daze, shoved the car into reverse.

The creature had been thrown off, just as she hoped it would, and it had crashed against the shield. She snapped on the headlights and was able to see the dark blood on the shield, and on the hood was the creature, writhing in obvious agony.

Good! she thought.

She slammed against the shield once more. The creature was flung from the hood and into the shield, then fell down past the grille of the car.

Good, you bitch!

Maggie shoved the car into reverse again, then she surged forward, stepping on the accelerator all the way, spraying gravel. "Hold on!" she shouted at everyone in the car. "Hold on!"

The Elder screamed—not because she was in so much pain, but because the lights were rushing toward her, and she knew she could not escape them. She tried to fly away, but her wings were broken, and besides, something was behind her, something was stopping her.

It took her a moment to realize what it was. It was the trap that she and The Little Ones had used to contain the humans. Now it was confining her.

She screamed again. The lights kept coming toward her.

Maggie slammed into the shield, then reversed the car until its headlights were spotlighting the heap below the dark, glistening smear of blood on the invisible barrier. She waited for the crumpled creature to move. A wing fluttered, then was still. She expected it to move again, but it didn't.

The air seemed so thick around her. She heard faint whimpering from the back seat and dimly wondered if it was Brice or the girls.

She continued to stare at the heap. It was wet with blood and misshapen.

It still didn't move.

She began to tremble.

"I think it's ... dead ... Maggie," she heard her husband say in his thick, slow voice beside her.

Numbly, she nodded. Yes, it was dead. She began to smile, then cry. Her body shook with convulsive sobs. She couldn't believe it. She had actually done it!

At last the nightmare was over.

CHAPTER THIRTY-THREE

Maggie entered the dark cylinder to find the controls that would remove the transparent shield. As she groped her way through the black chambers she wondered what the country, even the world, would say about this spacecraft. Or would the government hide this find from the public?

Would this be the first find? Or had there been others that were kept from public knowledge?

At last she found the control room and a large panel with red luminous dials, switches and levers. It did not look as complex as an airplane, which surprised her. She had expected something more elaborate. Then she reminded herself that the creatures were a lot like this craft of theirs—advanced, yet simple and crude.

There weren't even any windows in here, Maggie noted. This craft was like the interior of a cave, and once more she found herself wondering what kind of world the creatures had come from. Also, she wondered how the craft had managed to travel through space without windows. Had it been by means of computers and radar? Perhaps this vehicle was more complex than it looked.

She let her hand run lightly over the dials and levers, hesitant to touch or depress anything lest she activate something dangerous. The last thing in the world she wanted now was to find herself hurtling through infinite space. But then, she knew she'd never remove the shield if she didn't do anything.

Bracing herself, she flicked a switch. She listened carefully, waiting to hear the car horn that Lisa had promised to sound the instant Toni, pressing against the shield, found the barrier gone. At first the two girls had refused to cooperate. Toni had told Maggie she'd never speak to Lisa again. Their friendship was definitely over. Maggie couldn't blame her, but for now she needed their help. Once the shield was gone, they would be free to separate.

Now Maggie was hearing a deep rumble in the control room. Lift off? Quickly, she flicked the switch back. To her relief, the rumble ceased.

She tried turning a knob below a dial.
Nothing. She tried another knob. She heard
a soft clang and assumed a door had closed
in another chamber. She turned the knob
back to the start position and went on to
something else in the panel. At length she
heard the car horn, which was faint and
muffled. Relieved, she hurred out of the
tomblike cylinder.

Outside in the harsh sunlight, Keith was
waiting for her.

"We're free!" she exclaimed. To her
surprise, he did not seem elated. "We're
free!" she repeated, this time enunciating the
word.

"I'm not leaving with you . . . Maggie."

"What are you talking about?"

"You don't want me . . . anymore . . . You
haven't forgiven me . . . and . . ."

"Keith, we'll talk about this later. First, I
think we should get out of here—"

"No, Maggie . . . no . . . I'm not leaving with
you . . . There will be . . . too many questions."

Maggie knew he was right. There would be
a lot of questions, but she had tried not to
think about them. She wanted only to
concentrate on getting away from this place.

"I will be treated like . . . a freak . . .
Maggie," she heard him say. "And you don't
. . . love me anymore . . . Yes, I should leave."

"But where will you go?"

"I . . . don't know."

"What will you do?"

"Maybe I'll find work somewhere . . . change my name . . . be a janitor some place . . . or be a . . ." His voice trailed away as he failed to think of anything else.

"Keith, I can't let you go like this."

"You can't stay with me . . . either . . . Maggie . . . You can't accept it that I . . . was once dead."

Maggie looked away in frustration. He was right again, but she hadn't wanted to think about it now. It was a problem she'd intended to deal with later.

Down the driveway the car sounded its horn, urging her and Keith to hurry.

Toni will walk away from Lisa, she thought. The girls will probably never speak to each other again. It was sad, but simple. With Maggie and Keith it was different; it was not simple. It would be so hard to walk away.

"They will ask about you," she said at length, turning back to him. "What will I say?"

"You'll think of something . . . You always do . . . Besides, Toni doesn't love me anymore . . . either . . . and I saw how Brice looked at me . . . He is afraid of me now . . . He thinks I am a monster . . . I will never be close . . . to him again . . . And the others . . ." He did not finish, as though believing it did not matter.

"What about the authorities who'll demand answers? What will I tell them?"

"Tell them . . . the creatures got me . . . It

wouldn't be a lie . . ." He paused to think.
"And tell them . . . I was thrown into the lake
. . . Let them look for me."

"And will they find you?" Maggie asked,
as a heavy, cold feeling grew in her stomach.
She waited for an answer, but he gave her
none.

The car horn blared again.

"Oh, Keith, let's talk about this later."

He turned away from her and began to
walk toward the trees, where the woods were
deep.

"Keith!"

He stopped and looked back. "I've already
been dead," he told her, then continued
onward.

Maggie contemplated running after him,
but something stopped her. She wasn't
certain what it was, but she found herself
reluctant to respond. She stood without
moving, watching her husband disappear
into the darkness.

I've already been dead.

Now he would be walking among the
living. How far would he go before anyone
discovered the truth? Would he be
dangerous? She remembered the machinelike way he had killed the small creatures.
Somehow she knew he wouldn't. He had only
killed to protect the others and in self-
defense. Besides, she inwardly knew
something else—something that she should
stop, but couldn't.

His body would be found in the lake.

She continued to stare at the spot where he had disappeared. Repeatedly she told herself to go after him, and repeatedly she found herself unable to move. I do love you, she thought, and maybe someday I'll forgive you. But she was certain she'd never forget him.

After all, she was only human.

The car blared its horn again, and this time she didn't ignore it. She stared a moment longer into the darkness of the trees, then, steeling herself against the barrage of questions that she knew would come, she hurried toward the car and freedom.